THE DUKE'S KISS

(The Spare Lovers)

CAMIE GREGORY

E books/Books are not transferable. They cannot be sold, shared, or given away as it is an infringement on the copyright of this work.

This book is a work of fiction. The names, characters, places and incidents are products of the writer's imagination or have been used factiously and are not to be construed as real. Any resemblance to persons, living or dead, actual events, locale or organizations is entirely coincidental.

In Town Books

THE DUKE'S KISS
(The Spare Lovers)

ISBN-13:9780692513804

E book ISBN:

Editor: William Dyson

Book Cover Design: Michael Dyson
www.coroflot.com/guerrilla808

Copyright © 2015 Camie Gregory. All rights reserved. No part of this book may be used or reproduced in any manner whatsoever without written permission, except in the case of brief quotations embodied in critical articles and reviews.

DEDICATION

Dedicated to my husband,
who supported and encouraged me
to do what I love.

ACKNOWLEDGMENTS

To Mr. William Dyson,
my friend and my mentor who always
believed in me.

CHAPTER 1

IT HAS BEEN SIX MONTHS since they found me floating in the river, unconscious but barely alive.

Every morning I followed the same routine. I needed a few moments to grasp all of this. I tried to discern if this reality was at all plausible, or was my mind still clouded with the remnants of nightmares. I have had the strange feeling that I had been lost somewhere in time, far from the reality of my world, and I could not give any reason for it.

Perhaps I had been submerged in a deep dream, one that I could not understand and that was incomprehensible to me. But now, at this moment, this was my reality, even if I struggled so hard to accept it.

"To see you so much better gives me the utmost joy," said the
young man in front of me as he tried with a trembling hand to place his stethoscope over my dress.

I pulled the ribbons to the side and unveiled a good part of my chest so he could consult me. I was certain by now that he had seen me naked just by the hesitation in his eyes. "I see undeniable signs of healing. But I beg your forgiveness …"

His words completely diminished at the apparition of Lady Cooper. I was the mysterious guest at the summer cottage of none other than the famous Lady Stella Cooper. I knew who she was but she did not seem to remember me. We had met briefly before, at the DeSalles' ball last year in the fall, and at that time I wished never to be part of her company.

Strangely, but now, she was the only soul in the world who knew that I was not dead. But she could not tell anyone; neither could I.

"All right Clifton, what is the verdict," she questioned the young man, handing me a big cup of tea. I shook my head sharply – I did not like tea.

Doctor Clifton Cooper smiled patiently as he waited for his aunt to take a plunge and settle herself onto the love seat. Then he walked around the room until the moment I took a seat on the sofa and then he made his way across the carpet to sit beside me.

I was so accustomed by now to see this odd couple coming in my little parlor every morning and demanding for me to speak. Lady Cooper was short, a bit bulky for her height, with a very large upper body but parading her grandiose bust quite proudly. Her silver hair and her dominant dark colored eyes gave her an imposing, respectful allure.

Doctor Cooper was young, with a small frame; slim, with a pair of wonderful green eyes and an abundance of dark, curly hair. His delicate facial features were a perfect match with his whole demeanor – sensitive and soft spoken. He was barely twenty-four, but in my opinion, he knew his craft very well.

"My verdict still stands," answered the doctor in a confident tone of voice. "There is no visible damage to her vocal cords. I have no plausible cause for her speech impairment. She should be perfectly able to talk."

"Your verdict is no help – she is not talking." Unsatisfied, Lady Cooper gazed at her nephew who lowered his eyes, looking at the floor. She was a bit too harsh with him and I was not in agreement with her manners. Doctor Cooper leaned over to me, and placing his left hand on my chin, he turned my face toward him. His eyes were worried but imploring.

"Please my Lady, you must tell us what happened to you. I assure you that we understand your pain but we mean no harm. We must do right by you and find your family."

I had seen the compassion of his soul in his eyes and I believed him. I opened my mouth in an attempt to respond, but the words would not form, nor would they come alive. I shook my head again and I placed my palm on his shoulder. He took my hand and kissed it. This question was asked of me each time he visited, with the expectation of an answer that I could not provide. My memories were intact, but I wished they would vanish in the same way as my ability to speak.

I was told that the pneumonia had been severe and the fever that accompanied it lingered for a long time. Doctor Cooper – whose name I still could not attach to the word "doctor", pronounced that my body was otherwise healed. But the hurt from my memories was still present.

My hostess lifted her small hand and rang the bell, a sound that made the cook aware that she was ready for the breakfast. Then she swung her legs back and forth a few times, wrestling to get up before her nephew rose and rushed to help her.

"You should not be ashamed to tell us who you are, my dear girl," she mumbled as she collected her glasses. "We can conclude for ourselves that you are an educated young lady, most likely from a good family. We are not here to judge you. Perhaps you had a fainting spell; you collapsed, and fell in the river. The villagers who found you, brought you to us unconscious and caked in the mud of the river bank. Clifton fought hard to save your life. I am certain that your family deserves to know that you are alive …"

The desperate look frozen on my face interrupted her usual comment. Instantly I placed my hand on my chest as my breathing became irregular. Clifton jumped to my side and pressed his hand against my heart.

"My dear aunt, please be gentle. She still need more time to recover. She was almost dead, remember?" Clifton's soft voice became unusually raspy, a fact that made the wrong impression on his aunt.

"Do not worry about anything my dear," she assured me. "You are safe here, in my house. Doctor Cooper, I do believe that you have some business to attend elsewhere. You must go now. I promise you this young lady will be here upon your return."

The young man blushed abundantly but retired to the door, deeply bowing to each of us. His act of daily departure became another sad part of my life here at Fairfield Park. Miss Stella's good intentions were dangerously drilling into my soul, demanding an absolute defeat that would culminate with the divulging of my secrets.

But I should understand that. I was just a stranger to them, yet they saved my life and they embraced me. They did not even know my name. When I was not present, they called me the *Lady from the River*. Another motive, too, kept Lady Cooper trying to reach out to me. She was a writer of novels with unconventional characters, she had a curious nature, and it happened that she had some time to spare between her books.

I followed Lady Cooper down to the smaller dining area where it was a time honored tradition for her to have breakfast. I like this room because the sun is so bright and generous here. Catching a glimpse of myself in the large mirror above the fireplace, I was not satisfied with my appearance.

I was too pale and too slim. I was very hungry, so I accepted without complaint the large plate of fresh baked bread and ham that Mrs. Eustace generously lay in front of me. Between sipping coffee and long pauses after every bite, I managed to make a significant difference in the amount of the food that was left over on my plate.

After breakfast, we took a slow stroll in the garden. It was Lady Cooper's usual method to cool down after her meal, but I put my on bonnet and covered my shoulder with a shawl. September was a bit chilly this year, and all those tall trees guarding both sides of the long drive produced a very cool shade. I felt the coldness of the weather all the time, and the wind and rain frightened me.

The fresh air invaded my lungs too quickly, causing me to experience a sudden dizziness. I sat down on a bench at the end of a bed of dead flowers, wondering if I should blame the dizziness on the amount of time I was enclosed within my room or on the enormity of the food I just devoured.

"My nephew is very fond of you," stated Lady Cooper unexpectedly as she joined me. "Do not misjudge my words, I find nothing wrong with this notion, but I care a great deal about him – I do not want him hurt. You have a past that we are not aware of. You are so young and you must have a family, I am sure of it. Am I right so far?"

I nodded almost with indifference. By now my family considered me dead and buried somewhere. Why awaken the dead spirits?

"I can sense right now that Clifton is not indifferent to you either, but not in the same way," she continued. "I can only imagine that a handsome young girl such as you was not short of suitors. But if there is a promise made in your behalf by another, please do not keep it secret from Clifton."

Lady Stella Cooper remained quiet waiting for my answer. Oh, promises. At the moment I did not pity myself for what I had, only for what I had lost. From the time I was brought here, I started to cultivate my own philosophy and the overwhelming conclusion was that justice was done in my regard. I deserved what had happened to me. I actually found comfort and serenity in the fact that everyone thought of me as dead.

At first it was painful for me to try to imagine the amount of distress poured upon my family, but the secrets I held were better buried with my disappearance – and the memory of the man I love, too…

"Well, I can only imagine how terrible it would be if you are married," insisted Lady Cooper. I shook my head in denial. "All right then. I think I have a solution for all of this."

Saying this, we arose from the bench to walk again, but this time we returned to the cottage. My good hostess had a stubborn expression on her face. Holding tightly to my arm she guided me to the drawing room. I recognized it as her favorite place for her writing. She put paper and pen into my hand.

"Write it all on down my dear. It is time for you to become bold and confront the stress and the situation that brought you here into our home six months ago; we need to know who you are. I can assure you, there is nothing that can possible startle me – I have heard and seen many unusual things in my life."

I took the paper and the pen in my hands as they both were shaking. I moved slowly and sat in her massive chair trying to find a way out, a pertinent excuse to not disturb the phantoms I hold hidden in my soul.

"My nephew is a noble man," she continued, lying comfortable on the purple French sofa. "He is a son of a gentleman, yet he chose to have a vocation like the ordinary commoner and he employed himself to the betterment of people. My brother was aghast and turned his back on his youngest son. But I see things differently. I took him into my home and made him feel proud of his life and choice. Fairfield Park belongs to him now. You could have quite a decent living with him. Do this for Clifton. He will accept and endure anything coming from you."

Lady Cooper closed her eyes pretending to concentrate. Her lips moved without a sound, her hands laid restfully crossed over her chest in expectation. My fingers squeezed the pen with despair as nervously I started to write.

Dear Doctor Cooper,
Will you endure hearing this?

There is a curse following me – that of men's desire, lust and passion that enfolds me regardless of any rationality or logic. I brought it upon myself. And that eventually brought me here. No one can explain the murders, along with my own drowning. Oh, that one will be quite a dilemma.

I was born beautiful and talented, a notion so much sought after by every young girl in the world. I was born privileged, in a wonderful house, with a solid assurance and a fair inheritance. I was even engaged. Overnight I lost them all.

I was well educated, destined to have a wonderful and full life, as all my accomplishments and good heritage could produce, and allow me to ascend higher in my society. I had all that I needed to become a Lady. But it did not happen.

I was loved and adored by many young men. I was also stubborn, manipulative, selfish, but very generous and goodhearted. Now, perhaps you think that is all you need to know about me.

But pay attention: I must disappoint you. My demeanor was not proper, my lovers were not ordinary, and I turned someone into a killer.

My name is Cleona Somerton.

CHAPTER 2

April 4th, 1809

THIS DAY SHOULD HAVE BEEN my wedding day.

Mother was so quiet this morning. Mrs. Longwood carried a large trunk up to the attic that contained all of my possessions I was to take to start my new life with James Connelly. What girl would not be shocked to have her wedding ruined two weeks before it happened? What a cruel embarrassment it was to me, and to my family, for that matter.

And it was him, my first visitor that morning.

"Miss Cleona, I had Mr. Connelly wait in the parlor," said Betty, our youngest housemaid, running into my bedroom holding her breath. Her eyes were enormous and her face flashed with emotions, in the anticipation of the things about to happen. And indeed, many things had happened in our family for the past month.

Unfortunate things.

I could not believe that he dared to come here, today of all days, and expect to be welcomed. I grabbed the curtain forcefully with my both hands. I looked outside through the window and saw his horse he had left by the stables, as I tried to overcome the fast pace of my heart beat.

"It's all right," I declared boldly. "I need to speak my mind to him. Today is as good as any. Let him wait. Please ask Mrs. Longwood to come to my room."

For the thousandth time in the past month, my heart was in agony. Mr. Connelly's deliberate presence here on this particular day was obviously intended to hurt me even more. My feelings oscillated between coolness and despair. I struggled with bitterness, submerging my mind too deeply in these emotions. But I needed to stay focused and prepare to travel to London to Lady Winchester's ball.

Lady Edwina de Winchester was preparing to celebrate the coming out of her niece, Elizabeth Bowen, at the ball she was hosting. Elizabeth was only seventeen years of age and she was very rich. All of London agreed that she was quite a catch. Uncle Robert was lucky to be considered for an invitation to this ball, only because her Ladyship's affection for the military. My cousin, Louisa, was beside herself with excitement when she wrote to me about it last week. She included me in the invitation, and I struggled with it, but in the end I reluctantly agreed that would attend. My disgrace would most certainly be a known fact to that polished society.

I was a little jealous of Miss Bowen and her fortune; however, a web of intrigue was forming in my mind.

I had begun by immediately improving the looks of my wardrobe. There was no time left to acquire an entire set of clothing, and I was sure that no money would be at my disposal, so I had to ask Mrs. Longwood, our housekeeper, to help me save the situation.

First, I had to have many ribbons added to some of my so called prettier dresses, and then I had to make adjustments around the bust and waist, all the while having to listen to my rescuer's righteous indignation.

"Miss Cleona, if I keep cutting, your bosom will be showing quite disturbingly. Why do you want to torment these dresses?"

"I cannot wear these old things to a ball in London, absolutely not. I want to look good and attractive and my cleavage is beautiful – why not show it? My wardrobe is so plain, and it does not suit me anymore."

"Rubbish! It suited your style before ..."

"Yes, that was before, Mrs. Longwood," I interrupted her impatiently, "before I became penniless and homeless, and if I remember clearly, I was even engaged to be married. Now I have nothing!"

The incident regarding the loss of our estate hurt as much as James Connelly's betrayal of me. My brother, Cyril, had brought upon us a disastrous situation, which had influenced the judgment and wishes of my dear fiancé as he withdrew from our engagement.

Above all, everyone in the town of Chatham and in the countryside knew about his game of cards and the loss of our fortune. I did not know what disturbed me more: the fact that I was very young and already plagued with many tragedies, or the knowledge that people were talking foolishly and gossiping about me and my family.

"We can never recover from this embarrassment," I said laying all my dresses on the bed. "It has been a month since all this happened. By the end of the summer we have to relinquish possession of the property to the new owner. My poor mama, she must be in such distress, but she hides it well."

"She is concerned about you," answered Mrs. Longwood. "However, she ultimately forgave your brother for what he had done."

It would be very hard for me to judge my mother concerning her condoning my brother's action; I asked her to write to Cyril and demand that he accompany me to the ball. It was not in her character to ever voice her opinions or to expose her true feelings. He would never be a rogue in her eyes.

As Cyril, Cecilia, and I grew up, Mother was the rescuer between us and our vigilant and strict father, a former Colonel in the army, minimizing our frequent errors to the point of presenting them as future qualities. Father endured the compassion of her heart until she went about her homemaking duties, and then he would make sure that our iniquities received punishment.

Ultimately, our mother was so adored by us. She always tried to embrace us in her goodness, in which case my brother and I failed the test repeatedly. I was opinionated and always had an excuse for my unladylike demeanor at all times.

My sister, Cecilia, was a natural, however; the first born in the family, and eight years older than me. She had that quality of poise, intelligence, and amiability with no effort on her part. She had mastered the ability of engaging in interminable salon conversation, as was expected of a very bright young lady to do. She and Cyril, who is two years younger than her, were very close.

"You cannot fight against your fate," Mrs. Longwood said, changing the subject as she collected the pile of dresses. "I have said this so many times – when those damn mirrors started to break, they released the curse. It will not stop until the third soul is taken. Two are already gone – your uncle and your father both died in mysterious ways, *accidents*, as they were called. There are no such things as accidents."

"Yes, Mrs. Longwood," I replied trying to ignore her rambling, "and please have my dresses nicely done by the end of the week."

Mrs. Longwood always insisted that my uncle's and father's deaths were not accidents, but I had no understanding of the meaning of her words, and I did not believe in the existence of a curse. I sat on the edge of the bed while desperation was rising in my soul again, as I struggled not to cry.

"I believe that the loss of my inheritance ended any possibility for me to find a suitor again," I said to Mrs. Longwood as she was leaving the room. That represented my supreme concern. "Our dear neighbors, Mr. and Mrs. Parker, offered us shelter, but what will become of us? I must do something about it. But what is there for me to do?"

Bertha Longwood dropped my dresses on the floor and forced me to sit up, pushing me towards the mirror and pointing to my reflection in it. The girl looking back at me had a certain wild beauty, with perfect and symmetrical complexion, high cheek bones, very large blue eyes, full and deeply curved lips, and long blond hair that curled sensuously over her shoulders.

"Miss Cleona, you are more beautiful than is required to capture the attention of a gentleman. What is there for you to do? Upon my word, you can bring a man to madness if you would but put your mind to it."

"You are wrong, Mrs. Longwood. It seems to me that Mr. Connelly's affection for me did not stand the test. I have learned that as of yesterday he is newly engaged."

CHAPTER 3

MR. CONNELLY STOOD BY THE window, waiting for me, fingering his cravat nervously. He was a very handsome young man indeed, very well educated, and an aspiring composer. His family was not very well known, but the young Mr. Connelly had a great musical talent and he had high hopes of one day being employed at the court.

For now, the only title he deserved was to be my former fiancé. He did not move until I asked him to sit, and he thanked me very politely but lethargically. He was not generally a good dresser, but to my surprise, his attire today was very well put together this time – a dark blue suit and white shirt. His wide maroon cravat was tied in a bow, the fashion of the day. When he dared to lift his head and look at me, his brown eyes opened half way and I saw his manner had changed instantly to distress.

He tried to keep a dignified posture, but he looked pitiful; at this moment my resentment for him was rising. I watched him, wondering how I could possibly have been so tormented by this young man, and lost in love with him. I vowed then that never again would any man bestow such an affliction on me!

"Mr. Connelly, I believe your new fiancé would be unhappy to hear of your request to visit me, and I am not sure that I would disagree with her," I said. I started this statement coolly and my voice changed in intensity.

"Please," he replied, brushing his fingers through his reddish-blonde hair, "I need to tell you something…"

"It would accomplish nothing," I interrupted him, quite irritated. "There is no conversation that we could have that would be beneficial to me."

"But I need to explain my feelings for you …"

"Please understand that your feelings do not matter to me anymore. I have paid for the feelings I had for you. I once expected to spend a lifetime with you, but all of that is gone, now. You have no right to come here and seek me out – to attempt to explain anything, when I already know the answers."

"It is not what you believe," he said and his eyes began to fill with tears. I became somewhat curious, but I was determined to tell him all that I could about his despicable actions towards me.

"On the contrary, it is exactly what I believe. It has been made perfectly clear to me that your change of wishes in the association of your family to mine was solely because of our lost possessions…"

"The circumstances of that incident were very ambiguous to everyone," he said timidly. His hands were resting on his lap in a defensive posture.

"And naturally, no further investigation was made. If you had inquired further, you would have learned that we were deceitfully dispossessed…"

"I know!" he interrupted me. I looked at him, perplexed. I could not believe that he would know the whole truth. "There is this story circulating about how Colonel Radisson played a prank on your brother which concluded with the loss of your estate."

"And should I assume that the story of the prank would have affected you differently a month ago?"

"Perhaps not," he whispered, "but my parents are difficult

people with whom to trifle. I could not allow myself to be disinherited and risk both of us being penniless."

I stood up, enraged, and he followed me.

"Indeed, you could not" I said, ready to dismiss him, hurt and tired by our conversation that was going nowhere. "It appears to me that the final conclusion remains unchanged. So, please tell me what is that you want, and then leave my presence forever!"

"I am sorry for what happened to your family. It is horrible to be left with nothing. I just want you to know that you have my sincere sympathy."

His words made me angry and humiliated. So this was how he and most people think of me – helpless and pitiful; poor and futureless. He dared to approach me and bestow upon me his false apology and sympathy, only to make me understand that my misery was not forgotten. I suspected that Miss Linton had sent him to me, and coached him. And the poor stupid man thought he was doing right by me. But I kept my head high.

I stepped closer and looked into his eyes.

"Thank you, Mr. Connelly, but I can function quite nicely without you and your sympathy…"

"I love you," he said unexpectedly and his face became grave. He moved towards me with his arms opened in an attempt to reach my shoulders, but I stepped back.

"I beg your pardon," I said, and my eyes grew bigger, as I could not hide the surprise provoked by his unexpected confession.

"I still love you;" he continued, coming towards me. "That I cannot change, nor do I wish to. I cannot banish my feelings for you. I must confess to you my anguish and suffering."

Regardless of my anger for him at that very moment, a devious idea passed through my mind, a Machiavellian, ruthless plan. I wanted James Connelly to feel a great deal of uneasiness in his new and rushed engagement to this rich Miss Linton, for whom

I was abandoned. And that would be my own kind of revenge.

"You still love me? But you are engaged!"

"I cannot bear the fact that I was forced to give you away," he said and took my right hand and kissed it. "I am in pain, day and night. I beg you not to hate me."

But however well I could master some words to the point of incivility, cruelty is what I desired to deliver. Perhaps I should test a little Mrs. Longwood's predictions about my abilities to induce madness.

My mind triggered one memory of me and James Connelly, the second time we met again while we were attending Mr. Scott's picnic. He recognized me as the girl from the piano store and he followed me around that entire afternoon. I enjoyed his game, and at one point I attempted to hide from him. I ran into the woods and he ran after me. I proved to be a clumsy country girl during the chase and I fell to the ground, leaving half of my dress ripped off and hanging on the branch of a tree.

I was just an innocent girl of fifteen years old and he was just a very young man. My breasts were clearly showing through my transparent undergarment; I was unable to say a word to have him stop coming toward me.

But his eyes, as he gazed at me, were enormous. He took off his coat and offered it to me. I took it and I ran away to change my clothes, swearing to never see him again in my lifetime.

But the next day he was at my uncle's door in London, requesting my opinion about his music and to help with his composition. From that day on his eyes were always watching me, as if my dress was once again torn off.

"Tell me again, Mr. Connelly, do you still remember that little incident between you and me at Mr. Scott's picnic?" I asked him, smiling as pleasantly as I could.

"I do, very well ..." His eyes instantly and without hesitation, lowered their focus from my face to my chest.

"Well, then," I said touching his face and resting my fingers on his lips. "I want you never to forget it. Think at me always and of what you have lost. You may leave now. Good day, Mr. Connelly."

I curtsied and left him behind, speechless. Not being classy or civil was quite enjoyable, and I felt no guilt about it. No proper and well raised young woman would dare to bring up an embarrassing moment such as this, but I needed for him to remember it in order to spark the visual sight of my words. He would need a few minutes to ponder upon them and take them to heart. He would suffer some more, or return to his fiancé, whatever he wished.

I collapsed on the sofa in the parlor. The strength I felt earlier in the day was shaken a little, but this was temporary. My determination was unchanged. Nothing would change my mind now, about my new plan to be as attractive as possible and to make a grand entry at the ball. I knew with a certainty that James Connelly's love for me was useless and hopeless. For me, there was no going back.

I would have to complete my plan of having my dear brother redeem himself by doing the only decent thing left for both of us: marrying well. Of course, I had someone in mind for him, the perfect prospect. I could not see any reason for Cyril not to go along with this plan. Miss Elizabeth Bowen was young, related to the royals, and rich enough to repurchase Chatham Hill.

All Cyril had to his benefit at the moment was his handsome appearance, and I intended to use that to its fullest.

CHAPTER 4

EARLY THE NEXT MORNING I left for London. Saying goodbye to Mother was the most difficult thing I have ever done. I wished I was not leaving, but staying at home was not solving any of my problems. Mother and I would eventually be together at Stonebridge, the residence of Mr. and Mrs. Parker. I felt extremely tired, but I was making myself ready to venture into a new life, not knowing where and when I would find relief for my desperate situation.

Last night I did not sleep much. I had a strange dream that Uncle Edward came to visit me. Chatham Hill was empty and I was its sole resident. He was still young and handsome, dressed in the uniform of an army officer. I could not clearly see his face during his visit, but he did look familiar and I knew it was him. He did not want to stay for dinner, but he expected me to let him rest in Cyril's old apartment. Once inside the bedroom, he removed his coat, lay on the bed, and closed his eyes.

"I am exhausted and I wish to leave now. Please, do not hold me here anymore," he said to me.

With those words I awakened. I arose from my bed and ran down the hall. I opened the door to the apartment, but the room was empty. The dream was real to me; not a figment of my imagination. The bed seemed to be untouched and it was cold. Of course it would be cold; Uncle Edward died very long ago in a hunting accident while trying to teach Uncle Robert, my father's younger brother, how to use a shot gun. At that point, I was quite frightened by my own irrational behavior and my vivid imaginings, stirred by Mrs. Longwood's horrible predictions.

She and her husband were very old and they had been Uncle Edward's servants too – father inherited the two of them with the mansion. When we were very young, Mrs. Longwood would frighten us, Cecilia, Cyril, and me, with legends about ghosts and curses. She was firmly convinced that Chatham Hill was cursed when long ago, three mirrors in the mansion suddenly shattered without a reason.

Soon after that, my uncle died. A few years later my father, who had inherited the mansion, died too. Now, she was predicting that one more soul must be taken.

But back in my room, I could no longer fall asleep. The words of my uncle from my dream haunted me. I could not explain why they made such an impact on me, because they were not real and had not been spoken by a living person.

Then, without a reason, I reflected upon my life with all of the mental anguish and physical pain I had endured. When was this nightmare going to end if this was only the beginning? The past month was like a tale of terror that had turned real. Being exhausted was conquering me, but my spirit was restless.

The journey to London was longer than I had expected. The rain and the fog played a large part in the delay, and some of my fellow travelers were ill. But when the coach arrived at the station and I saw Louisa waiting for me in my uncle's carriage, I gathered all of my energy for her sake.

As we turned onto St. John Street, my attention was caught

by the shape and size of a small cathedral that was previously unknown to me.

"Is this church new or has it always been here? I cannot remember."

My cousin's demeanor turned exuberant as she was so eager to tell me about all of the changes that had occurred in the past two years during my absence. I braced myself to receive a great deal of information in the shortest amount of time.

"You are right, this is new. The Duke of Winchester built it last year. He is the eldest son of Lady Edwina de Winchester. He is a wonderful landlord, a philanthropist, a helper of the poor. All the people around here love him, although he is quiet and distant at times. It is too bad that he is not happy. His wife died four years ago."

"Oh, that is unfortunate!"

"Noble people have their share of pain and sorrow, as we all do," concluded my cousin. "But, looking on the bright side, he is the most eligible bachelor in town after the princes Edward and Adolphus."

"Louisa!"

My cousin was born exactly nine months after my birth. We look like sisters, both of us with blue eyes, blonde hair, and with fair skin that looks as if it came from a cream pitcher. Louisa was somewhat more fragile in stature, but she was determined and energetic.

"It is true, my dear. Why not admit it? You will see him at the ball, with all of those females chasing him, young and old."

"I am sure I will not encounter him at all, my dear. I do not have any such hope as this. How old is he?"

"Perhaps thirty-two. But he is so handsome…although he is also referred to as The Mysterious Duke."

"The Mysterious Duke? Why is that?"

"After he lost his wife, we do not see him too often in public, in London. But whenever he comes to the balls, he always looks sad, and mysterious like he wishes to be invisible. He does not dance at all because he is afraid of false encouragement. Some of the females become almost hysterical in his presence."

"Perhaps he loved his wife very much and he does not want to replace her or taint her memory. How did she die?"

"She was pregnant; that is all I know." Louisa's voice trembled without hiding the disappointment for the lack of knowledge about this important detail.

"Indeed, I pity him and I admire his steadfastness." I grabbed tight to my cousin arm. In that moment my heart was full of compassion and admiration for this man, a stranger to me, who possessed such a remarkable character.

"Some believe that he has the right to be married and be happy again, but he does not seem to entertain the idea," she continued smiling to me. "I think he desires some sort of absolution by being single and miserable."

"Perhaps it does not make it right with his heart. He must be left alone to choose for himself. I never expected Mother to ask my opinion or my permission in a matter such as this."

"But you have an opinion …"

My voice turned hoarse, sounding as rusty as an old gate hinge, and my whole attitude was bitter and unpleasant.

"Which I am ready to give, if asked. But I cannot assume I am the most qualified person to advise anyone in any way. At any rate, I disagree with strangers getting involved in others' affairs."

* * *

"Is there anything bothering you?" Louisa's smile disappeared. My unexpected angry outburst shocked her from her complacency. She put her arm around me and I regretted my harsh words. "I feel so much uneasiness in your answers, and this makes me aware that I am not very diplomatic now."

"Oh, Louisa! I am trying to pretend that I am courageous, but this conversation about the Duke's honorability arouses more anger in me against James Connelly. This is an expected reaction and it makes me even more hostile toward him. After his visit to me at Chatham Hill, I still feel this burning desire to punish him."

"I am certain he deserves it my dear," agreed Louisa, "because to continue to show you his affection, after breaking his engagement to you and becoming engaged to another, was senseless and cruel."

The whole time until dinner, Uncle Robert had that same undefined smile, while talking, reading or walking in and out of the house as we waited for Cyril. He resembled my father in so many ways, and that made him my favorite uncle. His retirement pension brings the family a decent income, enough to secure some money for his two daughters, Louisa and Caroline, and to pay Anna Henry, the governess, and Mrs. Topher, the cook. Still, although he was comfortably placed among the middle class of society, he managed to remain very much aloof from it.

I could not help myself but to wonder if he remembered anything about that day when his Uncle Edward died. At that time, he and my father were in their uncle's care and living at Chatham Hill.

I wavered in my immediate intention to inquire about that event; it happened so long ago and Uncle Robert had only been thirteen years old – his knowledge would be minimal.

Cyril arrived after we had sat down for dinner. I ran into his arms, forgetting my much tortured feelings that I had for him during the past weeks; I had not seen him since the scandal began. He was so affectionate to me and so clearly humble that in my heart I forgave him immediately. There was no way not to like Cyril, after being in his charming presence for just a few minutes, and this was what I was counting on.

Later that evening, I summoned my brother into the parlor. I did not allow him too much time to indulge in feelings of defeat and self-pity. Time was of the essence and I could not tolerate these feelings from him.

"Cyril," I said, forcing my brother to sit beside me on the sofa, "We need to form a plan to counteract the effect of the Colonel Radisson's despicable trick that forced you into signing over the estate papers of Chatham Hill to his nephew, Captain Clark."

"What a horrible charade," said my brother, a bit concerned about my wish to sit so close to him. When we were children that meant war. "Besides, I did not seriously think them capable of such an absurdity," he said as he waved his hands in a disappointed and defeated manner.

"This matter is very grave. Mother, you, and I are homeless and penniless. With the loss of Chatham Hill we have lost all of our income and I lost my fiancé. We did find promise of shelter with our dear Mr. and Mrs. Parker at Stonebridge, but we need a more stable environment. Captain Clark is giving us until September to vacate the premises."

"Cecilia will have us, and Uncle Robert, too."

I gazed at my brother with spite. I was right. By now, he had totally accepted our new situation as a definite life style, and he never bothered to be concerned about finding other means to overcome it.

"Certainly they will, but I am trying to make you understand that neither of these arrangements is acceptable – not for the entire length of our lives. Mother needs you; she needs your support, as you promised Father."

"What can I do? There is nothing I can do anymore." Cyril's voice was desperate but I was determined to convince him of my new plan. "You seem to have given a lot of thought to this. What you would you have me do?"

"As you know, tomorrow we are attending a ball at the mansion of Lady de Winchester."

"Cleona," interrupted my brother, "you *are* aware that we are not particularly invited."

"Yes, I am aware of that fact, Cyril, but Uncle Robert was invited and he is the head of the family. It is within his rights to bring with him any guest or guests he chooses, and he *will* ask us to attend. At the ball I want you to be extremely charming to Miss Elizabeth Bowen," I followed in a softer tone of voice, "She is very young and very rich. This would be a splendid match, do you not think?"

"Cleona, is this what you want of me?" My brother looked at me astonished and in denial. His dark blue eyes turned even darker for a moment. "To pursue a marriage with a rich girl I may not care for, all for the money and the social standing? My dear little sister, you know I will not consider …"

"Yes, you will!" I spoke in a low and forceful tone, and my foot vigorously stamped the floor. "You are the son of a gentleman and marriage is a part of life. It can be pleasant and gratifying, and I am sure that Miss Bowen is as good as any other. "

"But this is ridiculous! So, you expect me to marry no other but Miss Bowen? Why would you think she would have me, of all the other gentlemen in London?"

"Because she may be a sensitive lady and she may find you in need of assistance. Some women are very attracted to handsome, suffering young men, upon whom they can be their God-sent rescuer…"

"That is a humiliating prospect …" I was aware of it. But there was no more humiliation one could suffer than being fetched and shifted from one relative to another.

"Yes it is. But would you rather accept that the property which has been in our family for centuries was lost forever, so stupidly at a game of cards. Which of these prospects is more humiliating? We have an enemy, Cyril. It has been a known fact that Colonel Radisson has hated our father for many years, over a promotion he lost long ago. He blamed our father for it and swore revenge upon our family. He used Mr. Sutton to corner you and fall into his trap. We cannot bow down and disappear into nothingness. We owe this to our parents. My dear Cyril, the only revenge worthy of our enemies is to let them see that they failed, that they did not succeed."

"And my part in all this is to charm and tempt rich Miss Bowen into marriage?"

"I see you have an ironic turn. One of us will have to marry well. But you have the greatest chance of making my plan succeed, and I will help."

"Well, my dear, you have done half of the work already; you chose the bride. Let us pray that you will not be too disappointed if our lady does not turn out to be at all compassionate."

"She is not the only one you could pursue."

I wished I had not said that, but I considered the possibility.

"I assume my fate is sealed. Cleona, you have changed. I once had a very sweet and loving sister…"

"I grew up! I once had a fiancé, a home, and an inheritance. Now, all I have are enemies, but at the same time, I hope, a brother who is logical and who can still think rational thoughts. Think about what I have said and tell me if your little sister speaks nonsense. I will never again have a future of gratifying comfort, but you should not ignore the chance. Cyril, I need for you to understand: I depend upon you and Mother depends upon you. Chatham Hill is no more. I dare to hope for you, and pray that you will succeed. Without you, our family will be lost forever."

I had to face reality, however cruel; there was no turning back, now. I vowed that I would not leave London defeated. Someone, somehow, would be the one to put their hand out and pull us back from the abyss. That someone had to be our savior, and I prayed that her name was Miss Elizabeth Bowen.

CHAPTER 5

IT IS NOT EASY TO CHANGE your appearance with nothing more than old clothes that have been improved, but considering the qualification of my tailor, my appearance was beyond my expectations; although not as satisfactory as I would have liked, according to my own standards. Seeing my brother's and Louisa's reactions, I gathered that I had succeeded in rising above the plain and ordinary.

"I assume fashion has changed," said my brother offering me his arm.

My ball dress was faded but the gold ribbons around my bust gave it a complete new look. I also had to shorten the sleeves and take in a few inches from both sides of the skirt (perhaps a bit too much) because it barely allowed me to walk.

"I only wish to look different."

With the multitude of carriages ahead of us, we had a long walk to the front of the palace at the other end of Covington Street. The massive building was four stories high, made from dark colored brick, bold and impressive. The windows of every room seemed to be lit on both sides of the alley. I had never seen such a popular event like this one, and I was happy to enter with another large group, unobserved by the hostess who was greeting her guests at the main entrance.

As we entered on the right side of the hallway, Louisa recognized a few of the people and she introduced them to me by name. My uncle joined a group of other officers, and he quickly engaged with them about military affairs. I observed that the eyes of a few gentlemen were gazing at me in silent admiration.

One gentleman in particular was standing in the company of a few ladies but seemed absent from their conversation. He was handsome but not imposing. The light from above shone over his caramel color hair, catching my eyes with a very dignified posture and noble features. I thought I would like very much to meet him, and I smiled. He seemed to be puzzled by my interest but remained aloof and undisturbed.

I walked around the corridors, admiring the magnificent rooms with beautiful paintings and luxurious furniture. The expensive sofas and chairs were moved against the wall to allow the guests the liberty of walking and dancing. All of the ladies were splendidly dressed and were escorted by courteous gentlemen.

On one side of the palace was all the exquisite society, and to my left were all the military families with their more plain garments. For me it was natural to choose the right side of the palace. After I realized I was getting some attention and I had accomplished my goal to make myself somewhat attractive, my next task was to spot Miss Bowen and to be sure that Cyril was introduced to her. If I saw Mr. Connelly, I would do my best to avoid him because I would not wish to renew our acquaintance.

I felt so good and daring, with such high hopes of fulfilling my mission. At that point I believed that all was possible. But my first problem, I had to admit, troubled me very much. I did not know anyone there for a proper introduction required by the esteemed society – not even my uncle. The only advantage I had in this circumstance was to be anonymous in regard to my identity and my condition.

"Oh, look," said Louisa, "Lady Winston is coming towards us."

A tall, beautiful young woman with gorgeous red hair, full of grace and wearing an elegant silk and white lace dress, was coming straight toward us. I stopped from walking and followed her with my eyes.

"How do you know her?" I asked my all-knowing cousin.

"She is the widow of Lord Francis Winston. He died a year ago, after spending five years in the West Indies. It was an arranged marriage; she was only seventeen. Now she is in pursuit of the Duke of Winchester."

"Was she poor?" I asked intrigued.

"Not quite poor. She came from a good family, but her father lost a fortune in America and he came back penniless." This did not augur well with me – it seemed that we had some things in common, and she was potentially my competition. Perhaps she would sympathize with me since we both shared a similar social situation.

"I do not believe she is coming to speak with us." But I was wrong. She addressed my brother directly, completely ignoring Louisa and me.

"Sir! Lady de Winchester, our hostess, is anxious for you to pay your respects, along with your company. "

We followed her, amazed by the unexpected fortune of gaining access to an introduction to one of the most important people in London, unless she was calling for us to inquire about our shameful intrusion. I expected Lady Edwina de Winchester to be tall and grave, but to my eyes she appeared to be a tiny, fragile, but still beautiful lady with natural light brown hair still untarnished by the passing of time.

On her right, to my surprise, was none other than the handsome gentleman to whom I had smiled earlier. My brother made a deep bow. I curtsied, too, but my nerves were stretched beyond control. Were we about to pay the price for being infamous?

"Your Grace, Lady de Winchester, my deepest apologies," said my brother, with a quavering voice but keeping a straight posture. "My name is Cyril Somerton, at your service. May I introduce my sister, Miss Cleona Somerton and my cousin, Miss Louisa Somerton?"

Her eyes moved from my brother to Louisa but they rested a moment longer on me. Her face lightened with a generous smile. Louisa and I curtsied again. I liked her instantly.

"May I introduce to you my son," she said, "Lord Grayson Evington, Duke of Winchester, and your guide, Lady Winston?"

I could not believe that I was in the presence of the Duke of Winchester himself, the person with whom I already had so much admiration.

Meeting his eyes again, I felt embarrassed – my dress was too revealing, my hair was too loose, and my whole attire was nothing more than a cheap attempt to be elegant. But he did not take his eyes off of me. I found him to be more handsome then to my first glance, his light color hair and blue eyes was fascinating to me.

"Where is your residence, Mr. Somerton?" asked Lady de Winchester, focusing her attention on Cyril.

My brother looked at me alarmed.

"We previously resided at Chatham Hill, your Ladyship," I boldly answered in his stead, while waves of emotion washed over my face. There was no reason to hide or be reticent about our misfortune – sooner or later everyone would know and laugh behind our backs. At least now I could face the ones who would ridicule us.

"Previously? Did you move?" Her Ladyship's question was polite and unassuming.

"Under some unfortunate circumstances, your Ladyship," I barely whispered, "we will be forced from our home at the end of the summer."

"Lady de Winchester," Lady Winston interrupted, with an expression of surprise, "I am sure you remember their story. I believe it was Mr. Reeves who mentioned something about it." Then she turned to the Duke. "Your Grace, I hope you remember it!"

At that very moment, I began to dislike Lady Winston. Her manner was so cold and excessively proud. It was obvious that she was relishing the retelling of our unfortunate circumstances and the story was enjoyable to her.

"I did not pay too much attention to Mr. Reeves, I am afraid," answered the Duke of Winchester without looking at her. "I am sure the Somerton's situation is not ideal," he said to me. "I do hope you will find a proper replacement for Chatham Hill."

"Thank you, Your Grace, we already have," I answered with gratitude. The sound of his voice was grave, but soft and tranquil to my ear. "We are blessed to have wonderful friends in our neighbors, Mr. and Mrs. Parker, who offered us shelter at their residence in Stonebridge."

At that moment, Louisa excused herself to go and seek the company of her father. I believe she was more than a little embarrassed, afraid of seeing Cyril and me exposed and scrutinized.

"Perhaps you might describe to her Ladyship all of the circumstances surrounding Chatham Hill," asked Lady Winston with an unhidden cold smile, moving closer to the Duke of Winchester. Instead, he moved to a table, pretending to suddenly desire a glass of champagne. Embarrassed, Lady Winston continued to harass us.

"I am sure it is a very intriguing story; quite sad, I understand. It is very unpleasant to find oneself out on the street."

Lady de Winchester, fortunately, denied her companion's suggestion. Her delicate and small frame shook vehemently.

"I do not wish to hear it, my dear. This is not the place for such discussions. But I do wish to assure you, my dear friends that no one will be on the streets when I have so much room to spare."

"Your Ladyship is most gracious, considering that we are strangers to you," I said, gratefully bowing to her.

"Nonsense! I am very familiar with your family. Are you visiting in London?"

"At my uncle's home, Colonel Robert Somerton."

"Lovely! I will send all of you an invitation for dinner."

While I was having this pleasant conversation with Lady De Winchester, I was so happy and encouraged by her wonderful attitude that was so inexplicable to me. At that point, I was not in denial. The incident of my family's ruin had traveled to London, most likely circulated by none other than Colonel Radisson. By now, everyone surely knew that we were in desperate straits.

If we did not inspire mercy, then we surely inspired ridicule.

In the meantime, Mr. Cleaves, Miss Rowe, and Lord and Lady DeSalles, joined our group and the introductions continued. They, too, asked if we were 'those ones'. My brother tried to remain calm the whole time, but I felt so much uneasiness in his demeanor.

If the story that was circulating about us might be the one mentioned to me by James Connelly, none of these new people we encountered made unpleasant comments about it. My expectations were for the worst. But, as long as no one was laughing in our face, I was convinced that perhaps it had happened to others, before.

Actually, if it had not been for the spiteful comments of the dreadful Lady Winston, I could relax a little...

"Correct me if I am wrong," Lady Winston started again, sipping from a glass containing a red-orange punch. "Were you not engaged to be married to the talented Mr. Connelly? I think I just spotted him in the crowd, accompanied by his new fiancé.

What a pity that was all spoiled!"

Visibly, she had a hard time hiding her antipathy for me; but my full attention was given to our dear hostess. I was grateful for her sensible nature and for the reasonable attitude of her son. And for Mr. Connelly – I knew precisely where his thoughts would linger, and they were not on the woman by his side.

"This is not the forum to place all of Miss Somerton's misfortunes on display; she is very well aware of them," the Duke said impatiently.

"Certainly," agreed Lady DeSalles. "You poor child, you must try to forget him."

Lady Winston could not find a single soul to empathize with her insolence, and because she was risking the Duke of Winchester's disgust, she became less hostile. I was jubilant. This little victory and our acceptance by these noble people almost made me cry.

"Your Ladyship," I said to Lady de Winchester, "we are most anxious to meet the celebrated young lady of the evening. It would be a great honor to make the acquaintance of your niece."

"Oh, of course – Elizabeth. She is in the next room playing upon the fortepiano. I will send someone to fetch her. Gemma, dear, go bring Elizabeth to join our group. But I must warn you, Miss Somerton, she is quite timid."

Lady Winston left to bring Elizabeth to us, very unhappy to have been chosen to carry out this mission. I could hear someone playing the fortepiano, but the performance was not very good; however, I could not call it intolerable. In a few minutes, Lady Winston returned with a young brunette, tall and slim, who could very well be considered handsome.

My worries were gone – Cyril could easily like her. Immediately he caught Miss Bowen's attention. His gallantries flattered her and she smiled. Her aunt was quite surprised.

"I have to admit, Miss Bowen," said my brother putting on his charming smile, "I was quite enraptured to hear you perform upon the fortepiano so majestically. It was a very great accomplishment, indeed."

She was pleased, but she did not say much except to be thankful for his complement.

"Miss Somerton, do you play the fortepiano? Do you draw or do you speak French?" Lady de Winchester asked me.

"Yes, Your Grace," I answered politely, holding my back as straight as a plumb line. "My accomplishments are average, I suppose."

"I am sure they are good enough to keep me company."

"Thank you, your Ladyship, I would be most happy to oblige you."

"Have you considered how you will use your talents to ensure your survival?" asked Lady Winston, still in her aggressive mood. From the moment she observed the generous opening of my cleavage she could no longer strike a smile.

"What do you mean, Gemma?" inquired Lady DeSalles quite puzzled – and she was not the only one.

"Playing fortepiano, foreign languages, and good skills of drawing are common for governesses," was her victorious answer, placing her hands on her waist in an attractive posture. Her body was quite slim and attractive, but her dress did not do it justice.

Everyone became silent. Miss Rowe began to cough and Lady DeSalles blinked uncomfortably. I was sure that no one knew how to stop Lady Winston's hostile questions. But I had long foreseen this kind of venomous comments and I swore to behave like a lady, even if socially I was no longer considered one.

"Indeed, I had not considered that possibility," I said very calmly while my body felt a certain rise in temperature and the color of my complexion almost foretold a fainting spell. "I was under the impression that such talents are accomplishments that every well born young lady is taught to desire, and not simply tools to secure employment as a governess. If that is the case, I must praise my own governess, as she is a more accomplished lady than I."

"Bravo, my dear, the perfect answer," said Lady de Winchester clapping her little hands, relieved to have me still standing against my aggressor. "This tone of conversation is not to be borne. A lady is always a lady. Let us see if your talent as a dancer is to be considered. You would not refuse Lord Evington the next dance, would you?"

This time it was the Duke of Winchester's turn to panic. He looked to his mother, petrified by her proposal. His actions would have hurt me extremely, if I had not known the reason behind his behavior. Still, I jumped to his salvation.

"Oh, I have been made aware that Duke of Winchester does not enjoy dancing."

"Nonsense! Surely he will dance with you," insisted my hostess.

We both bowed to her Ladyship and left to go to the ballroom. Behind us, Lady Winston turned pale. Many people were stunned to see us lining for the dance. Everyone knew him, but I was unknown; however, I assumed I would not be unknown for long. As he escorted me to the dance floor, he kept quiet and I felt somewhat unwanted.

"Rest assured, Your Grace," I said softly, "you are not in a dangerous situation with me. You are safe."

"I do not understand," he responded, but he was visibly still uncomfortable.

"As you are aware, I am the infamous one here. There is no expectation for me to be involved with anyone at all or to have any pretenses."

"What made you think this? I certainly apologize to you if I have offended you in any way…" our hands united for the dance and for a second I felt their touch like a caress.

The orchestra started the music for the new dance that had been brought to England from the continent, the waltz, and he was close enough for me to see that his blue eyes were deeply immersed in sadness.

"You did not offend me in the least," I started to deny regretting to have started this conversation. "Your reputation made me a bit uncomfortable to force you to dance."

"Oh, my reputation … so what is said about me?"

"I would not know any of the details." It was too late to stop me from talking, pouring out my own opinion about him. "Certainly, this is my only chance to speak with you alone, and I must confess how much I respectfully admire you."

This time his right hand held mine firmly, and then it happened: he smiled at me. That smile was so pleasant that made me stumble as we moved around the dance floor.

"I will tell you, then," he said gently, "that I deserve no admiration. I am astonished that an amazing young lady such as you would have such feelings…"

"You also have the reputation of being a great and generous gentleman. I passed by the St. John Street church the other day."

"The Lord deserves to be praised by all of his people. I made that possible for them," he responded with a natural modesty.

"And the food they receive there every Sunday?"

"We will always have the poor with us."

"Thank you," I said softly. My hand rested on his arm and for a short moment I forgot about my pain.

"There is nothing for which to thank me."

"Yes, there is; for saving me from Lady Winston. One day I wish to have the chance to explain to you about my family's affairs. What has been made known to you is most likely not entirely accurate." My last words sounded desperate and unnecessary.

"Lady Winston is one person you can ignore, if you please," he said gently, holding my waist as we spun on the dance. "You are not required to give me any kind of report regarding your family. But I would be most happy to listen if you desired to talk about them."

The dance was over, but to my astonishment, Lord Evington's hand rested a few moments longer on my waist before he separated from me.

"Thank you for agreeing to dance with me, as uncomfortable as it must be for you…" He was a perfect gentleman and offered me his arm.

"It was my pleasure to dance with you Miss Somerton."

He brought me back to his mother's presence, but not rushing, excused himself, bowed to me and left. He was so civil, but so mysterious. On the other hand, I could not decipher him, nor could I understand why Lady de Winchester had insisted that he dance with me.

My brother was still in the company of Miss Bowen, along with some other gentlemen, but it was obvious that he was her favorite. Someone in the crowd was calling my name. I turned to see Louisa coming rapidly toward me, with shining eyes and large smile. She pulled me aside.

"Were you the one dancing with the Duke of Winchester?" she asked with juvenile giggling. Mr. Connelly saw you … he was there at the fortepiano and he saw you and the Duke. He was mortified. He still loves you, I could easily observe it."

"Sweet revenge! I am satisfied."

"How did you manage to dance with the Duke?" Louisa continued to ask, curious as always.

"Lady de Winchester strongly encouraged me."

"What?" My cousin's beautiful blue eyes were open to their

widest. "Do you mean to tell me her Ladyship asked you to dance with her son?"

"Yes dear, and she made him obey!" We both started to giggle.

"What an extraordinary stroke of good fortune," admitted my cousin, looking for a place to sit.

"Yes, it is. And it is not over. Look," I said and my head pointed to the opposite side of the room. "Cyril is very much liked by Miss Bowen. This is what I wished for. I can rest now. We are saved."

"You look happy and beautiful, Cleona. All the men in this room had their eyes on you and half of them want to marry you. You produced quite a stir; I have seen it from the other side of the ballroom."

For me it was not over. I asked Lady Edwina's permission to play her fortepiano and she encouraged me with no hesitation.

While waiting for the fortepiano to become open for a performance, I changed my mind a hundred times. It was when James Connelly, predicting my intensions, made his way to closely listen to me and observe my technique, that I realized I must follow my plan. I must not be weak and a coward – not now. By the middle of my performance of Haydn and Mozart pieces, I had a few ladies and gentlemen surrounding me. I played a new piece by a young composer from Austria named Beethoven. All eyes were on me.

This was my greatest opportunity. I would be noticed and someone would be capable of overlooking my situation, finding me desirable, and loving me. Indeed, I had little. But what I had would serve me well. I played with passion and emotion. When I finished playing, many of the guests applauded. Among them were the Duke of Winchester, the suffering Mr. Connelly, and another young man who had been in my shadow the whole evening.

Later, on the way out of the palace, I was holding my brother's arm. Suddenly, Cyril was trying to hurry my exit, but it was too late. A young man was in front of us, respectfully bowing.

Cyril had no choice. "Cleona, may I introduce Captain Clark?"

CHAPTER 6

MORE THAN A WEEK HAD PASSED since the ball without a dinner invitation from Lady de Winchester, giving me a great deal of time to become anxious and to keep revisiting my surprise encounter with Captain Clark. All of the wonderful events that took place at the ball began to blur in comparison to the final incident of my being so unusually introduced to Captain Clark.

If I had planned, hoped, and prayed for all the things that came true, I never gave any thought about ever meeting the most unwanted person in the world, in my estimation. I was not ready for it. Now, days later, I was ashamed of my behavior. Why did I run? Why did I not stay there and stand up to him face to face, as I did to James Connelly. Was I that weak?

At first, not knowing his true identity, I was pleased by Captain Clark's attention. What a horrible situation, though, to encourage someone you despise. It was so cruel of him not to come to me during the ball and make himself known. It would have ruined a wonderful evening, certainly, but my dignity would not have suffered.

Oh – that is correct – I had no dignity remaining, according to Lady Winston!

I wished that I could erase her and Captain Clark from my memory. But I certainly did not regret making the acquaintances of Lady Edwina, Lady DeSalles, the sweet Miss Rowe, and Miss Bowen. Grayson Evington de Winchester, the Duke, was a different story; he was well above anyone that I had ever hoped to meet one day. He was my most glorious acquaintance.

To keep me sane from all of the unhealthy pondering in my mind, I began to help Anna. But I was not very good at doing that, either.

"Miss Cleona, I think you are too agitated to do embroideries."

"I am not too patient in this particular matter," I admitted, happy not to have to pretend anymore. "I wish things could move faster, and then a moment later I want to stop time."

"It is a natural reaction to the recent events and expectations, but you are not the only one. For totally different reasons, Miss Louisa is very anxious these days."

"What you mean, Anna?"

"You should ask her. She is not telling me the entire truth."

"Is there something that is troubling her?" That would be quite unusual; nothing ever bothers Louisa.

"But you have seen her, very quiet and still. That is quite unusual."

"True, but perhaps she is not feeling well."

"Talk with her, Miss Cleona, please," insisted Miss Henry, with an imploring tone of voice. "This is serious."

Indeed, Louisa was spending too much time alone in her room. She had not joined me in endless discussions about the ball as she had before, but I was so preoccupied with my own worries, I did not observe her strange withdrawal. But if she was ill, why was she not confiding in me? Why was she not telling me what was wrong? I sought her out and found her in the drawing room, alone and sad.

"Louisa, are you hiding from me?" I asked, closing the door behind me.

"No. Why do you ask?" Her voice was nervous but her gaze seemed guilty.

"Anna just told me you are not acting like yourself, and I have to admit, my dear, that I was too selfish to see this myself. Please forgive me. You deserve my full attention."

"I wished to avoid you. I need your forgiveness."

"You have it, of course," I rushed to assure her while her words created a bit of uneasiness in my mind. "But there is nothing to forgive, right? You have not done anything wrong."

"I did. I did a horrible thing to you," cried my cousin. "You will not like it, and for that matter, you will never forgive me…"

"Let me be the judge of that, and do not prolong your answer. Louisa, please!"

"I have stepped over the boundaries of our relationship," she whispered and did not raise her face to me. "I was torn between the feelings of my heart and my devotion to you and our family. There, at the ball, I saw this handsome young man trying to get your attention, and I went to talk with him. He introduced himself as Mr. Rosedale. We actually danced twice, and I was impressed with him very much. I really liked him – well enough to have father invite him to dinner in a week. All the time I was with him, he asked about you. I did not learn his real name until the ball's end when he followed you outside. He was Captain Clark."

"Captain Clark?" His name stabbed me into my very soul.

"I knew you would be angry…"

"Louisa, I am shocked." More than shocked, I was becoming angry with my cousin. "I do not care that you danced with him, but inviting him for dinner! And when were you planning to tell me about it? When Captain Clark was knocking at the door and expected to be welcomed? What was your reasoning in of all this?"

"It is not an easy thing to talk about. I did not know who he was, and he was so charming, so well mannered. He was unknown even to my father, and there was no way to predict the possibility of such an encounter. Oh, I am so sorry."

"I believe you. I must have Cyril find him and cancel his invitation to our dinner immediately."

"He will be so disappointed!"

I turned to my cousin, exasperated.

"I do not trouble myself to care if he will be offended or not. I very much do not wish to have him here in Uncle Robert's home. Are you against my decision?"

"No, and yes." Her attitude changed to determination.

"Louisa!"

"I like him, Cleona," she said firmly. "I truly believe I that I am in love with him. My silly heart cannot separate the friend from the foe."

"It is too premature to accept this encounter as the seed of love," I said in denial. "It can very well be an overreaction to an amiable person, and that is all."

"Then why is it that I cannot make myself stop thinking of him? I avoided you because I was afraid of hostility…"

Louisa was now at the point of crying. Her voice was weak and her hands on the drawing board were shaking. As much as the whole idea of Louisa being in love was a surprise to me, I could not deny that Captain Clark was handsome enough to impress my young cousin. To me, however, he was an impertinent rogue who willingly attempted to penetrate the midst of our family and do more harm.

"My dear," I continue a bit more softly, "I believe him to be capable of inflicting more hardship. Nothing good is to be born of this. He is deceitful, as expected."

"I have talked with him, and he is nothing of the sort. Perhaps all he wanted was to meet you and to pay his respects."

"Meet me?" This time it was my turn to be astonished.

"Yes. All the time that I was falling in love with him, he was asking about you."

"For the obvious reasons, I would think. He wanted to boast in front of everyone that he owns our home."

"Cleona, please give him a chance," begged Louisa and her beautiful blue eyes were overcome with tears. "Let him come and dine with us and then, if you must, condemn him."

"Are you seriously suggesting this?"

"Yes. Please, do it for me."

What else could I add to my life? I have had tragedies, losses, heartbreaks, some encounters with ghosts, and now, something more Shakespearian. First, there was losing Chatham Hill, then losing a fiancé, seeing Uncle Edward's phantom, meeting and dancing with Duke de Winchester, and now having Captain Clark as our guest for dinner. I had lived it all and I had seen it all. Or so I thought.

* * *

That evening I had to tell my uncle and my brother about our future guest. They were puzzled.

"This is a most inconvenient event," said my uncle embarrassed. "I am unhappy about my role in the dinner invitation. When Louisa suggested it, I foolishly agreed. This is entirely my fault."

"It is not, Father. It is mine!" Louisa jumped to defend her father. "Captain Clark was not truthful to me and he hid his true name."

"Nonsense," I said. "He was tricky and deceitful. Now we have to deal with him and be civil."

"An easier way to solve this is by canceling our invitation," Uncle Robert said.

Louisa's eyes were imploring.

"Perhaps we should reconsider," I said thoughtfully. "I think it is time for us to take a closer look at the future owner of our estate. It is true, we should think of him as the enemy, but so far we know nothing about his character. We need to have a wider perspective regarding Captain Clark, and who knows; perhaps not all will be lost."

"Cleona that is not you talking – you hate this man," said Cyril amazed.

"Certainly. His coming here does not change my feelings toward him, but I am willing to take the chance to discover who we are up against."

Everyone else became quiet. I was in pain over the whole idea of meeting him, of having him so close to me, and of actually talking to him. This would have never happened if not for Louisa's irrational mind-set of being in love with him. I watched her closely and she still did not understand how this could happen. She smiled at me, always thankful and jolly.

How could this be happening?

CHAPTER 7

IN THE MORNING I WROTE to mother about the wonderful ball and so much about the Duke of Winchester. I missed Chatham Hill already, and the fact that I would be a stranger from it forever made me even more annoyed with our guest.

My stomach began to hurt, most likely from the anxiety I was feeling. I did not know how I would survive the day. Louisa was so excited to be seeing Captain Clark again, but I was not about to encourage her. She dressed up very nicely, and that was met with many sarcastic remarks from me. I could not comprehend her effort of looking attractive for him. To me, this was a most unpleasant notion.

When the doorbell rang, Louisa and I were both nervous. Indeed, Captain Clark was handsome, tall and well built, with an abundance of dark hair and flashing dark eyes. He was very polite and grateful for the dinner invitation. He addressed me and he expressed his deepest joy of having the honor of meeting me, as well as to revisit my brother.

He paid his respects to my uncle and he barely looked at Louisa. He was seated beside her at the dinner table, but not much conversation took place between the two. To my surprise,

I was the center of his attention. I hated to admit it, but his presence was not entirely overwhelming and his demeanor was tolerable. For the sake of civility, the words that I had prepared for him for so long were caught in my chest.

After dinner the men retired to Uncle Robert's library for cigars and brandy. Before the library door closed, Captain Clark turned to me and said, "Miss Somerton, may I have the honor of having a private audience with you this evening? I have news of the extreme importance that I need to share with you."

"Would not this news be better shared with me, rather than my sister?" asked Cyril a bit surprised.

"My apologies, Mr. Somerton, I did not intend to ignore you as the head of the family; however, my news is specific to her interests and nothing more."

This was the moment for which I was waiting.

"Certainly!" I accepted. "It is a wonderful evening for being out on the veranda."

Uncle's house did not have a garden or any other place where we could be far enough from the others. This suited my purposes well, as I did not care to have a great deal of privacy with him.

After three quarters of an hour, Captain Clark emerged from the library. He found me in the parlor with Louisa, and I joined him in the foyer to the veranda.

When the veranda door closed, I said, "Captain Clark – or perhaps I should address you as Mr. Rosedale – you have displayed such impertinence to come here, even for the pretext you declare to possess. I had not the need or the wish to ever meet you or to know you. I hope you did not have any expectations of me being civil. Our acquaintance is useless and preposterous. There is nothing you can change by apologizing, and I do not need to hear it. You and your family are the reason for destroying me and my family and you must understand: the only reason you are here is because someone dear to me believed in you and your worthiness. But, it all can end here and now…"

"I am unworthy to apologize to you, but I must," he said in a very polite way. "I want you to know that I had nothing to do with what happened on that day in March."

"Nonsense…" His attempt to deny his involvement in our decline made me very angry.

"Please, allow me to explain," he continued, stubbornly pretending not to notice my hateful attitude. "I am a frequent resident at my uncle's estate and I am familiar with his friends. When he called for me for a card game that day, I did not suspect anything untoward. He and his friends often play cards, and that day I only watched. I promise you, I did not know he was serious about the wager that was made until the next day."

"But you acknowledge signing the papers."

"I did sign indeed, thinking only that it was nothing but a game."

"A game which put my family into the streets and ruined our name forever. Do you have any idea what you have done with the lives of four people? I was born in a respectable place and now, because of you and your uncle, I must move to a work house. And to highlight of all of this, my fiancé recanted our engagement two weeks before our wedding. Is this something pleasant that you are hearing? Can you live knowing that, Captain Clark? Would you ever wish to see your sisters in this situation? Of course not. They are soon to move into the house that was built by my forefathers, where the Somerton's have resided for over a century."

My voice struggled to remain steady, but I was shaking. Moreover, I was angry with myself for my exclamation of how much hurt we had suffered. I resolved that I must be calm.

"And do you also know, Captain Clark, that your uncle stole our estate? That game was not real – it was all a charade, born of feelings of revenge that your uncle felt for my father. You cannot stand in front of me, proclaiming innocence, after admitting that you knew the entire truth."

"My dear Miss Somerton, I am a soldier," he declared proudly. "I have no need for an estate and I did not desire yours. I am not happy about this circumstance. It is not a welcome situation on my part. I will not rejoice in your unfortunate situation, and I wish to change whatever is possible to rectify."

I took a deep breath and moved closer to him. Until that moment we were still standing as I did not have the courtesy to invite him to sit. Perhaps Louisa was right; he might emerge as a reasonable person, and not just her seducer. Encouraged by my closeness, he continued.

"I need for you to know some details about my life so I can justify what I am going to say and declare further. My mother was Mr. Radisson's sister. My uncle was very much against her marrying my father, a struggling lawyer, but later he accepted the union because he loved me and my sisters. I am the second born in the family, the only son, and much was hoped for my behalf. My family was not considered poor, but my uncle helped very much in lean times.

"When I was eleven years of age, my father and mother left home to visit some relatives who were ill. They were drowned returning home, crossing an old bridge that collapsed over the Thames River. In that one moment, I lost both of my parents. I was an orphan. My mother's younger sister, Mrs. Rosedale, took us into her home and raised us with the help of Colonel Radisson. My youngest sister was not quite a year old. About four years ago, Mrs. Rosedale died, too.

"You must understand my attachment to my uncle. He was my spiritual father and most of my guidance throughout my life. I considered his advice for my career and I trusted him always. I have never believed him to be malicious or unfair; I respected him very much, and I still do."

"Captain Clark, I am sorry for your loss, but at this point your sincere biography cannot save this situation. I can see for myself that Colonel Radisson is your hero, but in my eyes he is just a villain." My uncivil sincerity did not bother him at all.

"I know how this appears to you, and I came to make amends."

"Sir, return the estate of Chatham Hill to my brother, the rightful owner. Nothing more or less is acceptable."

"I am afraid I cannot do that," he said a bit hesitant.

"You cannot?" My voice went few octaves higher. "You just declared that you would do whatever is possible!"

"And I will keep my word," he answered still very calm. "But returning Chatham Hill to your family is not possible. The morning that I found myself the owner of the estate, and with a clear mind, I read the ownership papers. They were written in such way that prohibits me or my inheritors from selling or donating Chatham Hill for the next one hundred years. My uncle wanted to be sure that the estate would be in our hands for a long time."

My hope was dashed forever with those words. I lost every interest in listening to Captain Clark anymore. He was no help and of no importance. I still had the deepest hatred for Colonel Radisson, and that would never change. I turned to leave, but the young man stepped in my way, to block my path.

"It is time for you to leave, Captain Clark. Our meeting is over. I hope you accomplished what you came here to do, assuming it was to see me and my sufferings and to reveal that you own Chatham Hill indefinitely. I cannot say that I have had the pleasure of meeting you."

"Madam, please, I did not finish…"

"Yes you did! Please do not tempt me to call for my uncle and my brother."

"I still need to reveal the secret behind my uncle's inexcusable action."

"There is no secret to be revealed, Captain Clark. Your uncle was jealous of my father's promotion and he swore revenge. I can only assure you that your uncle's attitude was an unjust and untrue depiction of my father's character. He was a brave and honorable man."

"That was not to my discretion and I have nothing to do with that notion."

"No? Then let me hear it." My patience was running out, but I decided to listen. Some sort of strange curiosity made me grant him this request. Perhaps the more I knew about my enemy, the better.

"Thank you, Madam. Again, after my unexpected and unwanted fortune, I became uneasy and restless about all that happened. I reconsidered my motives against my uncle's mad behavior and I felt ashamed. I have asked him about the meaning of all this. He reassured me that I should not worry, that it was all done for my own good. He did not appreciate my hesitation to claim Chatham Hill, but he accepted my condition to give you eight months to find a reasonable substitute for your home. That gave me time to discover the truth behind his actions. Miss Somerton, a promotion can be overlooked and forgotten, but the affairs of the heart are alive forever in some people."

It was his turn to take a quiet moment.

"I did not wish to tell you this unless it became absolutely necessary, and I am agonizing over it, but perhaps it will help. I found this old letter in Uncle's library. It is dated almost thirty years ago, written to a lady named Jane Milton. Let me read it to you:

My dear Jane,

I am in pain, a destructive pain, one that will send me to my grave. I do not understand why you keep avoiding my love. I love you so much, with a passion that I cannot contain, and you choose to ignore me, time after time, and you will not grant me forgiveness.

I will not let you go, never! My heart will love you always, even if you are marrying Charles Somerton. I will find you again, and you will be mine one day, I promise. Wait for my return.

Yours forever,
Thomas Radisson

I sat down by the time he finished reading. Nothing in the world could have surprised me more, but this and what he did next took me very much aback. He bowed on one knee in front of me.

"It seems that Uncle Thomas went on with his life and he married later on. I cannot change what happened long ago between our family members, but I know there is a connection that time or generations cannot break. Perhaps it was meant to be for us, too. The only way I can help is to offer you my heart and ask for the honor of your accepting my proposal of marriage."

My mouth was agape. I think I stared at him for many long minutes in a stupor before I could answer.

"Captain Clark, surely you do not expect an answer from me right away, because I do not have one to give. Please, do not disclose our conversation to anyone. And of course, we were complete strangers until an hour ago, so a rapid answer to your question would be madness. Sir, are you absolutely sure about …"

"I am positive, Miss Somerton, I give you my word. I know that declaring my feelings to you may not mean anything at the moment, for we just made our acquaintance, but you charm me already and I am infatuated with you. Miss Somerton, is there any hope for me, regarding my wish?"

"I cannot tell you, yet. I simply cannot tell you."

CHAPTER 8

SINCE CAPTAIN CLARK'S VISIT, MY relationship with Louisa had altered considerably. Of course, everyone expected a full explanation from me about his inquires, but all they received was the description of his deep apologies along with the details regarding his loss of his parents and his attachment to his uncle. I also added his discovery regarding the Chatham Hill property papers and admitted that our home was lost forever. I certainly wanted to end it there, but my dear cousin would not stop her questions. She wanted to know if I found him to be pleasant and tolerable. And I did, but not for her sake.

Captain Clark was correct about my knowing only what his uncle wanted to be known about his dislike of my father, as he hid the real reason. I now have to live with this knowledge, knowing that we are under the curse of revenge from someone from Mother's past – someone she did not choose to love, but who is ruining her family. Perhaps I should pay more attention to Mrs. Longwood.

Such a terrible thought.

Of all the ideas circulating in my mind, there was one with which I was unable to be happy: Captain Clark's marriage proposal. Was this an arranged scheme, or was it the nephew's own resolution and desire to conquer a territory forbidden by his uncle? If it was done for the nephew's sake, then Colonel Radisson would not win.

If, through me, we could have Chatham Hill back, Colonel Radisson would be at a disadvantage again.

So, I wondered, was I not a prey target myself? However bizarre, his proposal was dividing my thoughts, my heart, and my calculating plans. Here I was, with my whole world crashing down at my feet, but still flattered by a young man's attention. Yes, it feels good to be wanted, even by the most unlikely of people, making it seem more suspenseful.

Is spite of some danger and all of the lack of affection I felt for Captain Clark, I was not about to embrace a refusal of his proposal until I explored all of the arguments. I remembered taking an oath to do anything to regain possession of our residence, and that did not exclude a marriage.

If I expected Cyril to marry, then I should not be exempted. My great concern was only for my dear Louisa, who was hoping to manipulate my opinions about her beau in order to clear the way for his return to her. To me, her unstoppable conversation was torment. Still, how much pain would this produce in her if somehow I could not turn her against him?

* * *

Louisa and I went to the commercial section of London the next day to acquire new silverware and some fabric to make a new wardrobe for Caroline, who had just turned fifteen. As always, we passed the music store on St. Paul Street and I could not resist the temptation to go inside. Nothing had changed. Mr. Rolling was happy to see me and he invited me to play to my satisfaction on any of his fortepianos. He had an instrument similar to the one on which I was playing when I first encountered Mr. Connelly long ago.

I sat down to play and some sweet memories began to surface in my mind. It was true: I did fall deeply in love with James and I was so happy to be under his charming spell. And now, all was gone. I could not stop wondering what my life would be like now, as Mrs. Connelly, if he had loved me enough not to retreat. I would have a comfortable home, a secure place for Mother and Cyril, and fewer worries. I would never have learned about Colonel Radisson's sick love for Mother and I would not have to consider an unthinkable proposal of marriage from Captain Clark.

There was no reason to let my mind fester over my circumstance, now. Nothing was left, not even in my heart. There was nothing to which to go back. I stopped in the middle of the etude, took Louisa's arm, and quickly left the store.

"I suppose this was unpleasant for you," she said compassionately. "I am so sorry, my dear."

"Louisa, I need for you to listen to me," I begged of her. "Please, be the only owner of your feelings, and do not display them easily. I do not ever want to see you hurt."

"What are you trying to tell me?" she asked sincerely. "Are you afraid I have fallen in love?"

"You are declaring to be in love, even now. It is not a matter of my fear, but your choice to display your feelings."

"I understand." At that moment my cousin turned hostile. "This is all about Captain Clark. I do not believe that he is as despicable as his uncle, and we should not hold against him the fact that he is Colonel Radisson's nephew. I understand your feelings. They are rightfully held, but I cannot stop my mind from thinking of him and for my soul to want him."

I did not want to accept or deal with what I was hearing.

"Dear Louisa, do you see him sharing your affection?" I was appealing to her memory about their close encounters, having her to analyze those moments with a cold and rational mind. "I watched him while at dinner, and he did not pay any attention to you, considering that he danced with you twice at the ball."

"I am sure he has some affection for me. He just does not know it and he will not know it until I make it known to him. You should not judge by appearances."

"I do not judge, I said a bit irritated. "But I do not trust him or his future plans; they may not include marriage to you."

"No one knows. He is in charge, but it should not be considered impossible. Cleona, we are like sisters. Please, just let me hope. Will you despise me if marriage to Captain Clark should come to pass?"

"I will not alienate you, Louisa, and I am not worried for you if your wish were to became true, but I am terrified of what would happen if does not." And I was. This could be the right moment to confess to her, but I held back. "I do not wish to see you hurt. It would be far more easy for you to not to have any expectations. So far, it is only your heart speaking. Try to think more deeply."

"You have talked to him, and you saw him as a gentleman. I am not afraid he will hurt me, but is there something of which I should be aware? Did he mention to you that he might be engaged?"

"No, he did not."

How difficult it was to conceal certain details from the one for whom I care, but at the same time to tell the truth. How could I turn her against him or to diminish her wishes and still keep my secret?

"Why him, Louisa? There are so many other handsome gentlemen in London or in Kent. Why did you let your guard down for him?"

"I wish I had an answer for you, Cleona, but I do not know. I can see that this is a very unpleasant subject to you. Please, let us not discuss it further. If, in the future, my heart will be broken, so be it. I am aware of how much you have suffered for love, but I am ready for the pain, too. All I know is that I am very excited and joyful over the idea of falling in love, dreaming of marriage, all of that. This is every girl's ideal dream; mine is just more difficult to dream. However, think about it: our union will bring Chatham Hill back into the family. You should consider this to be a great benefit and be happy for me."

"There is no reason to be happy over such uncertainties. I am only being protective of you."

"You did change! You must recall the nights when you and I talked for hours about your love for James Connelly, and now, here I am getting the opposite reaction from you."

When we returned home, Louisa was sad about my stubborn attitude, and I could not stand to see her that way. Against my better judgment, I started to encourage her. But after a while I could not continue the pretense, so I ran to my room and lay on the bed, exasperated that she was not getting my hints.

A few minutes later, someone knocked at my door. Thinking it was Louisa, I did not answer, pretending to be asleep. I could not stand the tension between us any longer. But it was Cyril who was calling me from the hallway.

"Cleona, there is someone downstairs who is asking for you, with a message from Lady de Winchester!"

I jumped up and dressed in one minute, as best I could. I was thinking that this might be the expected dinner invitation. I selected one of my less annoying dresses and let my hair down again. Then, with all the calmness of which I was capable, I came down the staircase slowly but confidently. An older footman was waiting for me at the bottom of the stairs.

He bowed and asked, "Where is your trunk, Miss Somerton?"

"I beg your pardon?"

"Your luggage, madam. Her Ladyship is expecting you to

stay with her for a few days, as she was asking of you in her note."

"I shall return shortly."

I ran up the stairs, feverishly gathered up all of my clothes and packed them. I was going to spend some time with Lady de Winchester – me, a girl from country.

After all, being infamous is not always a disadvantage.

CHAPTER 9

THE BIG GRAND FORTEPIANO WAS positioned in the music room so that it opened to the living room and the massive spiral staircase. I agreed very much with this arrangement. As I remembered it from playing at the ball, the sound was carried up from the first floor and it could be heard throughout the entire palace. There I spent most of my time playing endlessly, since I came to Evington Palace.

    Mr. Bronson had brought me to the palace that evening, and Mrs. Petine had showed me my room. It was lovely; the tapestry was a soft color of gold with numerous cherubim's heads, but the curtains were only a plain solid shade of red. The chest was cherry, not a particularly an expensive piece, but still elegant. After I was somewhat settled in, Mrs. Petine asked me if I would like to tour the mansion with her in order to become familiar with its floor plan. After our tour and when I was on my own, I must confess that I was lost a few times.

    I had not seen my hostess during the first three days I was in the palace – only her maid and the doctor. Mrs. Petine reassured me that Lady de Winchester was growing stronger and returning to her health, but that it was more beneficial for her Ladyship's rehabilitation for me to not see her as yet. At my hostess's request, however, I practiced upon the pianoforte.

As I was waiting for my host to recuperate, I saw several people in the palace. One day I saw Lady Winston arrive as I was looking from my bedroom window. She saw me too, and then she left the palace shortly thereafter without acknowledging my presence.

Lord Frederick Evington, her Ladyship's youngest son, came to the music room and introduced himself to me. He is married and lives on an estate beyond the suburbs of London with his wife and seven children. On last Friday morning, Miss Elizabeth Bowen came to spend the day with me. I was grateful for this, and pleasantly surprised.

Miss Bowen was indeed a sweet young girl who is quiet and shy with strangers, but she was very comfortable with me. She had beautiful long black hair, a bit too thick, but her hairdresser was doing incredible work by keep it curly and soft. Her dress was quite elegant – white silk with small purple ribbons across the neck line.

My meeting with her at that moment provided an excellent opportunity to get to know her better. I managed to find out about her deepest feelings and it was possible to stir in her a wave of interest for my brother. Her dark eyes were sincere and curious and I liked her very much. She loved to read and I did enjoy playing for her delight, knowing that Lady Edwina was listening, too.

Our serene time was interrupted by an intruder, however – one who gave me chills and a nervous pain in my stomach: the Duke of Winchester. He was somewhat surprised by my presence when he walked into the music room, but his manner changed immediately and he was very polite and respectful.

My memory was filled with the scene of our dancing, his beautiful smile, and his warm hands almost caressing mine.

had to sit down quickly, aware of my wild and unholy thoughts. I fought to retain my calm, but my whole body denied my wishes. He remained serious, carrying on light conversation with his cousin about his mother's health. Then he turned to me, brushing his fingers thru his wavy blonde hair.

"Miss Somerton, what a pleasure it is to see you again. I was hoping that our prior encounter was not the last."

"Your Grace is very kind." I blushed.

I could not comprehend the short conversation we just had, and my mind was in turmoil again. What was it about this man I found so supreme, that it would stop my heart? The fact that he built a church? His devotion for his lost wife? Or his whole appearance, projecting the aura of being noble and untouchable.

This man seemed so perfect in every way, royal, good hearted, and widely sought after. He was here in the same room with me, almost within my reach, and all I could do was to be quiet and be tempted to find him human – because in my mind he was not.

Elizabeth took my place at the fortepiano. She had paid attention to my prior execution of the sonata, and she favored us with an extremely good performance of the composition. The Duke came closer to her and listened. I wished for another chance for his attention, but I had to be patient and wait.

"Very good, my dear cousin. You are working very hard to improve your playing, and I am very proud of you."

"It is not hard work, Lord Evington," admitted Elizabeth. "My little secret is to imitate Miss Somerton. I hope she will forgive me for such an intrusion."

"Miss Bowen, I am delighted to be an inspiration to you," I said, with all the calm I was capable, but my palms started to sweat.

"You are very modest in this matter," he said to me. "Your talent is extraordinary."

His complement made me blush again. I was very aware of the pleasant effect I always had on other people and the extremely amiable praise that had always been given to me. I have always made every attempt to receive these complements naturally and to not be affected and proud. Somehow, he saw this, too.

"It is not prudent to confess how easy it is for me to play," I replied. "I often wonder myself if it is truly a talent and if it is what purpose it should fulfill. I do play in our family gatherings and modestly take pride if I am accomplished, but I fear that my playing can simply be reduced to an entertaining tool. I wish to be more accomplished than this."

"This is a very deep reflection indeed, Miss Somerton," he said to me and the tone of his voice made me wish close my eyes and dream. "But your performance is more than this. When you play, it sounds nothing like a struggling commoner striving for accomplishment. Your performance is beyond pleasing. When you play, your music turns the spirit and unlocks the soul. The sound from that grand instrument is the very sound the composer wrote and meant for it to be. Do not disregard your talent, but deem it as high as it should be."

It was then that his mother called for him. He bowed, excused himself, and left the room.

The next morning Lady de Winchester came downstairs for breakfast. She was pale and somewhat weak, but in good spirits. The doctor joined us, primarily to be assured that she was well and safe. I did most of the talking, but she loved my rambling conversation. I wanted mostly to reassure her of my deepest gratitude for her invitation and my appreciation for her kindness. She did not promise to come for dinner, but instead she made sure I that I would have company.

Then, I was alone again. I made myself at home in the library for a while, trying to make up my mind as to what I should read, but I was not really concentrating on any of the many choices in the well-stocked library.

Later, when I played the fortepiano, I had a different attitude. I was not drawn to perfection anymore, but to the visionary approach of the composer. My goal was to reveal his emotions and tumult, his joy or sadness, all of his feelings, but none of the coldness that might be found in simply performing the notes.

At the same time, my mind was fighting for a severe dismissal of my path to madness. I had planted a seed in Elizabeth's unguarded heart and left it to blossom, with no regard for my brother's wishes. To me, they did not have the right to choose – neither Cyril nor Miss Bowen; Louisa or Mr. Clark.

I thought to myself that I did have an excuse. I did not choose this path deliberately; I was forced into it. Then why I should feel so covered with guilt and anxiety? It must only be the Duke of Winchester's influence. I could find no other explanation. It was him, putting me so high in his opinion, a place I did not deserve or earn.

I resolved that I must stay away from him and from playing the fortepiano like this anymore. It was too disturbing and I could not allow it – not now, when my plan was about to be fulfilled. Then, in just moments, I wished with all my heart to have him as a visitor again.

* * *

No one came to keep me company Saturday afternoon. Mrs. Petine joined me for dinner and then left me to be with her Ladyship for tea. Later, I sent a message to Lady Edwina de Winchester asking for permission to go church on Sunday morning.

The next morning, my good hostess had one of her carriages ready for me. I asked to be taken to the St. John Street church. The driver hesitated slightly, but then he agreed. I assumed that the reason for his hesitation was because it was an unusual route for him on that particular side of London.

We passed many people walking down the street, primarily men with their wives and children. They all seemed a little puzzled by my carriage, and they tried to give us as much room as possible. A few men were riding horses and they appeared to be better dressed. Perhaps some were clerks, or house servants, or even tradesmen and other professionals. Generally, all of these people were very plainly dressed in below average clothing, and all were going in the same direction: to the new church.

I entered the church feeling a little shy, but immediately a strong female hand pulled me in through the crowd and invited me to sit beside her and her child. She was a young woman, dressed simply but cleanly. She smiled and assured me that I was in a very good place, that it was easy to see and hear from this pew. I thanked her immediately for her timely assistance, wondering if there was any possibility that I might have known this person previously, or was she merely someone who was being nice to me.

Inside, the church was not extravagant, but it was a good size room, somehow quite plain, but with new oak pews and beautiful stained glass windows. I felt good, but in a moment I realized how strange I must appear to these people, with my elegant blue dress and my big hat, my blonde hair and fair skin, as I sat beside my new friend's worn brown dress and old bonnet. What was I thinking when I left the palace? Why did I not give any thought to this scene?

But it was too late now to change anything. I was accustomed to dressing nicely for church when I lived at Chatham Hill, and I even if I did not consider my wardrobe comparable with that of Lady Winston's, my clothing was superior on any scale relative to that of the people I chose to join this Sunday morning.

The preacher had a very simple and sensitive message. I had never heard a sermon quite like that. He was a young man, barely thirty, very tall and thin, with a deep, loud voice. When the service was completed, he came directly to me and presented himself.

"It is a pleasure to have you here, Miss Somerton. My name is Clive Warren. I see you have already met my wife, Emma, and this is my son, Grayson."

"Reverend Warren, I must thank you and your wife for a most gratifying morning," I said surprised by his welcome. "I would like to congratulate you for delivering such a triumphant sermon; it was quite accomplished. May I inquire as to how you know my name?"

"Certainly, madam. The Duke of Winchester recognized you as you arrived and he told me your name."

"Is he here?" Reverend Warren addressed him in accordance to his rank of nobility. My heart started to race again.

"He is here every Sunday morning, supervising the delivery of provisions for the supper later in the day. I suppose this explains the large attendance we have, even if only a handful of people remain for the evening service when all the food has been eaten."

I was a little distressed and I wanted to leave at that moment. This simple act of coming here to attend church was leading to an unwanted attachment to the Duke, but there was an undeniable pleasure of being in his presence.

"Miss Somerton, are you leaving?"

He was right behind me. I turned and curtsied, but I still kept my eyes lowered to his boots. In that moment, more than ever, I wanted to be somewhere else.

"Your Grace, I did not expect to find you here…"

He returned my bow and came very close to me. Reverend and Mrs. Warren bowed and left us to assist their daughters in the church dining hall, and we remained alone in the church foyer.

"Where else would I be if I were not here? And please, do not address me as you did – we are not strangers anymore. My name is Grayson Evington, and I am quite fond of my name. You may call me that if you choose. May I walk you to the carriage?"

I agreed only by nodding my head, certain that I would never dare to address him as he requested. This time I wanted to prevent any conversation that I would have enjoyed. I did not want to allow my spirit to turn to another disturbing and pathetic pattern of desire and interest. The admiration in my heart was growing deeper for this man.

"I did not expect to find you here, Miss Somerton! But it was a welcome surprise. I trust you did not feel out of place."

"Actually, yes, I did. In the future I should dress more modestly…"

His beautiful smile which I so much admired was a gift to me again. This serious man was finding my words humorous enough to change his demeanor for a few seconds. But I feared I might sound silly to him, and uncultured. I was so young and inexperienced; it filled me with trepidation to talk to such people of his high social rank.

"Your Grace, I beg your forgiveness for my words. I will make a greater effort to censor them."

He looked at me again, and deliberately made me look into his eyes.

"You seem to be frightened of me, and I am sad that you feel like that. I wish you would stop your worries about your image when you are in my presence and just be yourself. After all, we do have somewhat of a history together, like dancing and visiting…"

This time I smiled. He helped me to get into the carriage and he bowed again as I prepared to leave. But I could not let him go so soon.

"Your Grace, please don't leave…"

He turned back, astonished. But I could not dare to continue

— I had just made a terrible mistake. Addressing him in that manner was uncivil coming from someone like me, even if I had his approval. I felt that in the next second I would faint dead away in my effort to keep calm.

He saw my anxiety and asked me, "Is there something concerning you, madam?"

"Please, will you join me for a moment? I need to speak with you…respectfully."

He climbed inside the carriage and a few people looked at us curiously.

"My Lord, you once said that you would be willing to listen to me talk about my family's disgraces. I really need to talk with you concerning my situation because I constantly fear that your opinion of me will not remain high."

"Certainly, if you desire it."

"I know the timing for this is not right, but I am her Ladyship's guest. I will have numerous opportunities to meet with you again, and I am frightened. Rumors and false information about our so-called misfortune are circulating so quickly, and I am so confused. My speaking with you is not to increase our intimacy or friendship; I hardly deserve your attention. It is so much more important to me that you know the truth.

"My family's misfortunes happened because we have enemies who planned to ruin us, and they have succeeded through my brother's weak and vulnerable character. Before the year has passed, our estate will belong to someone else and my mother, brother and I will be forced to live dependent on friends' and relatives' mercy. It is very humiliating for me to admit that we lost everything, and to justify my brother's behavior to people who only see the results of his action and who blame him for it. I blamed him, too, for quite some time, and my soul was mired in spite. But now I realize that his only fault was to be unaware that someone is secretly full of hate for us, who thwarts us enough to lie and steal."

"Who is responsible for this atrocity?"

"I was told by a trusted friend that Colonel Radisson swore revenge against my father for being promoted over him in the military. Colonel Radisson was sure that this promotion should have been his and that my father received it unjustly. My brother, who was a guest in my sister's house, joined my brother-in-law and the Colonel for a game of cards. A friend of my family, dear Mr. Parker, believes that they gave my brother too much to drink and coerced him sign the release of the estate's property papers under the supervision of a lawyer named Mr. Tent. The property transfer is real; there is nothing about the transaction can be undone."

"Miss Somerton, these are truly people with indecent character. Your situation is grave and distressful. Please accept my deepest sorrow."

"Whatever awful rumor came to your attention," I continued, with my eyes fixed on the floor of the carriage all this time, "this is the entire truth. I am not in despair at this moment and I am not looking for sympathy from anyone, but I do not want my family's name to be sullied without any purpose and I do not wish to walk around in constant humiliation. I have the utmost regard of your opinion, as you know, and if I have offended you by my indiscretions, it was done only to gain access to your company without the restraint of an infamous reputation."

"My dear Miss Somerton I reassure you…" He tried to interrupt me but I just could not let go until my heart was free from my confession.

"My reputation will be infamous, perhaps forever, and I am aware of this. Some people's judgment of others is sometimes permanent, and I may not be able to recover. But you are important to me and to my state of mind, and I need for you to know all of this."

"Thank you for the trust, Miss Somerton. I honestly declare to be touched by your condition, as undeserved as it is. Please allow me to inquire after your wellbeing…"

"After the transfer of property, sometime in September, I am to reside with all of my family at Stonebridge, with our dear friends, Mr. and Mrs. Parker. They are our close neighbors. It will be a tolerable refuge until some other possibilities arise. Thank you very much for listening and for caring..."

I became quiet, as he did. I wished I could know what he was thinking – if my words did me justice or if they complicated our relationship even further. He looked at me, as if he were trying to gaze into my soul, and that frightened me even more.

There was so much that I omitted from my story because there was no point in his knowing all of the other complicating details, such as a thirty year old love story and the enemy's nephew's marriage proposal. I sat there waiting for his judgment, not knowing what he would say.

"Miss Somerton, please consider me your genuine friend, and please favor me with this one request: do not run away from me anymore. Treat me as you would your own brother or cousin, if that would be easier for you. Is there anything I can do for you?"

I shook my head and lowered my eyes once again. But yes, in fact he could do *everything* for me.

"Good day to you for now, Miss Somerton."

My carriage departed rapidly from the church, but he stood there watching me as I was leaving. At the time, I was not aware of his gaze as we drew away from the curb. I was simply happy and angry at the same time, and for a while, I was unable to recover from my weakness for him.

CHAPTER 10

I WAS NOT READY AS yet for a dinner gathering, but Lady de Winchester was determined to have one, now that she had fully recovered from her illness. I was told that the good lady loves visitors and dinners, and she does this quite often. For me was all too soon; I much preferred to spend all day with her and Mrs. Petine. It was very delightful to simply spend time in their company and listen to her Ladyship's stories – and she knew many.

My brother did not attend the dinner because he went with Uncle Robert to visit a friend in the country. I was quite angry with him; this was an excellent opportunity for him to spend some time with Miss Bowen in a smaller and more intimate setting.

She came to the dinner and she was very happy to see me again, after we had previously spent all that wonderful time together. I expressed my regrets on behalf of my brother for not attending the dinner and I was glad to see that she was disappointed. I reassured her that he would be obliged to visit her when he returned, if the opportunity presented itself. Of course, the DeSalle's ball was to be held the next week, and he and our uncle might not be back.

Lord and Lady DeSalles were at the dinner, and they brought

along their eleven year old son. He was a very handsome, sharp boy, and he was very attached to his mother. His younger brother, however, was left behind with his governess. Lady De-Salles wanted me to visit them at their home in the country before I returned to Chatham Hill, and of course, the invitation for their ball was initiated.

My dear friend Miss Catherine Rowe and Mr. Cleaves, her fiancé, passed the same invitation for me to spend some time at their estate after they married. Considering everything, I could have lived for a good year in the homes of these new and sensible friends. I was sure it would not come to that, but I would consider all of these invitations in order to keep these connections alive.

It did not take me long to realize that I hated Lady Winston as deeply as she most likely hated me. She brought along her friend, and after learning her friend's name, I well aware that I had created my own foe, because it was deliberate on Lady Winston's part who she had invited. Her friend's name was Miss Linton, none other than Mr. Connelly's fiancé.

Being civil is unnatural in situations of this nature, but I had to be. All eyes were turned on me when we were presented. Miss Linton was short and a little heavy, but she was not totally intolerable; she possessed an oval face with green eyes too close to the little nose shaped like a pear, and tiny lips that did not seem to move at all when she talked. Her dress was an expensive rose silk and her jewelry (too much to enumerate) paraded over her body and emphasized her vanity.

All of her finery was designed to dominate and intimidate me. I could feel it, and I was shocked to have the opportunity to meet her again so soon, in such a circumstance. My day was now in ruin, and I added James Connelly to my list of hated people once again.

That he was marrying her solely for her wealth should have

been punishment enough for him, and although this made me feel better, I was sure there was no love between them as he still declared to be in love with me. The fact that she stared at me nervously made me realize that my presence at the dinner was a complete surprise to her. She was overwhelmed by my appearance, as much as she had planned for it to be the other way around.

Mr. and Mrs. Rowe and their younger daughter, Miss Mary Rowe, Lord and Lady Bentley, and the Duke arrived last. I was determined to bear Miss Linton's unpleasantness, and I did not wish for Lord Evington's presence at all.

With all of the assurance from his part to not be afraid anymore and to treat him as a cousin or brother, there was something is his demeanor that left me perplexed. Many times, after our church encounter, I pondered why he chose the words 'cousin' and not 'friend'. Was it to indicate the significance of our age difference or was it because he did not need the caprice of considering someone like me to be a friend?

All in all, my explanations and rationalizations to myself was frippery. As a consequence, my attitude toward him was unchanged from the first time we had met. I simply continued to be uneasy in his presence.

To my benefit, I was seated four chairs away from him, on the same side of the table and not directly in his sight. My place was between Miss Mary and Lady Bentley and across the table from young Charles DeSalles and his mother. Lady Winston was seated across from Duke of Winchester, but not far enough away to not see me. This seating arrangement was contrary to my expectations. I anticipated that the Duke would take his place at the head of the other side of the table, as Lady Edwina did. To me, his sitting at the table as just another guest showed a deep respect for his mother and her status in the house.

The food was very well delivered with new and delicious delicacies, brought especially from the Far East, somewhere not specifically known to me. The conversation was going back and forth, over my head, and I hoped to not become involved. I felt that I was an outcast among them, but I did not care; their charm and their gentleness to me were priceless and useful.

For now, Lady Winston was busy talking with Miss Linton, and at the same time, attempting to stay focused in the attention of the Duke of Winchester. Considering her desperate efforts to make him like her, I considered myself lucky to have caught his attention without having made this attempt at all. I do pity her – it can be most dreadful to want someone's sentiment and to not manage to garner any admiration. The reputation of being indolent did not alarm her in the least and her privileged position in society made her excessively abusive in her quest. And I assumed that she found an easy target in me.

But why me? And why do I pity her more than hate her? She would kill me without remorse if she knew how I really felt about her. Even her mercenary attempt to disgrace my spirit by bringing Miss Linton into my presence was ruthless, and watching her struggle to be liked by Duke of Winchester was beyond agony.

I pray that I will never be like her. My pain that was provoked by losing my fiancé was a behind the scene ordeal and it was so intense as to change me forever, but I did let him go and I did not look back. I continued to enjoy my meal; after all, I am a force to be reckoned with. Lady Winston and Miss Linton were in for a surprise if they challenged me, and soon enough, she could not resist.

"You are very quiet, Miss Somerton," Lady Winston remarked. "We certainly miss your valuable opinions."

"I apologize, your Ladyship – I was not paying attention to the conversation. I would not be in position to comment on what was said."

"Miss Linton was asking if the fashions in Paris had changed this year, and did I believe that we in London were about to see something fantastic and amazing. What do you think about it?"

Almost everybody turned to me, waiting for an answer. The purple dress I was wearing had been transformed by Mrs. Longwood to show my shoulders and my neck, and tastefully, some cleavage. By pulling the skirt a bit toward the back, I was able to have my dress curve around my body. This was an attempt to show the form I possess, so feminine and attractive, and it made the Grecian style of the dress less boring. All of this was done by the good Mrs. Longwood, at my stubborn request, for one purpose only: to be seductive.

"I would know nothing about Parisian fashions," I answered, smiling. "Fashion is a bit different from where I live. I am just a country girl."

My answer was so unexpectedly humble that it surprised everyone, but it highly pleased my inquisitor.

"Oh, you are indeed!" Lady Winston jubilated. "That explains your lack of knowledge. I suppose you have someone to help you with your dress!"

That remark was made to humiliate me and I did blush. Miss Catherine wanted to say something but I replied faster.

"Are you referring to the fact that I am wearing my own creations, your Ladyship?"

The young females around me murmured in admiration. Lady Gemma's smile disappeared.

"You are actually ahead of your time, my dear," said Lady de Winchester.

"Not at all, Your Ladyship. Soon London's society will see more dresses like mine – perhaps in Paris, too."

"Why do you ladies trouble yourselves with everything from Paris?" the lady seated beside me asked. Lady Bentley was indeed dressed in very old fashion. "What about showing a little patriotism and seek after our own style. I believe there is very much talent here to launch our own unique fashions."

"Lady Bentley," answered Gemma, "we are not as tasteful as the French people are. Just because Miss Somerton has created some sort of questionable style as a girl from the country – as she has mentioned – does not mean anything. Her attire is not desirable or elegant, it is primarily only strange. No effort was put into her dress to emphasize the elegance or the sophistication of a high class lady. I am simply not as impressed as all of you are."

"You are right, Your Ladyship," I answered. "The style of my attire is not for a high class lady, as I do not profess to be. I hope my style of dress will not trouble you in the future."

"I like it," said Catherine. "Miss Somerton's dress is different and not unattractive. Secretly, all women want to show off their best parts."

"I see you have some admirers already," Lady Winston retorted. "Perhaps my prior recommendation should remain: it is a useful employment after all."

"Thank you for your kindness."

Mary and Catherine were laughing. Elizabeth listened without pleasure and Miss Linton enjoyed it. I stood my ground to be civil against the flurry of Lady Winston's rude and miserable comments. I had nothing to gain by adopting her frame of mind – at least, not now.

"You are amusing us, Gemma," said Catherine. "You are certainly not an expert in fashion yourself – you just buy what are the most expensive items in Piccadilly."

"This is true," replied Lady Winston proudly, "but I know for a fact the excellent quality for which I am paying. I was merely making some useful observations. What a pity it is that Miss Somerton's inspiration was produced under such unfortunate circumstances. That explains her lack of finesse. It must be awful for her."

"Miss Somerton has good, caring friends, Gemma. You

have no need to worry on her account." For the first time that evening I heard the Duke's voice.

"I am not worried, but I am not insensitive to her pain – she has lost a home, her inheritance, a fiancé..."

"My loss is Miss Linton's gain. I am sure she sees it that way." I answered quickly.

"Oh, Mr. Connelly is so lucky to have her," concluded Gemma as she foresaw more embarrassment for me. "As you see she is a very refined and proper young lady, and he is so fond of her. Don't you think it so, Miss Somerton?"

"I believe this to be true. He is in better hands. The moment he heard the news of my misfortune, his family intervened and ended our engagement. You are very fortunate indeed, Miss Linton."

The poor girl was turning various shades of red in her attempt to try to hide her feelings or to not say anything. She just let her friend speak on her behalf, hoping that Lady Winston would crush me undisputedly.

"Miss Linton has full knowledge of Mr. Connelly's reasons to become her fiancé," answered Gemma who understood my irony. "There are no issues about that. You had no choice regarding your brother, either. I understand that you and he get along very well, considering that he ruined your family so ridiculously by playing cards."

Suddenly, there was another moment of quietness. As she did at the ball, her merciless attempt to shame me and her endless hostility toward me made incapable any attempt from the others to stop her.

Not even him – the Almighty Duke. Or perhaps he believed her.

CHAPTER 11

I FELT GUILTY FOR GOING to the ball without my dear Louisa, but unlike Lady Edwina, Lady DeSalles was more selective with her invitation list. I missed my cousin and I was ready to return to Uncle Robert's home. I had been here in the palace for more than three weeks now, and it was time to end my visit – but not before I got the chance to have Cyril become more involved with Elizabeth. For now, I prayed that he would come to the ball and be with her.

Lady Edwina was late; by the time we arrived at the ball, most of the guests had arrived. The DeSalles palace was grandiose, as I had expected, with amazing paintings, expensive furniture and equally fantastic ornaments.

To my relief I spotted my brother walking around, probably trying to find me. We were both happy to see each other. I immediately told him that Elizabeth had expressed her wishes for him to pay his respects to her, and that she was impatient to renew their acquaintance. However, Cyril was hesitant.

"I am not sure it will be proper for me to intrude on her company…"

"It is no intrusion at all. She told me so herself."

"With a little help from you?"

"Cyril!" I did not appreciate his accusations even I feared they were true. "Why would you think she is insincere?"

"I do not imply that. It is a fact, though, that I am not a person in whom young ladies are interested."

"Nonsense!" My brother's lack of cooperation was annoying. "You are young, handsome, sensitive and a good hearted person. All of these are desirable qualities. If you add a little romance on the side, you are quite a catch."

"Did you forget my empty pockets?"

"No, I did not – I just ignored them. You must count your blessings and think hard. You do not have the luxury of having an unlimited amount of choices to make, anymore. And just look at her. She is sweet and pleasant, and she likes you, of all people!"

Elizabeth was still in her aunt's company when I took my brother to join them. My young friend was pleasantly surprised and she welcomed Cyril with a big smile.

"Mr. Somerton, it is a pleasure to see you again," she said, radiantly. "Did you have a pleasant trip to the country?"

"Very pleasant, indeed."

Elizabeth did not seem to need my help anymore as she took over my brother's company. All I hoped was that Cyril did not become too frightened or timid because of her status, and that he would raise himself up to her expectations. But seeing them together, my mind was eased; all of this was going according to my plan. The family who endured shame and ridicule would soon have a new life in London's social circles.

What could be greater than to have, Lady Edwina, who is the queen's confidant, and Lord Evington, the Duke of Winchester as relatives? What a change it would be, from a small estate in the country to access to the royal court!

I walked around without any purpose, enjoying the hidden desires I seem to provoke in most gentlemen, when someone came directly toward me calling my name. I could not believe my eyes! It was Captain Clark. In the time I was away from Uncle Robert's home, I had totally forgotten about him.

"What a pleasure it is to see you again, Miss Somerton. Please accept my apologies for not coming to see you sooner."

"Captain Clark! I did not expect to see you here." I answered to his greeting and his bowing, attempting to collect my unwanted emotions without being noticed.

"I am guest of Mr. Reeves. I was told that you would be here, and I could not fathom being absent from your presence."

"Captain Clark…" Suddenly I felt trapped and lost for words.

"Miss Somerton, I am not here to apply pressure to you in any way. I am willing to wait indefinitely for your answer to my proposal. My intention is simply to take this opportunity to make myself a little more familiar to you."

He was well dressed and his appearance was quite handsome in his new uniform. I did not dislike him at all. As I looked around the room, I could see that he was as well-mannered and as well dressed as any other high class gentlemen. He would make a good dance partner because he had shown himself to be friendly and fun. When I considered him to be the new owner of my home, and that he already desired me as his bride, I could only gain by accepting his company.

"I agree. And how you intended to accomplish your goal, sir?"

"By dancing with you, and only you, for the whole night. Yes, I know you think that is impossible, but I like a challenge."

"The only problem with this would be that it is not proper conduct, Captain Clark. I am sure you would not dare to challenge that."

"Passion can turn a man into a menace, so please be aware of me for the future."

I did like him. I saw in him stubbornness in achieving his

purpose, more like my attitude, but at the same time he was very humorous and pleasant. He definitely knew how to keep the company of a lady and to flatter her. Now I understood Louisa's sudden infatuation with him. Unfortunately, she was not the chosen one, and I felt guilty about accepting his intentions. That feeling held me in its grip until I found myself on the dance floor with him.

Captain Clark put a lot of effort in making me feel that I was the heart of his attention. Any young lady would like that, and I savored every minute of it. Yes, it was so wonderful to be courted and desired by a handsome, pleasant young man. At the Medley dance, Cyril danced with Elizabeth, and I could not describe his astonishment when he saw me dancing with Captain Clark. I smiled at him, hoping he would understand that he was not to worry and make a scene about it.

But Cyril was not the only one who was surprised. The Duke of Winchester was watching me from the side of the ballroom, quite intrigued by my indifference towards him and puzzled over my choice in a dance partner. We bowed to each other and to my astonishment, Lady Winston was not at his side. I could not account for her absence that evening. It was then that Mr. Connelly and I inevitably met on the turn of the dance.

After the first dance, I found Catherine and introduced her to Captain Clark. She found him to be agreeable, and then she congratulated me on my gown. She called it a nice compliment to my whole presence.

I was wearing my favorite white muslin dress, which happened to be my most provocative one. She was in the company of the famous Lady Stella Cooper. After the introductions were done, the infamous lady writer stared at me for a while, but a few moments later, I felt that she had lost any interest in me. Unlike Lady Winston, I did not want to be considered by her at all.

My brother and Miss Bowen came to my side too, and I managed to whisper to my brother that Captain Clark's company was very much accepted by me. He shook his head, but he left at Elizabeth's request to accompany her for a walk in the garden.

The moment that Captain Clark left me alone to go and pay his respects to Lady DeSalles, none other than James Connelly inquired of me about the next dance. But this time I was not in the spirit of accepting his company and I refused to dance; I may have been courteous at our previous encounter, but this was merely under the guise of revenge.

"Mr. Connelly, are you out of your mind?" I asked, trying to keep a reasonable distance from him. "I have seen you staring at me all evening; are you willingly trying to produce an unwanted public discussion?"

"You have told me not to forget you!"

His smile was proof enough of his state of mind. It was all about remembering the picnic and the mental lustful desire that memory brought upon him. I supposed that my silly remark gave him some sort of misleading hope.

"Miss Somerton, I know how this may appear, but for my own sake I must swallow my pride and repeat myself; I beg of you to not treat me with indifference. I am tormented by the memory of our love…"

"Mr. Connelly, by any measure of imagination you must not ask of me such a thing." This was the most inopportune time for him to declare his sentiments for me again.

"I dare to hope when I make this request of you. I am about to ruin my life and you are the one wonderful and meaningful part of my life. I am willing to take my chances. I do not care of what others may gossip…"

"May I remind you that you are engaged?"

"Of course but I consider you a very dear friend," he said

with a soft tone of voice, and I turned to him with a puzzled expression on my face. "Everything that I have accomplished in my music, so far, I owe to you", he continued. "I would like for you to consider me a friend as well…"

That was his way of safely asking me to not disregard him entirely and perhaps to allow him in my circle of friends, regardless of our awkward situation. I must admit that I could not understand his willingness to prolong his pain instead of choosing to forget me.

"Thank you, Mr. Connelly; I may very well do that. But now, look at my circle of friends, all of whom are of high rank in society. Nevertheless, I currently have a marriage proposal, and soon my family will be in the rightful possession of Chatham Hill once again. And there is more to be expected – an even closer relationship with the royals may be in sight. You must choose to stay apart from me, James. I am only your past but not your future."

Now, more than ever, I knew that I must prevail.

"I had you and I lost you," he whispered. "How can I live with that?"

James Connelly bowed to me and left, taking his sufferings with him. For the very first time, against my own will, in my silly heart, I felt sympathy for him. I was healing from the hurt he had caused me, and I had hope – but it appeared that there was no healing on his part.

From a window on an upper floor I had seen my brother and Elizabeth walking in the garden, and they both seemed very interested in each other. No matter who stirred the gossip about my family in a new direction, I was willing to keep my own promise. Marrying Captain Clark was my next step, but I had to be clever about it.

My dance partner found me again and for the first time I was quite delighted because of his presence. He felt my changed attitude, which made him extremely happy. He was close to being giddy and ridiculous. Not that it was necessary to seduce him, but I did everything for him to like me more, mostly responding to his smile and to his playfulness. People were beginning to remark about our closeness, but not many knew how awkward our alliance might be. After the dance, I did not think a walk in the park would be improper. It was a pleasant early summer evening, and some of the other guests came outside to enjoy it.

"You are a sprightly dancer, Captain Clark. I am impressed."

"I did try very hard to impress you and I am happy that this, at least, was accomplished. I am not sure that our last encounter three weeks ago did me any justice."

"You surprised me a bit tonight, but my cousin described you well. Do you remember Louisa? Actually, you are in her debt, because she was the one who extended to you the favor of the dinner invitation."

Curiosity spurred me to inquire about his opinion of the one who, so far, was in love with him. Even as I asked the question, I did not hope for a favorable answer.

"Oh yes, Miss Louisa Somerton. At first I thought she was you, but I was happy to be wrong. To be honest, you are more than I could ever hope for or imagine. I watched you all evening, and I am certain that I am in love with you."

"Be careful, Captain Clark, I may be tempted to believe you."

He took my hands and kissed them passionately. I felt nothing more than his lips touching my skin, but his declaration of love did so much good for my spirit.

"If I were to say 'yes' to your proposal of marriage," I started, softening my voice, "I must know that your uncle will not interfere. At this point, I am not positive that he is aware of your intentions. And, of course, I need to inform my family as well."

"Does this mean you are considering my proposal? Oh, Miss Somerton, I assure you that you have no worry in regard to my uncle. I will take care of the matter and he will not interfere, I promise."

"Answer me, Captain Clark, what prompted your desire to make this unusual proposal?" This question provoked in me a significant amount of stress for the past few days. "I am sure you did not merely wake up one morning, wanting to make this sort of concession to my family."

"You are right," he answered jovially as he offered me his arm for support. "But besides feeling unworthy to possess your home, I had the honor of meeting your sister, Cecilia. She is quite a handsome lady and I had no doubt that she would have a more handsome younger sister. Then, I was intrigued by my uncle's love for Mrs. Somerton.

"At first it was just curiosity to meet you as my uncle suggested, but to call upon you would not have been proper. I did not want to risk your hatred for me more than was already there or to have you avoid me. Week after week I realized I was falling in love with you without even knowing you; at the news of your broken engagement I was very close to falling sick from excitement. When I finally saw you at Lady Edwina's ball, I knew I had to do everything in my power to marry you."

I came to the conclusion that he had made himself lovesick over me. But how should I respond? I could not risk another failed engagement and more ridicule.

"What about your uncle? How will you tell him?"

"As simply as possible. He would not disagree."

"What if he did?" My heart was racing with emotions. "You could not ignore his wishes!"

"Why would he disagree? If he still has feelings for Mrs. Somerton, he would want to have easy access to her heart again. Our alliance would make this an ideal prospect."

"I am not sure that he cares about my mother anymore, when he would scheme to deliberately leave her penniless and in shame. What kind of love is that?"

"I understand your thinking very well. It did occur to me that his actions did not sustain his motives, unless he is planning to do something wonderful for your family…"

"That is absurd and you know it, Captain Clark! I need to know that you are not going to fail me and our future together by being timid with your uncle. I need for you to understand that I will come with a price, and that is for you to choose between him and me. Are you willing to go that far?"

We stopped by the fountain on the way back into the palace. Again he took my hands and kissed them passionately.

"You have my answer, Miss Somerton. Nothing will take you away from me, I promise. Chatham Hill is mine, and only mine. Soon it will be yours again, if you wish it

CHAPTER 12

THIRTY-FIVE YEARS AGO, MY father, Charles Somerton, inherited from his uncle, Edward Somerton, a decent sized property six miles away from a very important naval town called Chatham. My father was only sixteen years old at the time his uncle died. The inheritance was contested by Claude Somerton, Uncle Edward's cousin, but my father was within his rights according to the will of record.

Claude Somerton managed the property until my father turned twenty one. The house on the property was old and it was seemingly worthless, but the land would bring a comfortable living of five thousand a year. Father made the decision instantly. He would rebuild the house on the estate and he would move his family here.

A few years later that happened. The rebuilt mansion now sits on a high hill, three stories tall; large, but with a beautiful sense of proportion. The mansion was constructed of light colored stone with fine, immense windows. The Colonel was very proud of his project.

The road up to the mansion was not straight up the hill. It started straight, than began curving to the right, with a broad turn back to the left before it ended at the front of the house. Because there was not a lake or a river nearby, Father had an enormous pool dug in the back of the mansion, surrounded with fountains, statues and beautiful gardens on both sides. He named it Chatham Hill, after the nearby town of the same name.

When we moved to Chatham Hill from London, Colonel Robert Somerton, my father's younger brother, moved from the fort into our old house.

There is a six year age gap that exists between Louisa and her younger sister, Caroline. Soon after Caroline's birth, their mother died, leaving the two girls in the care of their father. Uncle Robert was on active duty at this time and was continually being transferred between England, India, and Egypt. As a consequence, our family at Chatham Hill grew overnight. Father brought Louisa and Caroline to Chatham Hill, in my opinion, just to clear his conscience about being the older brother and inheriting everything.

Caroline was placed in the care of Mrs. Henry, our nanny and governess, but shortly afterward Mrs. Henry died of a heart attack, according to Dr. Rowland, our family doctor. Mrs. Henry's daughter, Anna, who was only twenty-four at the time, gratefully accepted my father's offer to finish her schooling and replace her mother in our family.

Anna did not come alone. Her younger brother was now entirely in her care. William Henry was only seventeen, about the same age as my sister, Cecilia. With all of my cousins and us on the first floor and with Anna, William, and Mr. and Mrs. Longwood on the third floor, Chatham Hill was occupied to its capacity.

I do remember Father so clearly, riding his favorite big horse, Dune, side by side with Cyril and William Henry. Later, Father sent William off to school. William and Father had such a strong connection with the love for horses; William would have gladly accepted any job in our family. It was Cecilia's conviction, however, that he was above the inferior position of a house boy and horse groom. She persuaded Father to continue in his benefactor role as he did with William's older sister earlier.

It was sad to see William leaving for school in London, but it was not Anna whose eyes were filled with tears and who was hiding in her room, but my sister, Cecilia. I was only ten, then, and I did not understand much about what had possessed Cecilia to act in the way she did. My only thought was that her overreaction was because she was a weak and tender spirit.

That fall, we had our first ball in Chatham Hill to celebrate Cecilia's coming out into society. At eighteen, she was the most beautiful young lady in the room and many of the gentlemen were impressed by her. I could not accuse her of being too shy, but nothing would explain why she would deliberately excused herself from any other public appearances or gatherings from that day on.

The suitors for Cecilia came and went without a positive answer from her.

The next year, in the spring, William Henry returned to Chatham Hill for a visit, and we all found him to be remarkably well composed, to our great satisfaction. He delivered an eloquent speech of thankfulness to my father and stared at Cecilia the whole time. He only spent only a month with us, during which time my sister grew more beautiful and delightful – quite lively I do admit.

A closer examination of all the signs that were open to my discretion should have revealed a connection there, but my mind was occupied with something on my own. As had become routine, I was going to London with Louisa, Caroline and Anna, to spend the summer at Uncle Robert's house.

Our old house in London was now occupied only by Uncle Robert and his housekeeper. It was not in a very prominent part of city, but it afforded the perfect opportunity for us to take long walks to the best parts of London. We were, of course, accompanied by Anna. We would wander through the streets, admiring the buildings, mansions, palaces, and the stores. Our favorite place to go was Mr. Rolling's music store, where I actually met James Connelly for the first time. His father was purchasing a new fortepiano for him, and I remember how carefully he was inspecting each of them.

I was fifteen years of age and James was perhaps four years older than me. I was playing on the one instrument I considered my favorite. Mr. Rolling, being good friend with my uncle, did not mind our innocent company.

When James approached me, he asked my permission to try the instrument and I quickly gave him access to the keyboard, surprised by his handsome face and his good manners. He sat down on the bench, and in that moment, probably trying to impress me, he played beautifully the same piece with which I had been struggling.

I have never heard anyone so wonderfully gifted in executing so flawlessly and effortlessly such a difficult etude. I was so impressed. I could not even respond to his complement about my impeccable choice of the best instrument in the store. One hour later, he and the piano were gone, and my heart was gone with them.

Three months later, tragedy struck too soon. Father began to complain about an untreated wound that had become infected. Gangrene spread rapidly throughout his left leg. Dr. Rowland amputated his leg in order to save his life, but was too late; he died a month later.

I was only fifteen, and it was the saddest day of my life.

Life after Father's death was a slow descent into nothingness. We lost the pillar and the support of our family. Cyril was to inherit the estate, along with the promise that Chatham Hill would be mother's residence until her death. We, the girls, received an inheritance of five thousand each.

In the beginning we all cherished our solitude, but we found more perpetual peace in consoling each other. William Henry came for Father's funeral and expressed his sorrow and respectful gratitude to his benefactor. He remained at Chatham Hill into the summer to reassure us of his support, but by then I had left for London.

When I returned in early September, William announced the good news of his getting a pastorate somewhere in the north. He received all of our congratulations; however, when Cecilia looked at me, she appeared to be mortified.

Very soon after that, she accepted the proposal to marry Edgar Sutton. Cecilia was twenty-two and he was forty. So, with her marriage, she was gone.

Louisa was the next to leave our nest. For years, we all expected Uncle Robert to find a new wife and mistress of his household, but that never happened. Returning from a visit to London, Louisa told me that her father had recently returned from the recent war in France. He was sad and lonely, and the house had become such a morbid place. She was sixteen and she felt bold enough to take on the responsibilities of managing a household. Caroline was to move to London with her, and our governess would also move, at my mother insistence. We would not have accepted it in any other way. Anna was indispensable to them.

When I went to visit her, I was so impressed with her accomplishments. Everything was luminous and neat, a reflection of her taste for brightness and playfulness. Uncle Robert was unrecognizable from the last time I had seen him, visibly happy and content.

I confess that it was my malicious wish for Louisa's failure, but seeing all that she had accomplished, I buried my intent to convince her to come back to Chatham Hill. I had to be honest and embrace the family I lost and gained at the same time. I was merely feeling lonely and selfish for myself.

Indeed, Chatham Hill was the shelter and pride of my family. I loved the big entrance gallery with its dozen two storey high columns, masterfully carved and engraved, and the splendid staircase going up to the second floor. Such playful times Louisa and I would have with the solid oak balustrade. We would dare to bend over it recklessly, until Mrs. Henry would scream, very much displeased by our dangerous game.

But my favorite place was the small library, mine and Father's favorite place of all. It was not big, but it contained many volumes of the best literature and poetry that he loved and in which he delighted. His big leather chair was still there, almost waiting for its old master to return. When I was in that room, it was as if he never left. His presence was in everything he touched and did in this room, from the books he read and the letters he wrote, to the furniture and paintings. In here was all the blending, in such a comforting evidence, of his existence.

I would not let go of my home! I would do anything in my power to bring it back including marrying Captain Clark, the nephew of my enemy.

Mrs. Longwood was wrong – there was no curse upon my home.

CHAPTER 13

LOUISA'S SICKNESS HAD SHORTENED MY visit with Lady Edwina, but I was already longing to go back to Uncle Robert's house. I rushed to her bed, full of fear and remorse for all I had concealed from her or that I had her to sacrifice for me.

Uncle Robert, visibly worried, brought home a doctor who quarantined her room and kept us outside until he was certain that she was not contagious – he was afraid that Louisa might have contracted pneumonia. It was not pneumonia, to our relief, but an unfamiliar disease related to her blood and a persistent lack of nourishment that was still too dangerous for her fragile body.

Cyril came to tell me that he was invited to dine at Miss Bowen's house with her father that evening, but he was not sure if he should go if Louisa's condition was worsening. I encouraged him to go because we could do nothing for Louisa other than wait for her improvement. Finally, a sweet and expected victory! We could not start their relationship with his absence from such an important social gathering.

"She is going to recover soon, I am sure of it" I said hopefully. "What happened to her in my absence?"

"She was somewhat unhappy, to say the least," answered

Cyril, "and three days ago she left for London to see the marching parade. She has not been well since."

"But that was last Saturday, which was an extremely hot day!"

"She was gone for four hours. I did not know that she had planned to see the parade. Why she would do such a thing?"

I knew! Louisa was hoping to see Captain Clark in the ranks, I am sure. If he was in the parade, he had no idea that my cousin was looking for him. It is true, she does love him and she builds up dreams about him. I was about to destroy all of her fantasies, and not by myself. Captain Clark was a willing participant, innocent of knowing her feelings, but I was not.

But what could I do? He wanted me, he came looking for me, and he loved me before he met Louisa. This was all for my benefit, of course and I liked it – I could not deny it. What would happen to her when she found out? What would happen with our most precious friendship?

I loved my cousin and I was in such awful pain about what I was about to do, but I must go forward. If I gave up Captain Clark just for her, I would lose the opportunity to regain my home and my life would forever be in ruins. No one would ever want me as their wife, and I would die as an old maid. Even if Cyril married Elizabeth, I would be doomed by the curse of a shady scheme.

"My dear Cleona, you look so disturbed,' said my brother. "Are you feeling well?"

"No, Cyril, I am not."

My brother came to sit beside me and he took my hand. He was very worried about me and I had to tell him what was happening. I had been fighting for so long with myself, concerned with my own dreams, worries, plans, and plots. I expected so much from everyone, and primarily I expected the most from Cyril.

"Can you tell me? Is it Louisa?"

"I am distraught about Louisa, but it is not related to her sickness," I cried.

"I saw Captain Clark in your constant company at the ball. Did he threaten you in any way?"

"No, his company was welcomed. He actually behaved very well and I cannot complain."

"Why would you accept his company, then? And moreover, you danced with him all night. And you walked with him in the garden … quite strange. What is the problem? I thought he was the enemy…"

"It is his uncle who is our enemy, not him. I find him to be pleasant and civil."

"Pleasant and civil?" My brother was extremely surprised by my words. "Perhaps so, but why would you bother with him at all?"

"He was very nice when he was with me," I answered, stubbornly defending my opinions. "He paid me much respect and attention. In my condition, not too many other men would do so."

"What are you saying Cleona, that you only deserve attention from him? Look at you! You are the most amazing young lady I have ever seen…"

"Only because I am your sister…"

"No, it is because you are *you*. You are exuberant, talented, spirited, beautiful, full of life and very interesting. All the men I know are astonished by you. Why him?"

"He is in love with me. I know you are surprised, Cyril, but I need your support in what I am about to say. Please, my dear brother…"

Cyril looked at me in total disbelief. The hat that he had been holding in his hand as he was preparing to go out was thrown on the chair.

"He asked for my hand in marriage," I continued, ignoring his little outburst. "I did not say yes for now, but I am considering it."

"Cleona!"

"Cyril, please listen," I implored him. My attempt to convince my brother of my rationality was somewhat pathetic. "He is as good as anyone. I could be happy with him and have Chatham Hill back in our family. This is a desirable prospect, and I am aware of what I am doing."

"This is all my fault and you are paying for it."

"It is not your fault. I will not allow you to feel this way, ever."

"But it would be different…"

"I would still consider Captain Clark. He is indeed a remarkable young man. His only fault is to have such a horrible uncle."

"Are you sure? Cleona, I am concerned! I have already one sister married to an unworthy creature, and I do not want to have another one in that same condition."

"You have changed too, Cyril. You are much more mature."

"Our lives have been changed. I assume, then, that Captain Clark will require my permission?"

"There is no rush. He still must settle with his uncle."

"Are you implying that Colonel Radisson does not know his intentions? But this is impossible! Thomas is known for blindly obeying his uncle."

"I hope love will change that, for our own sake."

"Do you really want him? I am sorry! I am still debating in my mind if I should follow my instincts and do something to prevent this marriage."

"Please, do not make it harder than is. It is an enormous struggle for me. I have to hope that the nephew of my enemy will rescue me, and above all, I must tell my beloved cousin that the man with whom she is in love wishes to marry me."

Cyril was holding his head in his palms, refusing to listen to any more surprises. Welcome to my world, my brother.

"I urge you to leave now, Cyril. You cannot delay this dinner with Miss Bowen and her family. I will watch over Louisa."

Sometimes there is no joy in victory and all wars have innocent losses. I started to think like my father, believing that every catastrophe would bring sought after harmony.

When Cyril finally left, I attempted to see if I could get any good news from Louisa's doctor. He was optimistic, but he said it would take time for her to recover. I walked around the house, downstairs and upstairs, without finding anything to keep me occupied. Later, I began to play music.

Caroline came and stood by me at the fortepiano, and Anna brought us tea. Music made us all feel better. I began to play a song that Mr. Connelly had written for me long ago, but I could not remember all of it. To my surprise, Anna took Caroline's place and corrected me.

"How do you remember this song?"

"You used to play it all the time for Louisa. It is not that hard."

"It is hard, Anna! You are an extraordinary woman, and I want thank you for taking care of me and my family so well. All of my outstanding education is because of you."

"Except for the fact that you have the talent I could not give you," she answered. "It is you, Miss Cleona, it is only you, and I am so proud of your accomplishments."

"Anna, you could be so much more than our governess. Of course, I am grateful to you for choosing us."

"I am happy to be in your family. I would not have been anything had it not been for your father. My brother feels the same way. I do not aspire to anything more."

"Anna, do you remember when father died?" I asked of her suddenly. "He died because of the gangrene of his leg, is it true?"

I wanted someone's assurance that the facts I knew to be true, were true. Anna would not have any hidden motive to invent a different story. I would never want to start such a subject to Mrs. Longwood – I knew her opinion already.

"Yes, my dear. Your father died because of his wound."

"It was always my deepest fear that he would not come back from the war alive or he would be mortally wounded. And it happened." I hit a minor chord on the instrument and the sound of it made me sad.

"Colonel Somerton was not hurt in the war, my dear," said Anna softly. "I thought you knew."

Instantly I reached with my both hands for the edge of the fortepiano, holding my breath. My heart lapsed for a moment and my chest began to hurt.

"Are you aware of what had happened? I am embarrassed to say this, but at the time, some details escaped my attention. Please tell me."

The thought that my father could have been murdered made me sick to my stomach.

"All I know is that he returned from a trip to Miltonville shot in the leg, just above the knee. He declared to us that it was a silly accident – he was cleaning his gun, but I am certain that he never took his guns when traveled unless he attended one of those hunting events at Galveston. At first he ignored the wound, but it soon became infected…Oh! I hear the teakettle. I must go to the kitchen. Are you all right?"

I nodded. My hands fell off of the fortepiano, and I could play no more. Caroline wanted me to read to her or play cards. Then she wanted to show me all the drawings she had worked on for the past few weeks. None of her little suggestions for activities were appealing to me.

"I am so tired my dear. I must go and rest."

But I could not fall asleep. My mind was simply too busy. A

feeling of fear invaded my soul, the same fear I felt when a child, that Father would not come home from the war. But Father admitted that his wound was an accident. I have been such a superficial, ignorant girl and never bothered to ask for more particulars. I should not upon this subject any longer. Certainly Mrs. Longwood was wrong about it. Father shot himself by accident – it was not murder. Or was it?

But I would write to Cecilia for more information about Captain Clark and his uncle. I knew that she thought him to be tolerable, but how would she react to the idea of me marrying him? Cyril was right – Cecilia's marriage was awful and I wished to see her safe. I certainly would not want my husband to behave in the same manner as hers. Colonel Radisson was such a bad influence on her husband. I *would* have my revenge – I would marry his nephew!

My pillow was soft and warm. I closed my eyes, trying to remember Captain Clark's face. Would I ever be able to love him? Perhaps later, but not now. I had been in love with James Connelly because my heart was wide open for it, as Louisa's was now.

But Thomas Clark was better looking and more romantic than James. This decision should not be difficult, except I did not feel that I was ready for love, I was too afraid. But at last, someone loved me and I feel empowered.

Outside my door, I heard the doctor saying goodbye to Uncle Robert and the front door closed. After a few moments there was a complete silence. I fell asleep and dreamed something that was unpleasant and confusing.

CHAPTER 14

.ON A CHILLY, DRIZZLY SUNDAY morning I departed for the St. John Street church, a long walk I was willing to take. This time I dressed properly, putting on one of Louisa's old dresses and a small bonnet.

There was a chance I would encounter the Duke of Winchester, but I did not think he would recognize me dressed so plainly. My whole soul was battling between the love for my cousin and my own prosperity and protection. How was I to live through this?

Reverend Warren preached about casting our burden on Christ and at that moment I did what he asked. With all the humility of which I was capable, I asked for forgiveness and guidance. At that moment, I saw the Duke coming in from the back door. He took a seat immediately behind me. Now I had to pray that he would not notice me. But he was praying too, oblivious to the people around him.

My heart was beating so fast that I had to rise and leave before the service had ended. But in passing him, I did something bizarre and inexplicable: I touched his shoulder and took a seat next to him. He was quite surprised when he turned toward me; we sat there in silence for the rest of the service. It was the first time I had ever felt comfortable being close to him.

I watched the Duke from the corner of my eye and my heart was melting. He was none other than a suffering and tormented soul seeking deliverance. But how could this be so? He might still feel pain over the loss of a wife, but time will always heal a broken heart.

The Duke of Winchester was still the most desirable man in London – young, rich, and handsome. What hidden reason could there be to provoke him into such visible pain? My hands were restless and I had to restrain myself from touching him again – such inappropriate behavior in a church!

When the service was over, I left without a word, embarrassed at my intrusion into what were his most sensitive and private moments. He followed me immediately, but I just wanted to return to Uncle Robert's home.

"Miss Somerton! I hope you are not running away from me again."

"No, Your Grace, how could I?" I turned to him, but I could not force a smile.

"I was merely wondering. Here, we meet again. I am delighted to see you. Would you allow me to escort you home?"

"I am walking."

"My horse likes to walk, too."

The rain had passed to the east and the day had become clear and warm, so I removed my awful bonnet. Some people were passing us in a hurry to get to their homes, while some just strolled by, wanting to enjoy the beautiful, sunny day.

"You did not recognize me in these clothes, I assume." Oh Lord, such a silly notion. What was the matter with me?

"On the contrary," he answered and bowed. "I had no expectation of seeing you here and I was delighted that you had once again joined our congregation. May I inquire as to your cousin's health?"

"She is improving, thank you, sir." My hands started to perspire and I felt a bit dizzy.

"Last week at the ball I had to contain my belief that you disliked me…"

"Not at all. I was merely trying to avoid you." My stupid sincerity seemed to affect him, but in a different way.

"I thought we were settled in our friendship."

"No, we were not. I did indeed manage to explain to you my disastrous family situation and provoke compassion from you, but I am still incapable of being comfortable and tranquil with you."

"I regret this profoundly," he said, and his face turned pale.

He took my hand and kissed it.

Now I was surprised beyond description.

"I was most grateful for your attention," he continued and his beautiful smile mesmerized me. "There is nothing to forgive. I come to this church very often, not only in my duties for the people, but for my spiritual strength as well. Here I can unleash my soul and find peace, even if it only lasts for a short while. I may appear to be somewhat unsociable to you, and that is why you cannot find any compelling reason to be in my company."

"I am not actually avoiding you. For some reason, Lady Winston and I are not very civil in each other's presence. My logic is sophomoric when I am around you and her, and my opinions are indefensible. This makes no sense to you, does it?" I asked blushing.

"Actually it does," he rushed to agree with me. "She has a quite unpleasant demeanor."

"Very, I should say." I smiled too at the thought of Lady Winston's face if she were to hear us at his moment. "Your Grace, far be it from me to judge or even dare to have an opinion about your affairs, but to me, your tolerance for Lady Winston is bizarre. However, it is not at all uncommon. Perhaps my feeling of inferiority is blinding me."

"Please, allow me to explain."

"There is no need to do that, my Lord. Please forget that I brought this matter up – I have managed to embarrass myself once again. Perhaps I am the strange one, not Lady Winston. Look at me now, dressed as I am...and then, everywhere I appear, I am too flamboyant and opinionated. We should not be even talking or walking together."

"You are too severe with yourself, Miss Somerton. You are very beautiful, and I have the utmost admiration for you," he whispered to me.

I just could not hide my surprise; for a few moments I stood there, incapable of any response. There was no doubt in my mind that he was an absolute charmer and I was just another naive girl, so easy to deceive.

"You, Sir, are too much of a gentleman for me to believe that you not sincere. But I do not deserve your admiration. Besides, I am returning to Chatham Hill in a very short time. By then, you will forget about the country girl who made some funny remarks to you."

"Are you leaving London, so soon?" His voice changed a bit and I sense a bit of disappointment in his question. At that moment he started to walk even slower.

"It is time. As you know, my mother and I will have to vacate our house in September."

"Can you not stay here longer?" His questions and his train of thought did not make much sense to me.

"I have no reason to prolong my stay."

This time he was hesitant.

"Miss Catherine's wedding is in three weeks. I am sure she would like for you to be present. You two have developed a friendship and I can tell that she cherishes you."

"I did receive a wedding invitation but I can assure you, my absence will go unnoticed."

"Not by me. I would like the opportunity to see you more often."

"Your Grace!" I tried to maintain a dignified posture, but his answer struck me like lightening.

"I am sincere." His dark blue eyes were so intense as they gazed at me. "You are very charming to be around, so refreshing and a bit seductive. I have never encountered anyone like you in my life. I am becoming extremely attracted to you … more and more…"

"Please, Your Grace, do not say that. This is not the time or the place… I do not understand…"

"Neither do I, but these are my true feelings for you."

We walked quietly for the rest of the way; he, still hesitant to continue the conversation and me, too shocked to find anything intelligent to say. In front of my uncle's house, I thanked him and curtsied.

But before I knew it, he took my hand and kissed it softly then gently he laid it on his heart. My whole body started to shake.

I ran inside, speechless. I knew right away that I needed to keep away from the Duke of Winchester, to never see him again.

But that kiss changed everything. I was falling in love with him.

CHAPTER 15

ALL THE CANDLES IN THE candlesticks were beautifully lit. I did not see the reason for these candles, because it was still daylight, but Louisa insisted. Yesterday, we received a note in the mail from Captain Clark, announcing his special wish to be allowed to visit us and, if it were not to be considered uncivil, to bring a favorite guest.

Of course, I did not decline it and I followed with an invitation for dinner. It had been more than a month since his first visit to Uncle Robert's house and a week since our last encounter. My curiosity was profound – he should have already had that dreadful discussion with Colonel Radisson by now.

There is no need to say how Louisa's preparations were in the expectation of his arrival. All that morning, she and Anna changed all the drapes in the living room, dusted the big and heavy dining furniture, and polished the silver. Louisa and I had not talked about Captain Clark since I returned from Lady Edwina's palace, and she was grateful for my indifference to the subject.

The irony of all this was that we both had high expectations to emerge from his visit. If he was to be restricted by his uncle from marrying me, than I would remain silent about it. But if not, the curtain would soon rise, and all of this drama would necessarily unfold. I would have to reveal to Louisa my relationship with Captain Clark.

I did not volunteer to help in any way because I was too distracted by my own thoughts, but I craved so much to talk with Louisa again about my deepest feelings. This day would end one way or the other, but in the midst of it, I was not desperate anymore. In the past few days I was only halfway present to everyone around me, and no one seemed to understand, nor could they could suspect, the real reason.

I had seldom daydreamed in the past, but I was daydreaming now, and the subject of my excitement was the Duke of Winchester. If I could only undo my walk with him, us sitting together in the church, and the last words he had spoken to me, I would be able to regain my coolness again.

How could I remove these feelings growing inside me and totally devote myself to satisfying my pursuits and commitments?

Day after day I waited for him to write to me, that he denied all the words he had spoken to me and that he was asking for my forgiveness for his being improper and untruthful. But nothing arrived in the post except for Captain Clark's letter. What I struggled over was the little that he had omitted, that I was blowing out of proportion.

The fact that he admitted that he was attracted to me did not mean that he was in love with me; merely, his eyes were attracted to my person. And here I was instead, not attempting to guard my heart as I should have done. I was so affected, to the point of acting like my cousin.

It seemed peculiar to me to be in Captain Clark's presence again, and having my cousin between us. He did not come to dinner alone, but with his younger sister, Evelyn. Contrary to my expectation, she was a very pleasant girl. She immediately caught my attention and showered me with compliments.

To me, her behavior was an indirect answer to the issues

that Captain Clark and I must resolve. His attitude was inclining in the same direction and it made me anxious to have a more intimate conversation with him.

The atmosphere at the dinner table was pleasurable, the guests made all the necessary efforts to express their gratitude for being invited and for the special pleasure they found in our company. This time, Thomas was more attentive to Louisa, perhaps trying to win her as an ally for future encounters. She was ecstatic. But for most of the dinner his eyes were on me, unable to hide his favoritism. Uncle Robert seemed to have an enjoyable time and predicted that Captain Clark would have a splendid military future. The only person who was uncomfortable was Cyril, who had full knowledge of our unsettled situation and could not seem to relax.

After numerous attempts, I could find no pretext to speak with my guest privately, and considering the outcome of the evening, it would have been impossible to take him away from Louisa's sight.

But before they departed for the evening, Thomas managed to slip a note into my hand containing an invitation to visit him and his sister at Mr. Reeves' home.

* * *

I had a little trouble finding Mr. Reeves' home, hidden behind a multitude of trees down on Temple Street. As I approached from the adjoining alley, I was surprised to see a new mansion in such an old part of the town.

I did not use the carriage because that would have stirred too much curiosity from Louisa and I knew for a fact that my brother would never accept to chaperone me in that particular visit. This was an unprecedented adventure on my own – but at this point in my life, I was ready to take risks.

My horseback riding experience was close to nonexistent. My horse gave up on me half way to the entrance, and I was grateful to see Captain Clark running down the drive to welcome me. While we continue walking to the mansion, Thomas, now unrestricted by anyone's presence, took my hands again and kissed them passionately. A moment later, however, his manner became more reserved, triggered by the appearance of his sister.

Evelyn was only fourteen years of age. She was a little too tall for her age, but she was a very friendly and sweet young girl. What I was to soon discover was that she was so sincere in her opinions; one could not be prepared for them. Cecilia's letter about Captain Clark's sisters was still fresh in my memory, but Evelyn definitely possessed nothing malignant in her attitude. Once inside Mr. Reeves' mansion, she took over the conversation.

"Miss Somerton, what a pleasure it is to meet you again! I am sure you are not aware of it, but I admire your dress very much. I have never seen anyone's attire more interesting. And I should add that you are a very handsome lady yourself. It is no wonder that my brother loves you. May I draw your portrait, please?"

"Evelyn."

Captain Clark smiled, embarrassed for his sister's confession, and made visible efforts to curb her enthusiasm.

"This is the most exciting news for me," Evelyn interjected. "My brother will get married, and to such a beautiful lady. The last time, Miss Piketon tried unsuccessfully to win his heart. It was almost pathetic to see her attempts."

"Evelyn, please," insisted her brother. "Do not bore Miss Somerton with such odious stories."

"But it is true! My sister Miriam is Miss Piketon's friend. The poor girl is quite plain, but you resemble a duchess, Miss Somerton."

"Thank you, my dear," I said, smiling as I listened to her sweet and innocent rambling. But she continued to talk vivaciously, encouraged by my attention.

"Louisa is pretty, too! And so is Caroline! Mr. Somerton is quite handsome, too. I like everyone in your family. Would you like to see my drawings?"

"Yes, I would…"

"Evelyn, my dear, give Miss Somerton some time to relax," intervened Captain Clark perhaps surprised that his little sister took possession of his guest. "Would you not rather go and do an arrangement of your paintings so she can see them better?"

While, Evelyn was running upstairs to begin her little project, I inquired of Mr. Reeves' whereabouts.

"He is out of town visiting his brother, but he is returning tomorrow. Mr. Reeves was a very good friend of my late father. I remember coming here to his house quite often when I was a little boy. He never stopped inviting me to visit every year."

"He is a charming person, I suppose."

Thomas took my hand again and tried unsuccessfully to say something, but his whole body was talking to me. I did not feel in danger at all.

I was aware of two kinds of passions: one, calm, when one is content simply to be in the presence of the loved one, to breathe the same air, to adore and worship that person; and two, explosive, when one is under a constant spell and there is a burning desire to express your feelings by words and affectionate actions.

Captain Clark was in this second category, and to my surprise, I was drawn to it as well.

"I adore you, Miss Cleona. I am quite mad about you. I wish to find a more sophisticated way to prove my love for you…"

"I believe you, Captain Clark." My spirit wanted to delight so lavishly in his charming, uncalculated declarations. "I must confess I came here with the high expectation of the proof of love you could express on my behalf."

"And I have it! First, it was the most wonderful thing that had ever happened to me to see you coming here. I had doubted that my wishes would come true, even though you gave me your assurance. I had carried my mission to the end and the result, although somewhat hostile concerning my relationship with my uncle, is totally worth the price of having you as my wife."

"Captain Clark, I am most disturbed…Please tell me all," I asked, a bit nervous as I took a seat on a chair beside the fireplace.

"I cannot describe my uncle's stupor when I announced my engagement to you," he started, taking a seat across from me. "You were right; he did find my action abhorrent and he demanded my total disconnection from you. He was in total disagreement with my plan and he was quite furious with me. It was frightening – I had never seen him this way before. I stood my ground and declined to listen, and I challenged him to give me a logical explanation of his spiteful attitude towards your family."

My nerves were stretched to their highest point. Would revenge be the real reason behind Colonel Radisson's path of destruction? Could it been extended to murder?

"I continued by telling him how much I love you and there was nothing he could do – that you had accepted my hand. That information left him speechless for a while. All I could assume was that he was thinking of your mother's refusal. Then, I implored him not to make his cause my own. If he could not accept my choice, then we must separate our ways.

"He asked me if that was my absolute decision. My definite answer to him was 'yes'. I asked him if he could diminish his animosity toward your family and accept me and my engagement with you. He was silent. With no affirmative answer, from that day my uncle will be a stranger to me. I left his home with Evelyn, my beloved sister. My older sisters, Margaret and Miriam, will continue to stay with him."

Listening to Captain Clark, I could not believe that his uncle would actually never have foreseen this coming to him. All of this extraordinary courage that Captain Clark showed to prove his love for me should have stirred some strong feelings in my heart; however, I was still cautious and insecure. What would happen if he should regret his harshness to his uncle and run back to the enemy's arms, falling under Colonel Radisson's poisoning influence? It had only been a week since their departure and remorse could have settled in.

I had to keep Captain Clark's full attention and his focus on me.

"Captain Clark, I am so impressed with your fight with your uncle for me. It has sufficiently proved your devotion. I hardly deserve it, but I am terrified that you will change your mind and reinstate your relationship with your uncle. As you know by now, the two of us cannot coexist, and this is unfortunate. Nevertheless, I cannot ask you to make this sacrifice."

"It is willingly made, Miss Somerton," he said with determination, and that moment I liked him even more. "All I want is for you to become my wife. I cannot live the rest of my life under my uncle's dominion, fighting his battles."

"But he provided Chatham Hill for you!"

"A gift I did not request or want, and it is only fair that I give it back to you through the only way possible. My uncle perhaps did not know my character when he made sure that I was to keep the property indefinitely."

"You are a most sensible person, Captain Clark. Forgive me for my doubts. If you could only imagine what I have had to endure…"

This time he came so close, bowed, and kissed my forehead. I held my breath not knowing how to react.

"I understand. Please put your beautiful mind to rest. I have other news that will not be so welcomed by you, but I need to prepare you for it. My regiment will soon be transferred to Dover Port for the fall and winter. I am to leave during the first week in August and return in March. I am aware of the insensibility to ask you for a rushed wedding. If you would but wait for my return…"

"Of course," I answered without hesitation, barely realizing that I just given my agreement to marry him.

But such a long engagement would be only beneficial for me. I had so many loose ends to tie, especially Louisa and Mother.

"But you must be there to take possession of Chatham Hill in September. That is a month after your transfer date."

"I do not need to be there. You will be there for me."

"I do not understand," I said a bit confused.

"I ask you not to leave Chatham Hill, but to continue to live there until I return."

"But it would not be right to," I argued while my heart tingled with happiness.

"Please, do not refuse me; it is my engagement present for you. The only favor I ask is that you allow Evelyn to live there until my return. My sister and I are very close. She depends upon me for her care, and now in my absence, she will have no one. It was settled for her to accompany me to Chatham Hill and I hope her wish to live there will find favor with you. Sending her back to my uncle is not an option. Please, Miss Cleona. She is a lovely child and she already adores you."

"Of course I will have her. Thomas! I apologize, I meant Captain Clark. This is the most wonderful gift for me, to remain at home until your return. Thank you so much."

"It is a delight to hear you say my name," he said caressing my hair.

"It was improper…"

"Your other family members can stay also, if they wish to do so."

"What about the servants, will you keep them all?"

"Certainly! They know better than me how to run that big mansion."

I was so happy. I laughed and giggled, and my fiancé enjoyed every minute of my silly outburst. How could I not be happy? All that I had fought for was given back to me: my home, my reputation and a sacrificial love that I could not dismiss. I would not have to endure ridicule from anyone or be forced into an exile, or worse – considering how to go about finding a job.

Captain Clark accompanied me to the gate where my horse was waiting.

My big horse would not easily acquiesce and let me ride him again. I did not seem to be able to keep him still. After Thomas held him tight, I could not get up onto the saddle; my dress was too tight, unfit for such a purpose.

He came behind me to help. I felt his warm breath on my neck and on the skin of my back. I turned towards him and our lips touched, just for a second.

He kissed me again more daring and passionate but I was slow to respond – my mouth felt cold and unresponsive. He stepped back and looked into my eyes. It was when I realized that my new fiancé was determined not to fail in marring the woman he wanted as his uncle did. In the next moment, two strong hands were holding my waist and lifting me up. The horse impatiently moved away from him and galloped out onto the street.

Why was I not shaking and becoming breathless, as I was when the Duke of Winchester kissed my hand?

CHAPTER 16

"*WE ARE SAFE, MAMA*," I wrote, trying to combine as much information and details as I could about the recent development of my engagement to Thomas Clark. I did not omit his devotion to me and his separation from his uncle, and mostly, his immeasurable goodness toward us all. Now it was not necessary for us to leave Chatham Hill, ever.

Cyril was passing time in the room, irritated, waiting for the hour when we must depart for the Bowen palace where we were to have tea and dinner with Elizabeth and her father. This time we did not leave Louisa at home and she was happy to leave the house for the first time since her illness.

Lord Bowen was tall and heavily built. His personality was a strange combination of humor and sarcasm, but he was polite to the extreme. He took a long look at me, and that made me a little uncomfortable, but then I learned that his sight was bad and he would stare at people for a while. His attitude towards my brother was cordial and tolerant, and that was a gratifying moment for me.

Meanwhile, Elizabeth and her younger sister came to welcome us. My brother's reaction to the younger lady was quite alarming to me, but it went unnoticed by the others. At sixteen years of age, Rosemary was handsome, beautifully built, and over all, the master of a contagious smile. I remembered the remarks that Catherine Rowe had made about her – a very charming young lady, and her opinion that Rose, the wild flower, was a lot like me. I did not disagree.

Nevertheless, Cyril's attraction to her must be put to an end immediately. After some thought, this explained much of his absent minded behavior of late. If he preferred Rosemary over her older sister, we had a problem of major proportions.

I quickly reviewed the situation in my mind. I was convinced of the disadvantage of him waiting for the little sister to come out in society. And then, it was uncertain if she would prefer him as much as Elizabeth did. I watched her, expecting her to show signs of interest in Cyril, but she was composed, and she neither blushed nor hesitated. For the moment, an unshared affection from her was welcome until I had more proof and I could mentally process the entire situation.

What a vicious circle seemed to follow me, to have one issue settled and then to have it necessary to worry and pursue another. I still withheld the news of my engagement to Captain Clark from Louisa.

I was incapable of building my courage to face her sorrow and disappointment. How quickly would I deliver the dreadful news to her, and when was I to sever any thoughts that my brother might have, deep in his heart, of romantic feelings for Rosemary?

At five o'clock, tea was served and the conversation was lightened by the very pleasant appearance of Lady Edwina de Winchester. Her company was splendid as she entertained us with her charming little stories from the time of her youth.

One story in particular stood out. It was about one of the officers who were given the most challenging duty of guarding and protecting her and her sister by her father. She was only twelve years of age and her younger sister, Elizabeth's mother, was nine. They wanted to go and see the royal ball that was being held across the street at their uncle's palace. But theirs was not an easy task – they could not leave their home unobserved by their guardian, and if they ever managed to get to the royal ball, everyone would certainly observe two little girls running around unattended. Moreover, their parents would act upon their transgression very harshly.

"So," she continued, "I opened the door and took a look at our officer to assess his character. Would he be for us or against us? He was very young and handsome, at least in my childish eyes. For some reason, I knew he would play our game. When I explained to him what we wanted, he had us dressed nicely and he handed me a book of poems. He took us across the street to the palace where he announced a surprise: the reading of a poem dedicated to the honor of the hosts.

"Our parents were horrified to see us proudly march over through the crowd and loudly recite a poem that was unknown to everyone. During the recitation I kept my eyes fixed on my lovely new friend. It all ended well and we were loudly applauded. Our parents were angry with us and with the officer, but they knew who was to blame."

I could only imagine the young Edwina Nottingham trying to rule the whole world with her own special charm.

"You were quite the playful child, my dear sister," Lord Bowen remarked. "I assure you that this side of my wife's personality was totally hidden from me."

"She was more temperate, my dear brother."

"What happened to the officer?" I asked, sincerely curious.

"He continued to remain faithful to my father's house for the next ten years, until I married. I wanted to help advance his career, but he refused. He was my dear friend, being on my side during my wild years when I was growing up. I cared about him a great deal."

"What happened to him after you were married?" I was sincerely interested in this story as its familiarity intrigued me more.

"He retired to his estate in the country and gave up the military. Edward later died in a tragic hunting accident… It was only after his demise that I discovered who wrote the poems: he did. He loved to write and I believe he left an undiscovered legacy behind. As far as I know, his beloved nephew inherited his estate."

I did not dare to ask his name but an eerie revelation struck me – was she possibly speaking of none other but my great uncle, Edward Somerton? After we had our dinner, which was quite lavish, Elizabeth offered refreshments on the veranda, and I took the advantage of the guests' departure to stay behind with Lady Edwina.

"Lady de Winchester, would you find me intrusive if I asked you the last name of the officer who was your guardian?"

"Oh, my dear, I can see that your mind is seeking a certain answer from me which I am willing to give." Lady de Winchester sadly smiled, not to me but to her own memories. "I can remember a tormented time in my life when self-denying was expected as a gratifying edification. But learning to live by accepting yourself is a different battle. Edward Somerton loved me indeed, and for what it is worth, I loved him also. He was much older than me, a commoner, and I was very young. Naturally, I was not consulted when a promise was made on my behalf for marriage, but I did what was expected of me."

"Did you ever consider him?" This was another question that I had no control to withhold.

"Will you deign to judge me for it? There is no need. I did consider him. But eloping with him and bringing disgrace to my family was not a good option at that time. What is most detestable is that I did follow him to his house, and then I sent for the

Duke of Winchester to bring me back to the palace. My hurt made me grow insensible to my own heart and I considered dignity and honor the only rational approach to face my destiny."

"I dare to ask, were you unhappy?" I asked and my voice trembled.

"Certainly not! The Duke of Winchester was a wonderful man. We were happy together, and considering all things, we had a wonderful life."

"But…"

"Why do you think is a 'but' there?"

I turned red, embarrassed, forgetting with whom I was talking. But Lady Edwina smiled back to me.

"The Duke was not Edward Somerton. I had seen Edward after I married. I sent him numerous invitations to court – and sometimes he came. My husband delighted in going hunting with him at times, always on opposite teams, except for that day when he died. The Duke was the one who brought me the terrible news that Edward had been accidently shot by his younger nephew; I believe he was only thirteen at the time, while trying to teach him to hunt. I was devastated – of course. I could say that l loved him until his death."

The fact that for the first time ever I was told about this version of Uncle Edward's death involving the actions and the guilt of my dear Uncle Robert was shocking and painful, to say the least. More, the embarrassment of such knowledge made me remain quiet and apathetic. Surely, because this happened more than thirty years ago and uncle was just a young boy, perhaps he was not too affected by the memories of such horrible accident.

Indeed – what a tragedy befell our family. But it was over now – no more of it.

Certainly, this fully explained Lady de Winchester's kindness and generosity to me and my brother. In my mind, I could go back in time and see the young and playful Edwina being in love with the young and handsome officer, Edward Somerton. What a fiery but impossible love they must have had, and how sadly life ended for Edward, unable to live life to the fullest with the one he truly loved.

Here I was, engaged to a man for whom I possessed no strong feelings of love and, I must confess, it did not concern me. His love for me would compensate for my lack love for him, but would it be sufficient to bring us both happiness? The more I reflected upon the subject, the more convinced I became of its rationality.

On the veranda a reflection of my feelings was occurring. Cyril was torn between the sweet and quiet Elizabeth and the vivacious, lovely Rosemary.

"That one is like me, do you not think so?" said Lady Edwina about her younger niece. "You should come for dinner again my dear, perhaps tomorrow. No, not tomorrow, forgive me. I must be back here – the Simmons' are coming for dinner. Their son, Frederick, is good friend of Elizabeth's. Would you be free on the Saturday after?"

"Saturday is certainly agreeable, Your Ladyship. May I bring my cousin, Louisa?"

"Of course my dear. I will not invite Gemma, I promise."

"Why you did not mention my uncle previously? I have delighted in so many of your stories, but this one was beyond my expectations."

"Oh my dear, I have an old mind and I recall the old stories. I have a guilty pleasure in telling them. Edward Somerton was my love that I kept in secret."

While we were returning home, we were all quiet. Only Louisa attempted to begin a conversation, but she did not find fertile ground in either Cyril or me. I could not stop thinking of the dream I had about my uncle, Edward Somerton. I remembered his words to me and our disturbing encounter in the library.

Of one thing I was certain: my uncle was not an outstanding poet or writer – he was simply a young man who was in love and who was in pain.

I could proudly reassure him that I did everything in my power to preserve his lifetime of treasures that he left for the next generation. How could I not be satisfied? I had a new fiancé who was very much in love with me, I had stirred the interest of a Duke, and my former fiancé continues to hold hidden desires for me while being ridiculously matched.

CHAPTER 17

AT HOME, UNCLE ROBERT WAS not alone. When we entered the house, a man whom I recognize as being Reverend Warren came directly toward me.

"Reverend Warren!"

"Miss Somerton, my apologies for calling so late, but I did not know where else I could go." His face showed distress while his whole appearance was in disorder.

"Is everything all right at home? Your wife and children…"

"They are very well, thank you," he rushed to answer. "However, we have a situation that has arisen at the church and I need your help."

"I will do anything in my power to help you," I answered in doubt that I could be the right person to provide any service to this righteous man.

"I would have asked the Duke of Winchester, but he is away from London and I do not know any other people from high society. We have a guest: a young lady, very well dressed and groomed who I am sure has a high rank in society. I found her unconscious on the church steps this morning. She is ill, but I cannot afford a good doctor."

"Cyril, go fetch Doctor Cole immediately! I will pay his fee," said Uncle Robert, as generous as always.

"Thank you so much, sir. Miss Somerton, I wish you to accompany me to my home because there may be the chance that you will recognize this young lady and I can locate her family."

"Certainly I will come, but the chance is quite slim that I will know her. Louisa, please do not come with us, you have only now recovered. Cyril will take care of me."

I followed Reverend Warren through town to his house, which was situated on a very narrow and dark street in lower London – a location that projected a feeling of uneasiness on my part. The rain had begun again. I felt the need to take a deep breath before entering the house, after an interminable thirty minutes of fast walking.

Cyril was to meet us here with the doctor, but I was not sure he could possibly find us in the dark. Someone came outside to meet us with a dim and minuscule candle.

I entered into the small hallway and from there I saw only two doors: one was wide open and in this room, Reverend Warren's children and wife were sitting around a small table. The room did not have much furniture, but there were two beds, a kitchen stove, and a few benches. He opened the other door for me. It was the same size as the other, with two more beds, three chairs, and no other furniture.

In one of the beds a young lady was lying, and my first impression of her was that she was very ill with a fever. I did not go too close to her because I was convinced that I could not recognize her and I feared contracting her disease. Shortly thereafter, my brother and Doctor Cole came into the room, and the doctor asked us to leave.

I saw Cyril looking around the small room as we were waiting and I felt his surprise and discomfort for being in such poor environment. I could not discern if he was shocked or upset by the reality of discovering how most poor people lived in comparison with us. But I did not feel discomfort in this house, not in the slightest.

I went to help Emma boil water and to light more candles for the doctor. I disliked the Warren's situation, but I loved this family. Little Grayson came and showed me his wooden horse and begged to be kissed.

The doctor eventually emerged with uncertain news: the young lady was weak and could not be moved for a while. Her fever was not high, but she was suffering from malnutrition and she was not out of danger. It was best, for now, that the Warren children be kept away from that room. Doctor Cole said that he would return tomorrow and could judge the situation better at that time.

The door to the room where the stranger was sleeping had been left halfway open and the room was semi-dark. I saw her again – this time with her head turned toward the door. I observed her for a moment and then I grabbed my brother's arm, terrified.

"Oh my Lord! Cyril, this is Hannah, Hannah Connelly. How could this be possible?"

"Are you sure?"

"Absolutely positive."

"At least now we can find her family." Mr. Warren was relieved and grateful for my discovery. "They are sure to be searching for her."

* * *

The next morning before breakfast I returned to Reverend Warren's house, in need of some answers and seeking an opportunity to confirm my belief about the patient's identity. My brother could not find the strength to accompany me and he excused himself from the return visit with a very incriminating reason. His weakness was not a surprise to me and in all of this, the dreadful experience of last night crushed his perspective of reality. He could not continue to deny his foolish view of the world – society was not fair to good, hearted people.

It was true, however. Hannah Connelly was there, ill and away from her comfortable home, finding refuge in the most unlikely place of all. I knew she could not stay there too long. This family was not capable of sustaining another soul, especially one more that needed this much attention. I brought all of this to Doctor Cole's attention, who agreed.

"I can tell you that she will survive here until tomorrow. After that, you must take her somewhere else, a secure location where she can receive complete rest and good nutrition."

"I will alert her family, they are known to me…"

"Please, no…" Hannah's weak voice was calling for us.

I wanted to go to her but the doctor stopped me. Through the slightly open door I tried to talk to her.

"Hannah, it is me, Cleona. You are in my friends' house, but I need to take you to your home, my dear. You are very ill…"

"Cleona, I recognized your voice…I cannot go home, please…"

"Why not?" Her reluctance to return home astonished me.

"I ran away…they wanted to hurt me…"

"Hannah that cannot be true…"

"It *is* true…please, promise me…not home…"

Those were her last words before she lost consciousness again. The doctor went to her and closed the door behind him. I remained in the hallway, but I could not leave as yet, because I was very puzzled by Hannah's plea. I could blame her illogical request on the fever, but she did not appear to be delirious to me; she seemed to be very aware of my presence and my identity. But her fear of going home was as real as her presence in this home, and I did not want to do anything that would continue to harm her.

I had never cared for James' parents. I had always considered them to be cold and ignorant. It would not be a stretch of the imagination to consider them treating their daughter so cruelly that she had no other choice but exile herself. For the moment, however, my immediate worry was to find her a suitable place until I had a full explanation of why she was in this predicament.

* * *

After only one afternoon of visiting Lady Edwina de Winchester and divulging to her my latest dilemma, she enthusiastically allowed me to put Hannah in the room in which I had stayed. Once she was in the clean and fresh smelling bed, Hannah looked at me gratefully. She whispered her gratitude to Reverend Warren, who left the palace satisfied that he had the opportunity to help someone. He bowed to me, but I returned his bow. He was greatly surprised at this, but in my opinion he deserved so much more.

"Hannah, you can rest now and recuperate," I comforted her, still standing in the open door.

"I ran away because they wanted me to marry Mr. Collins...I could not do that! I had rather die..."

"Mr. Collins? The old Mr. Collins? Is he not your father's friend? But he is married!"

"His wife died a year ago. He has children who are my age...I cannot...they do not understand...I hate them..."

"Oh, Hannah, your parents love you," I tried to reassure her. "Give them time and they will understand..." I lied, regretting it as soon as I spoke the words.

"They say I must marry Mr. Collins or they will disown me...please...help me..."

"You are safe here," I promised her. My friend's strength to stand against her parents' detestable decision raised a certain degree of my own powers to act on her behalf. "I will help, I promise. Now, you rest and be at peace, and I will see you tomorrow."

Lady de Winchester shook her head in disbelief. Hannah's little drama was quite a good source to keep my dear Lady's spirit aroused and lively.

CHAPTER 18

MORE THAN TEN MINUTES PASSED before Mrs. Connelly asked me if I would like to have some tea, which I gracefully refused.

"Your visit to us is very much a surprise."

"I only stopped to inquire about Hannah."

"Oh! Certainly!"

All the way to the Connelly home I had doubted whether my visit would be accepted by this rigid and unfriendly woman. She was calm but she seemed to be very disconnected from the outside world. For the first time I realized how much she was involved in her family's affairs, enough to control everything and demand that things be done according to her will. It was no mystery now, how quickly she changed her opinion of me and took charge. At this time, her feelings for me were very unfavorable and she could not find too many subjects for conversation.

"Hannah is not at home, and I am sure you could not possibly have any legitimate reason for seeing her."

"On the contrary, Mrs. Connelly, I was hoping that she would accompany me to have tea with Lady de Winchester."

Yes, her character was not a challenge to me. She was a snob and if I may be truthful, she was so vain, almost irritating and detestable; but this was my opinion and we had a checkered history together. Now, her small eyes were examining me, trying to make sense of my answer.

"You are having tea with a Duchess?"

"Yes madam, I am very well acquainted with Lady de Winchester, and as you know, she and the queen are sisters…"

"I know that! I simply do not understand why she would have an interest in you." Her direct insult shook my sprit but was just for a moment.

"What are you saying, Mrs. Connelly?"

"You know – your family scandal. I am sure that it is notorious."

"Oh, that. It is a pleasure for me to inform you that Chatham Hill will belong to my family once again, and that my brother and I have several friends in very high society. Actually, Cyril is to be engaged to Miss Elizabeth Bowen in a short time."

I was lying ferociously and my hostess was making every effort to keep up with me, and to not faint under these unexpected revelations. Her face changed from bright red to deep purple, and for me, seeing her wounded composure was a mean victory.

"Oh! Well, our children are engaged very well…"

"Yes, I have heard. I offer you and Mr. Connelly my congratulations. Miss Linton has a good assurance of an inheritance, and I am sure that James must love her very much to desire marriage with her."

"Marriage requires not only love, but also comfort and respect. Miss Linton is very respectable…"

"I suppose at one time that James had true affection for me…"

"Your family was respectable – at least we so believed. We did what was the best for our son when those circumstances were altered. I trust you are not upset regarding the outcome of your engagement."

"Oh, I am not, in the least. I have a much better situation, now."

My answer was repulsive to her. She stood quietly for more than a minute.

"Miss Somerton," she said in an aggressive tone of voice, "I do not want you to be associated with my son anymore. You must understand how much I disagree with recent rumors about you two…"

"I do not understand. What rumors are there? I am not *'associated'* with your son at all."

"Since you came to London, James has spoken of you constantly at home and in public; this behavior makes some people suspicious about his feelings for you. This is quite disturbing to his fiancé. I am not aware of anything going on between the two of you, but should there be, I forbid it!"

"Mrs. Connelly, you cannot forbid something does not exist." I wished not to be this cruel but I could not resist. "And if Mr. Connelly still aspires after my friendship and has affection for me, it is not for you to interfere beyond your past actions. Your remarks are very insulting and churlish to me. I should leave immediately."

"Do not inquire regarding Hannah, either – she is engaged, too…"

"To Mr. Collins?"

"Yes, to Mr. Collins. He is a very distinguished… How do you know this when the prospective union was decided only a week ago?"

We were both standing close to the entrance door.

"Rumor spreads quickly, madam. Perhaps you should be very well aware of the fact that there are whispers regarding your family in all the palaces of London. Does Hannah respect Mr. Collins, too?"

"Do not mock me, young miss. I am not to be trifled with."

"I had higher expectations for her, Mrs. Connelly – Hannah is a better person than to be betrothed to an old gentleman her father's age."

"Hannah is not your worry; I decide what is best for my daughter. Hannah will marry Mr. Collins and nothing can change that. You go now – you are not welcome here any longer."

"I do not wish to return. Good day, Mrs. Connelly."

I left, but boiling with anger for lowering myself to her level. What an impossible woman! But she was wrong. Hannah *had* become my worry and I would not allow her to be destroyed by a marriage that she despised, if I could help it. Her parents had no information about where she could be and they did not show any concern about her disappearance.

Hannah was right – she could not go home, not until she was the one who would decide upon her marriage. However unsuitable her engagement might be, she must be the one to accept the situation and possess the full ability to be in control of her life.

I had heard many times about arranged marriages, and I had no reason to consider my own future marriage as one. Mine was in accordance with my free will, to accept what was coming to me, and it was not forced upon me by anyone.

* * *

Back at Lady Edwina's palace, my brother and Louisa were waiting for me, eager to know everything about my little adventure into such hostile environment. It was not good news, as they expected. That being said, our family just grew by one more member.

It was so good to see Catherine Rowe, happy and beautiful, so ready for her own wedding. Lady Bentley came to talk with me and Lady DeSalles, and to congratulate me for my big heart in rescuing Miss Connelly. I supposed my dear Lady De Winchester had told everyone, and I became somewhat agitated.

"Oh, please, your Ladyship, do not tell anyone else about Miss Connelly. She asked me in the most pain and distress to help her maintain a safe shelter…"

"Do not worry my dear, her presence here is a total secret," responded Lady DeSalles, so kind, as usual. "No one wants to see her hurt any further. I will honor yours and Miss Connelly's wishes."

Hannah came downstairs to join us for dinner. She looked well and happy, and she gave me a hug before joining Louisa and Mary Rowe at the end of the table, far from us so they could talk and giggle. I was only a year older than them, but I felt so much more mature and serious. Had I just been relegated to the older lady's group, or would I join them only after I was married?

Perhaps so. That would be an interesting change – my curiosity was whetted about which of their varying subjects I would find entertaining. One of them would be children, I was sure.

Still captivated with that thought, I did not notice when the Duke of Winchester was seated to my left. His voice saluting me produced such anxiety in my emotions, and my heart began to beat rapidly. I turned to him in complete amazement, incapable of a response.

In spite of our numerous conversations and his assurance, I found myself agonizing about our relationship again in his presence, displeased by my weakness and my uncontrollable feelings. It had been more than three weeks since our last encounter and by now I knew very well that I would be obliged to push him far away from my mind. During this time I was overwhelmed by Captain Clark's love for me and our engagement, but my soul was invisibly attached to his memory. And this was the man who asked me to treat him as a brother or a cousin in order to accept him as a friend.

"Duke of Winchester," all I could do was to murmur his name.

"My apologies," he said smiling. 'Did I startle you again?"

"Yes, Your Grace, you did."

I could not even lie to him, me – the master of lying. Very infrequently have I ever found myself at such a loss for words, when more and more I was becoming more impertinent and uncivil? My face must have been pale, for Louisa looked at me in wonder from across the table.

However, my response was not very well received and it quieted the Duke for some time. I was in some pain and discomfort, attempting to ignore his presence, but I was quite aware of the strong tension between us. I was so thankful that everyone's attention was on my dear Hannah.

I was the first to leave the dinner table. I ran to the fortepiano, my only place of refuge and strength. As I played, the sound of music calmed my restless spirit and restored my heart. Now I was ready to confront him and I was confident that I would not show any tell-tale emotions. I played for a few minutes and with a rare courage I looked straight into his eyes the whole time.

So painfully I wanted him to come closer so I could breathe in his presence. It was sweet torment – the battle between falling in love with him and the impossibility of it following my heart.

"Bach," I started the conversation about what I was playing, "Not J. S. Bach, but his son, Johann Christian. I fell in love with him when I was nine. He was actually my first love."

"It is unfortunate that he died so young. Should I hold any hope of your giving your heart away so easily, Miss Somerton?"

We both smiled. I was not frightened anymore…

"Perhaps, if they are composers. Ironically, the two I loved did not return my love. But I love Mozart, too."

"Ah, the Pergolesi Fantasy. It is beautiful when you play. You change music so easily. How do you do it?"

"I do not know," I answer blushing but pretending to be modest, "perhaps it is not that hard. What about this one," I asked changing the composition.

"Let me guess: Haydn, Piano Sonata in G Major."

"G Minor, Your Grace."

"Oh, than I lost the game. Am I to be punished?" His smile was so attractive; my whole soul was in torment on that moment.

"We are not playing a game," I giggled happy. He seemed to approve of my silly discharge.

"I am trying to take you away from the fortepiano. Would you accompany me for a walk?"

I could not refuse, but leaving the fortepiano was always difficult and I was hesitant. This time there were only two persons who witnessed our departure: Lady Edwina and Louisa.

* * *

The palace garden was immense. During the time I spent here, I did not have the courage to explore its every corner because of the danger of becoming lost. He guided me into an alley where I had never been. The rose bushes, all in bloom, were absolutely wonderful.

"This is beautiful. I have never seen this section of the garden. Why is this place so far…?"

"I did this arrangement. I should say, this is my little garden. My mother was generous to keep it and the gardeners still attend to it. It has been so long ago…"

"I love the roses. This is the most amazing garden I have ever seen…"

"You are generous with me, as always. I am still puzzled as to how you change from respect and admiration to being frightened of me. I must have done something wrong. Could it have been my dancing?"

The thorns of one a yellow rose became attached to my dress. He cut the rose from its bush and offered it to me after stripping the stem with his penknife.

"You are so like this rose, beautiful and untouchable, and I am the poor gardener. I have been attempting to get to you through the thorns. Will you allow me to find a way to your heart?"

"Your Grace…"

"Please do not refer to me in that manner; it is too formal and I do not accept it. I see you are somewhat afraid of me, even now…"

I took a deep breath. What was about to be said, must be said.

"I am not. I am not afraid of *you*. I am afraid of the Duke of Winchester, who is inexplicably interested in someone like me. There are boundaries between us that are not meant not to be crossed."

"Why should I not be allowed to have an interest in you?" His question was sincere. Would I choose to answer in the same way and lay bare the ugly reality of my world?

"An interest in me would cause so many complications. As I mentioned before, I am just a simple country girl, naïve and immature. We have nothing in common and it is better for us to remain simply acquaintances to avoid a scandal. Besides, everyone thinks you are going to marry Lady Winston and I am not among her favorites; in that case, our friendship must cease."

"I am not going to marry her. That is only a rumor." His answer made me jubilant, although it was wrong for me to feel this way.

"I should also say that you are the only person who is capable of handling her."

"Lady Winston only loves herself," admitted the Duke. "Miss Somerton, I do not wish to continue on the subject of her any longer. I... I am trying to confess my feelings for *you* and I feel lost. I cannot seem make you understand..."

My whole body shook, seemingly invaded by that strange fear. Was it true or was it only my imagination? Was he about to declare something that was so impossible? But against all logic, my impulses and desires took over.

"What is there to understand, my Lord?"

His face was so close to mine, and I had to step back.

"Since the first day I saw you, I could not stop thinking of you. You may be naïve and immature but this is what my soul desires – a refreshing breeze of vitality. I have continually felt trapped by your memory and by your music. Then, somehow, you became afraid of me. And I must tell you, it was for a good reason, because my feelings for you became dangerous. Nothing like this has ever happened to me. I cannot attempt to explain myself to you. I have lost all of my will power..."

"You are merely attracted to me and," I murmured, fascinated by his declarations, "this is all...and it is my fault. Please forgive me."

"Perhaps I let myself be seduced by you, but I like it, you did nothing wrong..."

"I did everything wrong! It is all wrong! The two of us being here is wrong! My Lord, you cannot allow this, please! Think: you are such a powerful man in rank, the cousin to the king, a benefactor. The whole world is at your feet. You cannot allow such feelings to arise for someone like me. I am not a desirable person..."

I stopped, more frightened than ever. At this juncture, "love" was the only word I had not heard from him. My fragile soul was so hungry for his love, regardless of possessing the affection of my fiancé.

Would I dare to stop him?

"I am so in love with you that I cannot even breathe," he

continued coming closer to me. "You must believe me; I know how to look beyond physical attraction. There is a beautiful person inside you, and I can see it deeply in your heart."

"No, you cannot," I continued stubbornly, but just a step away from fainting. "Do you want to know the truth about me? I am very insensible, manipulative, I lie, and I am selfish. You must understand that a girl of my social status would never dare to believe that someone of your stature as being seriously seeking a relationship. If I leave London and you do not see me again, I will shortly be forgotten."

"You do not believe me? Are you running away again?" The Duke of Winchester laid his hands on my shoulder in an attempt to hold me still.

"I only run from your motives which are becoming apparent. Sir, we need to return."

"I do love you and I desire you. You have brought me to life again. My soul and my body have attached themselves to you since the day we met, and that attachment grows stronger with every moment we spend in each other's presence. Can you not see it?"

"It is not right," I insisted but my soul burned with happiness and agony.

"Nothing can possibly be more right. Will you not love me in return?"

I could say nothing about the one motive that surpassed them all: I was engaged to be married in order to regain Chatham Hill. I started walking back to the house, hoping he would do the same and this would be the end of our conversation.

But he ran after me and pulled me into his arms. He kissed me violently, then gently, and to my unexpected surprise, my reaction was that I was kissing him as much he was kissing me. I devoured his lips.

Our tongues danced rhythmically together, and his lips were

floating from my mouth to my chest in a continuing search for possession and satisfaction. My dress's cleavage was quite low and I felt my breasts pushing against his chest, looking for a way out while the nipples were puckered and begging for his attention I felt a sensation I have never felt before, of a soft pain in my lower abdomen. It was not a real pain. It was an awakening in my whole body, provoked by the man I was in love with.

I felt his kiss. At that moment, Captain Clark's kiss was nothing but a memory of a passing cold wind.

I wished the moment would never end, but Lady Edwina was calling for us. We had to return. Everyone was preparing to go home, and Cyril and Louisa were waiting for me in the carriage.

"You love me too, please do not deny it," he whispered in my ear as he helped me climb the stairs.

"Good bye, Your Grace." I took a seat beside my brother, still gripping the yellow rose tightly in my hand. I wanted to acknowledge his last remark, but this was not the time or the place.

Louisa was first to comment.

"Your face is so blushed. Oh, and what a beautiful rose! Did the Duke of Winchester give it to you? If you ask me, my dear, I think he likes you very much."

CHAPTER 19

HOW BITTERSWEET MY LIFE HAS been this past week. For days I lived in ecstasy. I was happy to know that the Duke of Winchester adored and desired me beyond civility – *me!*

It was impossible to sleep the entire night after I arrived home that evening. For the next few days this moment was still so intense in my memory. I would touch his imaginary face and try to kiss him again. Then, a letter from him came on Monday.

"My dear Miss Somerton,

A letter of apology from me to you is well deserved and it is one I should convey. On the contrary, I am to be forgiven only for my manners. At this time they were severely compromised. But I am not to be forgiven for my feelings for you. I expressed them so poorly and you are not yet convinced of my love. I find myself whispering your name, dreaming of our next encounter, and I am more than anxious to hold you in my arms again. Once more I dream of tasting the flavor of your lips. Please give me more opportunities to declare my love. Will you still run away, or will you give me a sign of your affection once more?

Yours undeniably,

G. Evington de Winchester."

I read the note innumerable times. Each time it was fresh and I renewed it in my heart. What could possibly have changed in this great man's mind, to abandon everything he stood for? His unchanged attachment to his deceased wife and his gentlemanly composure, always so calculated and superior, were ignored in order to unleash his feelings so openly and so passionately!

Did he truly love me or was he only infatuated with me, my youth and my beauty?

My heart would not let me be in denial. I was definitely and absolutely in love with him, from the moment he smiled at me when we were dancing – or perhaps earlier, when his eyes followed me at the ball. No, it was earlier than that, from the moment I first heard his name.

So many times that day, I sat down to answer to his letter. Sometimes my response would be passionate, but many times I thought to answer with an uncalled for coldness. But I finished none of them – it would not have been proper to write, as we were not in a relationship. How could I be so irresponsible as to conceal from him the hurtful truth of my engagement? Why would I choose to prolong his agony of falling in love with me when our love was already condemned?

Was it because of fear that he would do the right thing, casting away his feelings for me? Yes, his honor would override his conscience, and soon my memory would dissolve from his mind, along with my existence. Then, I would be the only one remaining who was in love. And if I were just a passing flame, I was confident that my efforts to reject him were sufficient throughout our entire conversation. If an answer to his letter was not forthcoming, his interest in me would fade and it all would end.

It has been said that rejection produces more passion and I was about to see if this proverb was going to be confirmed in the Duke's reaction and future attitude towards me. Beyond my desires, the truth was unchanged. Our relationship would never survive in our society. Then, why do I wish it so hard even now when my future is established?

But beyond my delirium, and the memory of our passionate kiss, I felt so guilty to have betrayed my moral duty towards Captain Clark. Then, as always, I found an excuse that was not worthy of my offense. I attempted to justify my betrayal of him by telling myself that he had a growing attachment to my cousin. Or so I thought.

Captain Clark came to dinner a few times, and he was welcomed by everyone but me. Here I was, miserable and guilty, culpable of loving another man while I was engaged to another.

How could I explain me to myself, the one whose logic and interests were above the weak and troubled creature I had become? If I chose to suppress my love, I knew what was ahead in my future: tears of remorse and pain, for I had experienced that before.

If I should surrender to temptation, releasing my heart to delirious passion, all that I had accomplished so far – for myself, for my family, for my father and for my uncle – would be lost. Chatham Hill was within my reach and I could not let it go. I could not lose the man who would willingly abandon everything for me. I had given him my word and I must follow through.

What I had to abandon was the most wonderful moment of my life, when my prince kissed me and asked to love him in return.

With all the catastrophes pointed at me once more, I decided to bring Hannah to Uncle Robert's house, eliminating any possibility that I would meet the Duke again – at least, not until Catherine's wedding. There, I would be surrounded by a multitude of people and he would not attempt to engage me in any conversation of our love for each other.

I moved into Louisa's room, allowing Hannah to again occupy my old room, as she did at the palace of Lady de Winchester.

Hannah was relieved and grateful. Contrary to my expectations, she was bored and lonely at Lady Edwina's home and she did not find her Ladyship's company exciting.

That Wednesday evening, we had a large gathering for dinner. Captain Clark came, along with Evelyn. He was pleasant and charming as always, and I stared at him constantly, hoping that he would save me once more. My attention pleased him and through all of the dinner he was showing his emotions, but both of us were careful to avoid stirring the suspicions of Louisa.

Yes, his love for me was genuine. I had no reason to ruin everything because I felt more love for someone else.

What is it about the human heart that it can be so unsettled? Is love a reflection of what delights the eyes, or is it a majestically formulated combination of harmony, beauty, need, and attraction. In retrospect, my love for James Connelly was buried, along with a slice of painful memory.

Thomas Clark was young and handsome, so what was stopping me? Why did I feel so little affection for him? Was it because the Duke of Winchester was the first man I saw who I respected, then admired, then loved? Was he the only man who had all of these qualities? Was Captain Clark totally devoid of them?

Captain Clark took the occasion of the dinner to announce to everyone his imminent departure to Dover Port. This was news that I had expected, but it troubled Louisa. Then, she reminded Uncle Robert of his old friend, Colonel Weston, who still resided near the port. Uncle made the commitment that he would write to his friend immediately and attempt to make Captain Clark's stay in Dover Port a little more comfortable.

Louisa was quite satisfied with her little role, especially when she received my fiancé's gratitude. It became apparent that underneath his adoration for me, Louisa's feelings for him did not hinder his manners and attendance to her.

I did not answer the Duke of Winchester's letter, but every day I expected another one from him. Our house was quite lively, with the four young ladies, so no one noticed my affliction. A week passed, and the only letter that arrived at Uncle Robert's house was from Elizabeth's father, demanding an audience with Cyril on Thursday. I was surprised when Cyril summoned me into the library. My brother never opened a conversation unless provoked. His first words to me were rambling and unorganized.

"Cyril, I cannot understand you…"

"Since my coming here," he started agitated, "I have followed your directions and I have done what you asked of me. Now, I am trapped in this impossible situation and I do not know how to resolve it. And you cannot possibly help."

"Are you angry with me, because that would be well deserved," I said holding my tears.

"I am not angry with you," he replied into a softer tone of voice. "None of this started because of you, but you inherited father's practical intelligence and I admire your strength in handling all of this. I am a weak link in your chain of plans."

"Cyril, you know very well that I would never ask of you what I would not be willing to do myself, by example."

"I am certain of it. You are marrying Captain Clark in order to bring the estate back to our family. You are paying the consequences for my mistakes. I am in distress because a proposal of marriage is expected from me and I do not have the will to deliver it. What other choice do I have? If my mind could stay as rational as yours, I would be flattered to be acknowledged by this esteemed young lady, but besides feeling so unworthy, I am exasperated by it. My heart chooses differently."

"I know. You are in love with the younger of the sisters, Rosemary."

"Cleona, nothing escapes you!" he exclaimed astonished.

"You are not hard to fathom. If I can hazard a guess, I assume that Sir Bowen has his reasons for having you to commit to Elizabeth."

"True. Have no doubt; I know what is expected of me. But I am unable to pretend to possess this feeling of love when I do not have it. It does not make the situation right."

"Lord Bowen must be in full knowledge of Elizabeth's own feeling for you. And you should be aware, she did not lack gentlemen who were interested in her and who would have called upon her. Francis Simmons is one that I know of, and his persistence in being in her graces is not to be dismissed."

"But she favors me."

"I can only advise you to not take this lightly. You may not have a second chance. Rosemary is beautiful, but does she share your affection? I am afraid not."

"She is too young for me now, but I hope…my mind and my thoughts are full of desires for her…when I am around her I can only picture her in my arms…"

"You are a gentleman, Cyril! You cannot allow the harboring of such forbidden thoughts. Do not pursue a caprice…"

"A man's heart is full of hidden desires, Cleona! I am certain that even the Duke of Winchester cannot retain from desiring you!"

His attempt to dig deeper into my weaknesses and to use them to assuage his conscience provoked me. There were no similarities between our situations. I was ready for my battles, while he was sitting there quietly, tormenting a small book with his hands. His lost and desperate expression helped to bring about reconciliation with me for his harsh and painful words. I had no right to force him into such a marriage, but there was no other choice. For a ravished family like ours, rising above our circumstances was the only possible way to regain our position and our dignity.

"Everything comes with a price, Cyril, if you do not want to see your loved ones sent to the poor house. We are only a step away from being Reverend Warren's neighbors if we abandon our goals. Just think: Elizabeth finds you agreeable and desirable, and her father is sensitive to this."

"What about you, Cleona?"

"I am, as you know, engaged to Captain Clark. He wrote a letter to mother and soon he will come …"

"No, I mean you and the Duke of Winchester!"

"There is no such thing," I denied vehemently, "we have no relationship such as that. The only thing that I must consider is Captain Clark. Without him there is no more me, Mother, or Chatham Hill."

"But the Duke of Winchester could change everything for us! He is beyond comparison…"

"Yes, he is indeed, except his help is not necessary. I owe it to Father and to Uncle Edward Somerton. If it is within my power, I will regain our inheritance."

"You do not owe anything to anybody."

"Perhaps this is so, but you do, my dear brother. Chatham Hill was once yours and it will be ours again. I am disappointed that you find no consolation in my sacrifice to marry Captain Clark."

* * *

My conversation with my brother on this subject was over, but this deep unhappiness we both felt lingered with me throughout the night. How different, how serene and relaxing would our lives have been without the interferences of the Duke of Winchester and Rosemary Bowen into them! Yet, I should not be critical of them, for it was our hearts that were unguarded.

Louisa complained about me as an unsettled bed companion

and she was ready for my departure.

On Thursday night I waited for Cyril's return. He came home late, and surprised by my presence, struggled to smile.

"What is it, Cyril?"

"I must disappoint you again, my dear sister. I was certain that Lord Bowen would corner me into admitting my intentions for his daughter, but instead he delivered an apology for her being still too young and unprepared for a marriage. What an unpleasant expectation! I am perplexed! What should I do now?"

"Have you spoken with Elizabeth?"

"She was not there. The strangest thing is, I do not feel relieved, as I thought I would be. Do you suppose my vanity is hurt? I was so sure of myself."

"Have you declared your feelings to Miss Bowen? She may be sure of hers but she may feel insecure of yours. You have never showed her more affection than to her sister, I assume. You cannot return with me to Chatham Hill until this is resolved, and I do not have the necessary time at my disposal to turn her attention to you, again. Don't you see it? Elizabeth is a romantic; she expects more from the man with whom she is in love."

"Am I rejected by her?"

"Perhaps not, but there is a fine line between being charming and showing love."

"You are charming and seductive too!"

"Stop there! Your charm is not working with me. You see, Cyril, we have so much in common! To me it is the same: I need Captain Clark – I am grateful for his love and for saving me. He is handsome and pleasant, and it is not difficult to give him just enough attention to believe that he is loved and admired."

"Will you do this for the rest of your life?"

"I see him as a gift, as someone who will do anything to make me happy. Elizabeth will do the same for you. By the time Rosemary grows up, you will be older and she will have forgotten you."

"You may be right, although I hate to admit it. I may be penniless but I am still a gentleman. I must win Elizabeth back – I cannot lose that connection! What a fool I was!"

My brother's distress over his lost love was soon overpowered by a new desire to gain the interest and eternal love of someone who he believed, now, was rightfully his. I did sleep better that night. Cyril was confused at times but he was not going to need my guidance anymore – his mission was well established.

* * *

At breakfast Louisa brought a letter that had arrived for me. When I opened it, I trembled again. It was from Lord Evington.

"My dear Miss Somerton,
I refuse to believe you are ignoring me. I know your soul; there is an undeniable connection of our hearts and spirits. Please give me a moment of your precious time tomorrow and aid my mind in healing."

"What is it?" she asked. "What is happening with you, my dear?"

I missed so much confiding my heart's longings and desires with my dear cousin, but lately I had completely locked away that opportunity. I feared that the subject of Captain Clark would arise again and she would be confessing her love for him.

"Please forgive me, Louisa, I cannot discuss it at the moment."

The moment of truth had arrived: either I acknowledged it now or I never would. Before I returned to Chatham Hill, it was imperative that I make a confession to Louisa and to somehow make the Duke understand my torment in this twisted situation.

Christ said that the truth will make you free, and I was desperately in need to be free.

CHAPTER 20

IT TURNED OUT TO BE a very beautiful summer morning for Miss Catherine's wedding: not a cloud in the sky, and just the right temperature for the outside ball that followed the church ceremony. The bride was indeed delightful and her dress was exquisite; at least, I was told that she liked it very much. All of the work that I put into it had paid off once again. Lady Winston immediately recognized my handiwork and she was unhappy, but this time, I did not care.

I had arranged with Captain Clark to leave with Louisa and me to attend Miss Catherine's wedding. More than pleasing Louisa, I needed him as a guardian.

What a beautiful and sunny day it was. I put a lot of effort in my dress for it to be revealing and for my curly hair to flow freely onto my shoulders, refusing to follow the all too boring hair fashion that was common.

After the ceremony I saw the Duke of Winchester outside, waiting for his ride to Mr. Cleaves' home for the ball. He was not alone. Lady Winston, my nemesis, was with him. I cannot describe the feeling of jealousy that permeated my body.

I could not overcome that feeling for a several moments. The presence of the two together was intolerable to me. How was this happening when he assured me that he was totally uninterested in her? And why was I jealous over someone with whom I have no right?

He saw me too, but he did nothing more than to bow to me. Oh, how I desperately wished to be uncivil, to run to Gemma and have her read the love letters he had written to me. What a satisfying moment that would have been.

Captain Clark interrupted my imaginary battle by offering his arm to help me board the carriage. This gesture did not go unseen by the Duke of Winchester. I did something more, then, taking a big chance that I might be observed by Louisa: I leaned over to Captain Clark's face and thanked him with a sweet whisper.

I had made one man happy and had disturbed another. But then, I became agitated, because of the pressure of guilt. He had the right to have anyone with him that he chose, and I had behaved in such a tawdry manner.

At the Cleaves house, all of the festivities were outside, and the orchestra was situated on the first floor balcony. It was a splendid arrangement of tables, chairs, and flowers by the garden. We had refreshments and everyone was free to walk around in the garden. I did not leave Captain Clark's side.

To my dismay, James Connelly came to greet us; the two men were polite to each other but clearly, both were barely hiding some degree of animosity. Lady Winston smiled at us coldly; what an awkward situation. I am sure Miss Linton had informed her of her fiancé's indiscretions.

Perhaps this would be one more gossiping event for a bored social gathering at my expense.

Later when the Duke attempted to come and speak with me, I asked my partner to enjoy a garden stroll – but to my surprise, he first accepted an invitation to dance with my cousin, because of her unusual persistence.

"Will you do me the honor of accepting a dance with me,

Miss Somerton?" inquired the Duke of Winchester.

I curtsied in agreement. How different were his polite manners compared with the wildness of his love. Our entrance produced quite a stir and a few people began to whisper their shocked remarks about us. The dance was slow enough to allow close conversation.

"You never dance, Your Grace! Your attention to me at this reception will not be beneficial to your reputation."

"What is it you are trying to tell me? My heart is crushed to see you with that officer. Who is he?"

"It does not matter…"

"This cannot be," he demanded. "Is he the one considered by you? It must be my fault for taking so long to express my sentiments to you…"

"It is not your fault. The only proper time that would have mattered was at our very first dance, but then, there was no passion for me in your heart…"

"That is the precise moment I fell in love with you. I should have known better – a beautiful lady like you would find someone else so quickly. I am not sure I will be able to accept your rejection so easily."

"I am to leave for Chatham Hill tomorrow. I have no intention to ever return; there will be one less infamous person in London. But our paths will never cross again. Think clearly, Your Grace, I must remove myself from all of this intrigue."

"Think clearly you ask of me?" His voice was strong and irritated. A few dancers turned to stare at us. "I cannot hide or contain my passion for you. You cannot leave me forever and not share this passion I feel for you."

"I must, sir," I begged him, but my heart fluttering inside my chest was burning with pain. "Please, allow me to leave."

The dance had ended, but he was still holding my hand. Captain Clark was visibly unpleasantly surprised by the Duke's attention to me.

* * *

That evening in the bedroom, before my departure for Chatham Hill, Louisa was sad too, but she attempted to hide it. I knew she was sad, but more sorrow was to come her way. I watched her as she brushed her beautiful hair, trying to pretend there was nothing wrong. At that moment, if Captain Clark had not been attached to Chatham Hill, I would have easily passed him on to her. I was slowly tormenting my soul, trying to prepare myself for her grief, and I started to weep. She saw my tears that I could no longer contain and came to sit with me.

"Cleona! What is it? Will you never talk to me, ever again?"

"Louisa, I do not deserve your compassion. I have changed, but I have become a villain to everyone around me. I am not a good person anymore, my dear – I am constantly hurting people."

"I cannot believe such thing. But I do know for a fact that you broke someone's heart this afternoon. Is this what your tears are about? I saw the Duke trying desperately to win your graces, and that is why I took Captain Clark away for the dance! The Duke of Winchester is, without a doubt, very interested in you."

"Yes, except we are totally unsuitable…I do not deserve his attention."

"Did the Duke suggest that, dear? He is in love with you. Everybody could see it – he was not hiding that from anyone. And he danced with you again! You are the only one he has ever danced with since his wife died! He loves you…"

"I *know* he loves me and I love him too," I cried. "I have been in love with him from the moment we met at the ball!"

"But this is so wonderful!" she exclaimed pleasantly surprised. "You should be so happy! I am most happy for you!"

"I cannot be happy – I cannot bear it! We cannot be together. He is Lord Grayson Evington, the Duke of Winchester, the King's first cousin, and I am only a simple country girl. Oh Louisa, please forgive me."

"Forgive you for what? You do not make sense..."

"You have been like a sister to me, and more," I continued building more courage. "I have spent all of my life with you, more time than with my own sister. I desperately need to tell you this."

"Cleona, please, what is it?" Louisa's eyes were larger than usual.

"I am engaged to Captain Clark," I said, but I did not dare to look at her. "He asked me to marry him the first day he came to Uncle Robert's house for dinner."

"Cleona! What ... what are you saying?"

She was aghast. At that moment, all the color in her face was fading away. The news she was hearing was terrible and I feared she would collapse into unconsciousness. But she was still awake, albeit horrified.

"I could not tell you sooner because I am so much aware of your own feelings for him. I am not insensible to that, but I could not deny the opportunity he offered me to remain at Chatham Hill. I do not expect you to understand. I know that I have become a monster in your eyes. All I want is for you to understand that he had fallen in love with me long before he met you, or me, for that matter. He came to London with only one purpose in mind: to find me and marry me. Still, none of that matters, now. You are devastated, and now, everyone I love is hurt."

"But you do not love him..." she barely whispered.

"You were so right about him: he is a wonderful person, and our family future is in his hands. I have a duty to do my best to make him happy, to return his love..."

"He does love you, isn't that it?"

"He told me that he fell in love with me by thinking and dreaming about me all the time," I answered carefully. I felt her disappointment and pain. "Such a manner of behavior was quite strange, but then, he was happy. I turned out to be as handsome as he had hoped."

"Imagine that…"

"This is so awkward isn't it?"

Then, to my complete surprise, Louisa began to laugh.

"I do not think he would be happy if you had resembled Miss Linton, do you think?"

We were both laughing.

"You were always beautiful, Cleona," she said while her laugh transformed in to tears.

"You are the most beautiful one, Louisa, but you need to be brave. Will you forgive me, my dear? Please, I beg you."

"My whole world is upside down," she said after a moment of silence. "All of my hopes are gone, perhaps forever. There is nothing I can do to change a thing, now, unless I continue to humiliate myself. My feelings for Captain Clark must be over, but I have nothing for which to forgive you. He did not come for me, he came only for you. The signs were always in front of me, and I just refused to admit it. You tried to warn me, but I did not listen."

"You must know that I did not want to hurt you."

"I know, but still it hurts – it hurts so badly!"

"I know my dear, I know." I ran to her and hugged her tight. "I must keep my promise to Captain Clark. You should not think that this is easy for me, that I must face you with this atrocity. And I have no way out. You and the Duke will suffer, but soon your pain will be eased and the both of you will marry someone else you will find to love."

"A true love never ends, never! If two people love each other, that love is twice the stronger, and it will not be broken."

Louisa's words brought me to tears. I collapsed on my bed face down, frustrated.

"But I am not right for the Duke and, I cannot accept his love, regardless of Captain Clark. I am a commoner and he is a royal. At first his attention was so pleasing to me and I allowed it in order to punish Lady Winston – at least, so I thought. But it was I who was punished by falling in love with him. It is entirely my fault! This cannot be!"

"Why are you so severe with yourself?" my cousin stubbornly continued. "None of that matters to him. You are the daughter of good people and you come from a good family. Why should you not be right for him?"

"Oh, Louisa, look at where we are. Our family is constantly the subject of gossip. Everyone knows what has happened to us and how undignified we became. This is a man who is in line for the throne and who dines with royalty. He cannot marry a commoner, for he would be ridiculed in his society, and I could not allow that. But it does not matter anymore. Our future has ended before it could begin."

"I am so sorry for you, my dear."

"Louisa, this is why I adore you! I hurt you only moments before, and now you are worried about me…"

"Please write to me often, my dear."

We talked and discussed more throughout the night, but we made peace with each other, despite all the hostility that we had shared for months. There was nothing hysterical in her demeanor and our bond was unshaken.

CHAPTER 21

HOME AGAIN!

What a wonderful feeling it was to be home again at my beloved Chatham Hill. I had been gone for over two months – months that seemed to drag into years. I hugged my mother for a few long minutes and then I jumped into Mrs. Longwood's arms. I wanted them to know immediately that they were safe in this home, and they were to be happy. Then, I left Evelyn and Hannah in their care and I hid in my favorite place: the library.

There, in the safe where I keep Father's entire letter, I added two more. I laid the memory of my love with the other eternals, forever to keep and cherish.

I did not reveal many details to the Duke of Winchester, and I am not sure if he was interested in hearing them. He was distraught, in denial of the fact that he had to release me without having the opportunity to share our love.

Here I was, loved by two wonderful men, but overwhelmed by the radical decisions I was forced to make. I left the wedding reception holding Captain Clark's arm, believing that I had forever lost the man with whom I am truly in love. Yes, I left the Duke of Winchester behind, in the same world in which I found him, a place where I did not belong.

Dinner at Chatham Hill was a joy. Hannah was happy to be so welcomed, but Evelyn was the heart of the conversation and her immediate attachment to mother and Mrs. Longwood was commendable. As with Caroline, she had lost her mother when she was an infant. She was raised by an aunt, but she lost her, too.

The other aunt, to my understanding, was not able or willing to take on the task of bringing up Evelyn, so she was forced to live with her brother, a single man. Now, she was surrounded by adult females, ready to pamper and adore her.

Mother was watching us as we interacted and I believe, for the moment, that she was intrigued by our guests – one who was to become my sister-in-law, and the other who almost became one. The past and the future of my relations were here in my house, finding shelter.

I was also sure that my decision to marry Captain Clark was the reason for her quite visible uneasiness, but we did not have the opportunity to talk more intimately until the next day. After breakfast, Hannah and Evelyn expressed their desire to roam around the property and Betty, Mrs. Longwood's niece, was given the duty of serving as their guide.

I could never admit to my mother that my decisions about Captain Clark and the Duke of Winchester had inflicted deep suffering in me and how much I had struggled in my soul when I assured her about my imminent wedding and my expected happiness.

"Mama, I can only imagine how surprised you must be, but this was such a miracle, to meet Captain Clark in London and for him to propose marriage with me. Chatham Hill is ours, again, and we are not without hope."

"Cleona, my dear, are you absolutely certain that you wish to marry this young man whom you hardly know?"

"Yes! He is as good as any. But, in his defense, he is a good man and he loves me."

Something inside Mother's spirit was becoming very troubled and I wondered if she would ever admit or confess to me about her relationship with Thomas Radisson. More mysterious to me was the fact that this soft and delicate women, who forgave so easily and never got upset, was ever capable of resenting someone so drastically. Of course, knowing Colonel Radisson, it would not be difficult to see him as a very unpleasant man.

"It so evident, Mama that this is enormous news for you and you do not want to see me fail as before, but everything is different, now. Captain Clark is the master here and we have nothing. He has proved to be so generous with me, and I believe him to be sincere. However, if there is anything I should know about him or his family, please do not hesitate to tell me."

"Do you have any feelings for him? I am sorry, perhaps my question is too insensible, but I would not want you to marry him just because of our circumstance…"

She was drinking her coffee slowly and indifferently. As I have done before, I had to boldly ask questions and make strong statements in order to have mother unfold her thoughts. I was curious and determined to pursue the truth, hoping that there would be no obstacles.

"Yes, I do have feelings for him. He told me he had nothing to do with the odious manner of his uncle's involvement in deceiving Cyril, and he did abandon his family for me. That is extraordinary! Don't you think so, Mama?"

"Indeed! That is very commendable," she whispered.

"Are you against our marriage? I am guilty of taking it upon myself to accept him without consulting with you, but I did not think you would be displeased."

"His affiliation with a man like Colonel Radisson is what I dislike. As you know from Mr. Parker, he was your father's bitter enemy. I cannot be so quickly comfortable with such a situation."

"Are we to be afraid of Colonel Radisson's future wrath? What more is there to expect from him?"

"Forgive me, my dear. I may just be thinking foolishly. Our family has been through the strain of disaster, and I coped as well I could, but the one thing I could not endure was for you to be unhappy."

I turned to the window and looked outside. How much happiness was I seeing there? I had imagined myself as happy and content at Chatham Hill, with Mother and everyone I loved, but what guarantee did I have now that it would happen? It could easily happen, were it not for the Duke of Winchester.

How much struggle would be necessary to erase his love and memory from my heart and mind? Only when that was accomplished would I ever find peace, and perhaps happiness – and a slight chance to love my husband.

It would have been so easy to tell mother about my love for Lord Evington, about his adoring letters and the affection he had shown to me, but here was a woman who would not deliberately open her heart to me and release her pain and her secrets. She was obscure to me, as was my sister Cecilia's imprudent marriage. But mother knew that.

So, until all these mysteries were revealed, I must keep my own secrets.

"I will be all right, Mother. Captain Clark is very amiable and you will find him very agreeable, I promise."

"His younger sister is lovely, at least. I suppose I am worried for nothing."

"Mother, it is so good to be back at Chatham Hill. You would not believe the stories I have to tell you about Uncle Edward and Lady Edwina."

I talked for an hour about all the exciting details between the two of them and abut his unfortunate end in a hunting accident;

I expressed my regret that their love was condemned to nonexistence.

"Mother do you have any knowledge about Uncle Edward's death? Who was the person that accidently shot him?" I asked rapidly changing the subject.

Mother's face changed to an expression of consternation. She dropped her napkin on the floor but made no attempt to collect it.

"You should not listen to Mrs. Longwood my dear, her stories about the curse…"

"Lady Winchester mentioned it. Was it Uncle Robert?"

Mother smiled, but she answered very slowly and carefully.

"It was believed to be an accident, my dear, but your uncle has no recollection of being involved in that particular event. You should not be mindful of these things."

After she left to attend to her chores, I waited for Hannah to come back so I could show her the libraries. Evelyn had already taken over the immense and beautiful drawing room. But whatever hint had I given to my mother, made her more nervous and more quiet than usual.

Indeed, I should not ask about these sad things anymore; most likely the truth was distorted. I would have no great joy to think that my dear Uncle Robert, Louisa's father, provoked the death of a family member. Such a tragic incident! If it should be true it was very sad – but in my heart I refused to believe it.

CHAPTER 22

I COULD NOT FATHOM IN my mind the number of letters that arrived last week and I put aside, reading only the few that mattered to me. What a weak mind I still had; every evening I would stay in the library reading the notes from Lord Evington, tormenting my soul with the sorrow and regret of a lost love. The only consolation I had in my defense was that even if I were not engaged, I could not possibly accept a relationship with him.

The first letter I read was from my dear sister, Cecilia.

"My dearest Cleona,

I must tell you personally that I did not find your engagement with Captain Clark surprising at all. So many times when he was visiting us, he inquired about you and I am sure that he pondered over and over the possibility of your union with him. But I must not hide from you the fact that his uncle is very much against your marriage and the two of them parted in disagreement. One good thing has come out of this: Colonel Radisson and his nieces are not visiting so often anymore.

My opinion of Captain Clark is still stands, and his sister, Evelyn, is very sweet. I commend you for taking care of her. About the other matter you asked – as far as I recall, Colonel Radisson was at war in France at the time of father's death.

I wish you happiness with all my heart, but I mostly rejoice in the fact that you are back at home and you are there to stay. And to finish my confession, in your absence I did try to convince Mother to come and stay with me. I feel uneasy about such a strong refusal from her, but I am aware that my husband is not very amiable. I hope her desire to see her grandson growing up will change her mind. I beg you to talk with her, my dear. I need her and I need you too.

I miss the both of you so much. It has been a year since I have seen you and so many things have happened. Please come and visit with me soon. In the fall, Mr. Sutton leaves for his hunting trip with Colonel Radisson and we will have more time to spend together. Please come. I am waiting for your response."

It was very clear to me why my mother did not want to be anywhere near Colonel Radisson. She was paying a dear price for not seeing her daughter and her only grandson. But knowing the truth behind it, I had no heart to question her any longer about this matter. I was considering going alone for a visit with Cecilia, even though I felt so much animosity against her husband and his neighbor.

"I am sad and I grow restless every day", was Louisa's letter. *"The house is empty without you, and Caroline is misbehaving again. She constantly requests permission to come and stay with you. What I should do? I am looking forward to Evelyn joining us in October, so I will have some time to go places. I need to be far away from my own thoughts.*

Miss Catherine invited me for a visit yesterday and I gladly accepted. I do not see Cyril too often; he is always on some sort of trip. Yesterday he dined with Mr. Reeves, a very nice elderly gentleman. Mr. Reeves is friends with Captain Clark, more than just being acquaintances, and he is very fond of you as his protégé's fiancé. It is strange; did the two of you ever meet?"

I stopped reading her letter and moved on to Captain Clark's letter.

"My dear Cleona,

When I left for Dover Port, I left my heart behind in your loving hands. I am truly happy and I do not deserve it. But more than being so in love with you, I am in deep agony for being so far from you for so long. It is no use for me to count the days until I will see you again; there are too, too many. The only thing that keeps me functioning sanely is the thought of you waiting for me at our future home. I will always love Chatham Hill because it brought you to me, and I love you dearly for accepting me.

Yours truly,
Thomas Clark."

No emotion stirred in my heart from his affectionate letter and I felt enormous guilt because of that. If I should dare to think of our future together, I might foresee my feelings for him growing considerably and in time, return his love. Isn't that what I always planned to do? I need patience and much self-denying control.

It was Hannah who interrupted the endless lamentation of my mind and soul. She looked frightened and she was breathless.

"Oh, forgive me for interrupting you, Cleona. I need to talk with you."

"Come in, my dear, and sit down," I invited her. "You are only interrupting my wayward thoughts. Are you all right? Is something troubling you?"

"No and yes. But before I tell you what is on my mind, I came to apologize for being so uncivil. I had not come to you sooner to express my gratitude to you and your uncle for taking care of me, when you consider our past. I hope instead that you do not find my behavior unjustifiable and that you accept my explanations."

"My dear Hannah, please do not make yourself uneasy. I love having you here at Chatham Hill and I am so thankful to have been the one who helped you. If you wish to tell me what troubles you that will be your own choice. I will always listen to you, and you have my word that what you say will be held in confidence"

"Cleona, my parents are determined to have me marry Mr. Collins, but I have refused. For a week I begged my father to reconsider their decision and to not force me into such an impossible situation, but they refused to listen. Can you imagine! I have known this gentleman since I was born and his wife would sing me songs when I was small. Even the thought of such a union is insufferable. My life had started to become a nightmare, and I had to remedy the situation."

"I am so sorry. What prompted such a radical choice of suitor by your parents?"

"Mr. Collins' father died a month ago and supposedly he is to inherit the title of baronet, as he will become Sir Collins. My parents are grossly impressed by that and wished all that felicity and good fortune upon me, and there were no words of imploring I could bestow upon them to change their minds."

"I believe I am quite aware of their stubbornness," I said smiling. "Hannah, you are most welcome to stay here for as long as you wish."

"Oh, Cleona, when I ran away from home, I was helpless. I hid for days in that big church on St. Paul Street until I realized I was in danger of dying of starvation. No one came in there for so long, so I left, wandering on strange, unknown streets, lost and destitute. Perhaps at that point I looked like a commoner who had become unconscious from excess drink, because someone lifted me up and laid me on Reverend Warren's church steps. But I did not care. In my mind, it was better for me to be dead than to be back at home. That evening, when you came to see me, I felt so guilty. Why would you help me after my family treated you so unfairly? But you did help me and I thank you for your aid."

"I did not consider the past at all when I invited you in with my family. For me, you are not only James' sister, but you are also Hannah, my dear friend. We did get along so well and we had so much in common…"

"This is true, I always liked you so much! My brother loves you, too…"

"That does not matter anymore," I said quickly. The sensitive subject of James love for me must remain unopened.

"It matters to him. He loved you greatly, and when my parents asked him to write you that awful letter, he was very much against it, but he had no choice. I had the choice to run away, but he did not have that choice. I want you to know that. He could not stop talking about you. Poor Miss Linton was so disappointed by his comments and she strived so hard to ignore them."

"Why he would do such thing, to hurt Miss Linton in that way?"

"It was his very rude way to revolt against his engagement and his future wife, as well as our parent's wickedness. Somehow a scandal is imminent. By now they will begin to look for me and if they find me here, their feelings toward you might not be so harsh."

"That is possible," I agreed with her logic. "But you are the only one who will decide when you will leave."

"Where could I go?" Hanna's eyes became watery. "I have no one to take me, and who would understand me."

"Hannah, I promise, you are safe here with me."

"I am not safe here anymore! James is waiting for you in the living room."

I rose from my chair, quite unpleasantly surprised by the news of his visit. It had been quite some time since he had been a guest here and in all truth, I found his late admission of admiration for me rather gratifying. Hannah's big brown eyes were looking at me, imploring.

"Does James know you are here?"

"I believe he saw me coming into this office. Cleona, I cannot hide for long. My father is a very angry, horrible man, and if he learns I am here, he will bring his wrath upon Chatham Hill. I must obey him."

"No, you must not," I said firmly. "You stay here, and do not come out of this room until I call for you."

My hair was up from being in the garden the whole morning, cutting roses for the dinner table. I removed the scarf from around my neck, hoping that my shallow dress would be attractive enough. Hannah pulled the dress away from my shoulders in the attempt to help me show more of my breasts. I let my hair down and tried to make its curls more full by twisting them around my fingers.

"How do I look?" I asked, quite a silly question.

"Lovely! But my brother already has much affection for you, and the sight of you will make him fall that much more in love with you."

"We shall see. This time I need his affection more than before…"

"What are you going to do? Oh, forgive me for having you to do this for me."

Instantly she understood my intent to fight for her freedom in any way possible, and that would include preying on her brother's feelings for me.

"You deserve it Hannah," I said to her. "You are a courageous young lady, and I feel that anything I can do to help you is worth the effort. Wish me luck, but more important, stay here and pray. I need it."

As James Connelly ran to hold me in his arms, I pulled away from him as quickly as I could; however, his attitude was not altered.

"How is everyone at your home, Mr. Connelly," I asked very

cordially, remembering that our last encounter did not end in his favor.

"My parents are tolerable, considering our present situation." His voice was lifeless and dull. "I am to meet my father at my uncle's house tomorrow night and Chatham Hill was on my way. I wish to congratulate you on your engagement."

"That is so considerate of you and I am impressed," I said surprised that the news about my new situation reached him already. "How did you learn about it?"

"Oh, just a minute ago I spoke with Mrs. Longwood. She was so eager to deliver the news."

"So, I should think you came to visit me without being aware of my engagement?" I asked, astonished.

"Yes, and I am very excited about meeting you again. My mother made me aware of your visit to our home in London last month and once again that gave me hope."

"I should not have treated you so coldly," I said, a bit hesitant." It was only the effect of my unwillingness to grant you forgiveness. You must understand the dissatisfaction and the other harsh emotions I had suffered. I am certain that you had suffered too."

"Yes I did suffer and I deserve it," he said with a sad smile. "It would make me so happy to know that you do not hate me anymore."

I smiled and got up from my chair to go sit beside James, praying that Jesus would forgive me for my iniquities. His past afflictions on me and his lack of spine were now forgotten, but judging him for pursuing a fortuitous marriage, would bring judgment on me for encouraging my own brother and myself to undertake the same task.

"Those things are all in the past, now, Mr. Connelly. We are friends, remember!"

"My mind is telling me that it is so wrong to wish it," he said whispering, "but I wish it with every fiber of my soul. My heart would give anything, to have you back in my life again. I am so burdened by my expected future…"

"James, if is not your will…"

"It is not my will, nor is it my choice." His voice became vehement. "But I do not have a choice! I cannot stop thinking how my life would have been so different with you, for us to interact together – I, writing beautiful music and you, playing it divinely. I am still so in love with you, perhaps more than before…what can I do?"

"James, we both are engaged! We cannot turn back the hands of time."

He nodded but his struggle to accept loosing me softened my heart.

"Please tell me the truth – is Hannah here with you? I thought I had seen her…"

"Yes, she is here," I admitted with prudence. "She has been my guest for the past three weeks."

"Did you know that she ran away from home?"

"She ran away, rather than be forced to marry Mr. Collins! I perfectly understand this, and she is very welcome here."

"Oh, Miss Cleona, I have been so worried about her. Of course my parents are extremely angry with her and they are determined to find her. I must take her home with me."

"She does not wish it, James. You must think rationally."

"Rationally?" James looked at me perplexed. "At this moment my father is going around to all of our relatives and acquaintances in the quest of finding her. That is where I have been for the past two weeks, aiding my father in his search, and I am to meet him tomorrow. My family will not allow such scandal."

"Would you rather have her go back and be unhappy and miserable for the rest of her life?" I asked him harshly. James did not seem capable to open his mind to other possibilities.

"But what other choice does she have? She will be destitute…"

"She made her choice when she had the courage to take a stand and leave home. I found her when she was rescued, half dead on the steps of St. John's church. At the moment she is not concerned about any inheritance. That is worthless to her."

"She is indeed so courageous, and she is only seventeen. I could not do what she did. But what will I tell father?"

"Nothing at all. You did not know she was here when you came to visit me. If you do not tell, Chatham Hill will be the last place on earth for him to look. Please, James. Your sister has the opportunity to break free from your parents. Do not take this away from her. Please, do it for me ... prove that you still love me."

I took his hand in mine, forcing him to listen and to answer, knowing his tendency to slip into indifference. At this point, I felt bound to keep his feelings alive for me, for Hannah's sake – his attraction to me was harmless. Besides, in my mind he still had the right to love me; we *were* engaged to be married at one time.

"Oh, my dear Miss Cleona, please believe in my love for you. But I am so afraid I am not good at lying …"

"James, you must remain quiet about your sister," I insisted, forcing him to look into my eyes. I touched his lips again with the tips of my fingers, and he closed his eyes and smiled.

"I remember our first kiss last Christmas, when we got engaged…"

"James, please focus on our plan," I asked him hoping that my pleasant demeanor towards him won Hannah an ally.

"All right. For how long must I pretend? What will become of her?"

"Hannah will be in my care for as long as she chooses. And I am thinking, it may be only until Mr. Collins remarries someone else. That will not be very long – he seems to be very eager to do so."

"He does, does he not?"

We both laughed. I encouraged his senseless passionate conduct even though I knew that it was not right to do so. But I have known him for three years now. He was not a stranger to me but someone who many times I dreamed of sharing love and home together. He was my spare, tormented soul.

"Would you like to stay for dinner?"

That evening Mr. Connelly remained for dinner. Mother was astonished. Even to her, the personification of kindness, my demeanor was out of ordinary. To her, my actions may have had a certain explanation, but there was none that she fully understood.

I did persuade James to keep his sister's presence in our home a secret, and so far we had no reason to fear that he would lose ground with his family and confess. Hannah was weary and agitated for the first week but then she started to gain a little more faith in her brother's character.

We had spent a pleasant evening in James' company and I did not regret it. He played his latest sonata for us and he was happy to be in my company and that of his sister. Nevertheless, it was a sad time for him when the moment came for him to say goodbye, as it was for me and Hannah. He was to return to his family, to his falsely happy life with Miss Linton and their engagement, and perhaps to never encounter this opportunity to relive an important part of his past again.

His unhappiness was intolerable.

CHAPTER 23

SINCE I WAS A LITTLE girl I hated the ordeal of traveling to my Uncle George's home. Uncle George was my mother's older brother. I did not mind the four hour's drive there as much as I minded the whole idea of being in the company of such annoying relatives. Mother did everything possible with us, the children, to foster a more civil attitude toward our younger cousins. But it was unanimous – we did not care for them at all.

We liked our Uncle George, but he was just a lonely shadow dominated by his uncultured and strong willed wife, Susan. Beautiful, but mean and soulless, she took over the command of Miltonville and alienated all of his friends and family under the constant suspicion that people had taken advantage of him.

But apart from thinking of her as a despot, she was hard to please and she constantly criticized everyone. The only weakness in her life was her two sons, both of whom were about my age. They were particularly educated by her with the same insensible, sarcastic manners. As they grew older, their level of rudeness and arrogance became effortless. Yes, perhaps Mother enjoyed going to see her brother, but for the rest of us it was a sacrifice.

Christmas was not the reason for us to be on the road to

Miltonville again, but it was the letter from Uncle George regarding his beloved wife's failing health. This did not come as a surprise to us, for Aunt Susan had struggled with her health for the past five months. Uncle George wanted us to be present in his home very much as encouragement to Aunt Susan, but I strongly believed that a second motive for us to visit them was for his relief. Poor Uncle George was the one who was in deeper need. Impaired or not, Aunt Susan would be fierce.

I wished I could have brought Evelyn or Hannah along, because Mother was not amiable company anymore. I wished I could make her talk to me, to release all of the troubles and secrets of her soul, so we could tear down the invisible wall that had been built between us – the construction of which that started with my engagement to Captain Clark.

For the first time in my life I saw Mother in a different way. She was not the simple, happy, loving, and serene woman that I had grown to know. She had become someone with a mysterious past that no one knew, but a past that was following her with a vengeance. I was aware of her hidden suffering, and I pondered over the temptation of whether to force her to talk as we rode, or to wait for a more appropriate time, which might never come.

Certainly, I was culpable in part for creating these unusual circumstances. The whole blame was mine for provoking her past and my future to meet. One almost destroyed us, and the other was our salvation. Mother's past and my future were the result of some terrible secrets that I wished with all my heart to unveil.

I also could not help but wonder if Father knew about her past with Colonel Radisson. It was not uncommon in our society for some engagements to be broken or friendships to deteriorate, with no reason except for such vicious revenge as the one that Colonel Radisson preyed upon us. It is true; I was honest in remembering my own idea of taking revenge on Mr. Connelly not long ago.

We stopped twice along the way, and my impatience grew larger. It was late in the afternoon when we arrived at Miltonville, the estate of my Uncle, George Milton. The servants came to help us unload when we arrived, but none of our relatives were there to greet us. To me, this situation was more than acceptable. I did not wish to have to see them at all.

Later we were shown the way to Aunt Susan's quarters. There, my uncle and the cousins were sitting quietly, staring at the walls and at their beloved, who was incapable of talking to us.

I was frightened when I saw Aunt Susan's pale face and her unhidden suffering. Her dark eyes were looking elsewhere, to a far place that was unseen or unsearched by us. I had never liked her, and I could never understand her bitterness and her unpleasant manners. But all of that was nonexistent in this sad and tired body I was now seeing, one who was awaiting absolution.

She opened her eyes. She saw me, and a glance of recognition provoked a weak and incomprehensible sound from deep inside her body. For the past six months she had been incapable of communicating with anyone, and moreover, she had slowly lost the power to discern her family's faces or names. Of course, the doctor and everyone present found that little movement of recognition of me as an extraordinary improvement; to me, however, it was as if someone who had been dead for six months had suddenly returned to life.

Soon after looking in on Aunt Susan, Mother and I retired to our room. We did not think that our vanishing act might be interpreted as indifference by my good cousins. I was not able to produce more spontaneous sympathy than I already had when it was involuntarily stirred by aunt's unexpected reaction. Later that day, to our surprise, Uncle George and the twins accompanied us for dinner. He looked so tired and pitiful.

"Thank you for coming, dear Jane. It is a great relief to have you here again. My dear Susan would enjoy your company, too. I am sure of it."

"My dear brother, I am here for you."

"Cleona, you look so much like your mother did when she was your age. You are a precious and handsome young lady!"

"Thank you Uncle George. It is so kind of you to see me in that way."

"What you think of George and Joseph?" he asked of me. "They turned out well too, did they not?"

For the first time in five years I turned to them, to take a more curious look at the otherwise well-known characters. Now they were tall, not identical and not disagreeable. In fact, I can be honest and agree that they had changed their appearances and they were now a bit more handsome. They smiled at me, intimidated by my daring search of them.

"I very much agree, Uncle George."

Dinner was simple and quite humble, but everyone seemed too preoccupied to care. The conversation was carried primarily by my uncle, who posted a detailed report on his wife's failing condition. Soon after dessert, he and mother rose from the table and excused themselves for leaving us, and for being absent for tea and coffee. I just assumed that they were going out to enjoy an evening walk in the garden.

"Do not be alarmed, cousin", said George. "I believe Father wanted to show Aunt Jane all the improvements he had done to the estate over the years. The deterioration of this old house was too visible."

"The effort that Father made for improvement was great, but the results are minimal", Joseph responded appearing to be bored. "There is nothing about this property to brag on."

"Maybe they wanted to have some privacy … so they can discuss certain things."

"You think so? And from whom are they hiding? Mother

could care less," said Joseph with a harsh indifference.

"Perhaps he will tell his sister the truth about Mother," George said.

"George, you are beginning to sound ridiculous…"

"You know that Father cannot keep it hidden anymore. He will confess all his sins!"

"That is nonsense! No one knows with certainty what happened that day. It all started because Aunt Jane's so called catastrophe…"

"Gentlemen!"

My cousins were ignoring me completely and an all too familiar argument was happening, this time between the two.

"My apologies, Cleona," said Joseph. "I am sure that you are unpleasantly surprised by our conversation."

"Tell me Joseph, and not to deviate too much from the subject of your arguing, but my curiosity is raised very high. What is the significance of your disagreement?"

"It is only a reflection of our tribulation, my cousin. Our family has plenty of secrets and sins. There is nothing for which you should concern yourself."

"Joseph, I advise the two of you to adjust your attitude toward us. This disagreement is about your aunt, who would consistently bring us here each year in the attempt to spread some otherwise nonexistent affection between us all. Do not dare to offend her or me again."

My listeners were speechless, and moreover, I achieved my goal to repress their absurd desire of contradictory arguments. My strong words were more powerful and violent than George and Joseph could endure. As I expected, George was the one who was quicker to respond.

"It all started six months ago, with the dreadful news of your misfortune. Cyril had lost everything you possessed and he brought all of you to the stage of being homeless and destitute.

Father wrote to your mother immediately, offering assistance and shelter. Mother was very much against this. You may not be aware of it, but when their parents died, they left a good portion of this property – land and the Bristol cottage – to Aunt Jane, but she never was able to possess it. When she married your father, she barely received four thousand pounds as her inheritance."

"My mother does know? Are you telling me that for the past thirty years you used Mother's inheritance and offered nothing, even when we were about to be without a home?"

"Aunt Jane had some knowledge of it," responded Joseph with guilt. "It was your father who first came upon the information. He came here before his death, trying to convince my Father to relinquish possession. He and Father fought pretty badly that evening. Mother was so shaken with fear that Father would give in that she almost had a heart attack. I felt sorry for her. Later that evening he left to attend one of his sporting affairs, and I was glad to see him gone and spare my mother from such sufferings."

"You were just under her twisted influence," commented George. "But Father was completely overwhelmed with guilt when you lost everything, and he wanted to share with Aunt Jane the last will and testament. But mother would not allow it! She took the papers and threw them into the fireplace. The next thing we knew, Father became so angry that he pushed Mother away from the fire in an effort to recover them. She fell and when she hit her head on the fireplace hearth, she could not regain consciousness for more than four hours. From that point, Mother began to lose her health."

* * *

Aunt Susan died on Sunday morning. Consoling Uncle George was a very difficult task that Mother took upon herself with a deep sense of compassion and persuasion. I knew then that his grieving process would be long and difficult. There was so much to overcome and knowing all the details of her so called accident, it would be difficult for him to cope with the past or future.

George and Joseph were more withdrawn from their father and the rest of us than usual. Despite all of the hard feelings I had against these deceitful people, the loss of their mother abruptly interrupted their way of life, and all that they ever knew and loved. I could relate to that.

Nothing was required of me that afternoon, and I decided to take a long and refreshing walk to Bristol Cottage, the second house on the property, located half a mile to the south. The sun was not too warm, creating a beautiful late summer day. I was very much affected by the new information that I had learned, and I was disgusted by my Aunt Susan's selfish and unjust conduct.

I cannot write strong enough words to express the indifference and lack of sensibility that was shown to us from my own family through the years. It was too late, now, for bringing a proper order to things. All that could have been proven was now lost.

At this time the cottage was occupied, because Uncle George rented it to Aunt Susan's cousin. The cottage was far too small and inadequate to be compared with Chatham Hill. It was only two stories high, with six living quarters and three rooms in the back for servants. But in that time of despair, it would have made a monumental difference to us.

I heard a sound behind me, and to my surprise it was my mother who had followed me on horseback. I experienced trepidation over her daring act, because it was not in her nature to take such a challenge upon herself. Mother was always terrified of riding horses.

"Mother, what are doing here?"

She got off the horse and ran to me.

"I saw you walking in this direction, but you were too far away to hear me calling. I actually wanted to accompany you."

"But why did you get on the horse? It is dangerous!"

"This one is very calm. Now, why are you here?"

"What do you mean, Mama? Why should I not come here? I have been here before, when I was a child."

I argued with myself over whether or not I should discuss the truth about her brother to her, but mainly I hoped that he had cleared his conscience on his own. Poor Mother – how much these circumstances would distress her sensitive soul.

"I must tell you immediately about my decision to remain with your uncle. You must be aware by now about my right to own this property and I intend to request the possession of it."

"Mother, I am so sorry for the way they treated you. I see Uncle George was truthful after all, but he was a little too late. There is no proof now of the will. It is all destroyed."

"There is no need for one. Your uncle knew the wish of our father and he will not deny it. When I married your father, he did not care about my inheritance. I was promised a wonderful home of my own, and Charles kept his promise. I was blessed. Then, upon our last Christmas trip before your father died, he stumbled upon some papers stating my father's will for me to inherit Bristol cottage. He told me about it, expecting me to take action. You must understand me now, my dear – my brother's happiness was more important to me than claiming my inheritance. It was not difficult to know Susan's greedy character, but George loved her unconditionally. My persistence in pursuing the matter would have brought such a disturbance and turmoil in his life and marriage that it was not worth it for me. But your father thought differently. He left to meet with your Uncle George to persuade him to do what was right but your uncle declined. Then I became a bit distracted because your father returned home two days later, shot in the leg. Personally, I considered the matter closed."

"Mama why I was not told the manner Father was hurt?"

"I supposed I was wrong to consider that you need not know. That evening, he was a guest at your uncle George here at Miltonville when he shot himself in the leg cleaning a pistol. He was too proud to allow such a notion be known by others, so we kept it discreet.

"Your Father never brought up the subject again."

My memory triggered a conversation with Anna about her doubt that Father carried his guns with him unless he traveled to hunt, but I could not demand from Mother to admit to me the truth in this matter. I wondered why his other trip was held in even more secrecy.

"I will return home very soon Mama. Should I understand that I will return without you?"

"Yes, my dear. I gave a lot of consideration to my decision. It is my heart's desire to live here at Bristol Cottage as my father meant for it to be. George will make the necessary arrangements for the tenants to move out. As of tomorrow, he will see to having all the necessary papers in place. It will be a pleasant place once again."

"I understand, Mama."

Mother was willing to give up Chatham Hill for something that would raise her spirit and restore her dignity. Indeed, I did understand and I agreed. She will be independent and secure, and as horrible as it may sound; only the death of Aunt Susan made this possible.

CHAPTER 24

THE RAIN DID NOT STOP for five days. I enjoyed a little freedom from Evelyn, who was determined to paint my portrait. She had me to pose for her for four long hours each day, and I had done this for the past week. But it was all done in crayon and all she had to do was to add colors.

When I looked at it I was so impressed by the talent this young girl had. She actually painted me more beautifully than I truly was, and it was perhaps too angelic for my own taste. At the first opportunity, I would make changes in the little artist's proud achievement.

No one joined me for tea that afternoon, and that was quite unusual. I was curious as to why all the people who lived at Chatham Hill would remove themselves from our daily social gathering. Or perhaps, I could see the reason in front of my face. I noticed that a number of books were missing from the library and I assumed that everyone choose solace. I followed their example by getting myself comfortable in the office.

Uncle Edward's books were my delight since I discovered them upon my return from London: poems and little stories, all written for the benefit of his own pleasure, but with the absence of gratifying love. Time after time I turned my head to take a furtive look at his portrait, and our eyes always met as if we were both in the same world. Each time this happened, his deep eyes would frighten me. I could almost feel his struggle to overcome love and continue to live without it, making suffering and sorrow an all too frequent companion.

I could not ease my heart from the pain of restraining my feelings from the one I loved and lost in a moment, and many nights I spent sleepless while pondering over the circumstances. Everyone in my family, including me, banished love.

Mother was still withholding secrets from me and had feelings for my enemy; my sister, Cecilia, was a mystery to me; and my future was unknown. I could not recover from the path I chose, I was taking a narrow road, stripped off any vitality.

The sound of the rain splashing against the window was relaxing. Then, I heard the noise of a horse galloping through the water, and I was confused by that. I was sure that Mr. Parker, who promised to bring Dune back to Chatham Hill, would not commit to traveling in such dreadful weather.

But my hearing was not playing tricks on me. It was confirmed by the dogs barking nervously and Mr. Longwood's short conversation with someone. At this time a visitor would be quite a tolerable excitement, but who could it be? After about fifteen minutes, Betty and Mrs. Longwood came to announce the visitor, and they both talked at the same time.

"It is most unusual to have someone fight this horrible rain and to come from so far..." started Mrs. Longwood.

"I had him to wait for you in the parlor, Miss Cleona..." continued Betty.

"I had him change clothes, first. He was soaked to the skin..."

"I am afraid Mr. Cyril's clothes do not do him justice..."

"I will take care of him..."

My heart beat anxiously.

"Who is it?" I asked. "Who is the gentleman? Is it Mr. Parker or Mr. James Connelly?"

They both shook their heads.

"Oh my Lord, is it Mr. Connelly, Hannah's father? Find out…"

Again, the same reaction.

"Miss Cleona, he introduced himself as the Duke of Winchester…" gave up Betty.

"Who?"

It was not ordinary at all to have someone with that name as your visitor, but in truth I admit that I wished at that moment I could lie down on the floor, close my eyes, and drift into a deep sleep. An absolute weakness overwhelmed my whole body and I found myself incapable of movement.

"Will you decline to see him, my dear?"

Mrs. Longwood's voice was thoughtfully softer. I wished I could say, "*Yes, I decline*." But I could not. I asked Mrs. Longwood to see to our visitor's comfort and to tell him that I would join him momentarily.

"Good, because he will have to remain overnight at Chatham Hill," she murmured. "We cannot have him leave in this terrible weather!"

They were both looking at me, expecting further instructions.

"Miss Cleona, you look as if you have seen a ghost! Are you all right?" dared Betty to ask.

"Yes, I am quite all right, except that this man's visit was not expected."

"I will see to his comfort and then prepare the guest bedroom. Go along, my dear, he is waiting! Betty, go fetch Mr. Longwood. I need him to start the fire so our visitor will not catch cold."

I still could not move with any amount of ease, but I slowly followed Mrs. Longwood's shadow. I dragged my feet into the corridor, which at that point seemed immeasurable.

He stood by the window, watching the rain and listening for my coming. Immediately he turned to me.

My feelings were indescribable! How could happiness and misery coexist simultaneously and in such intensity?

I could not discern which one was stronger! He bowed to me deeply, but I could not say anything, and moreover, I trembled almost uncontrollably. I made a tremendous effort to play the role of one who is indifferent.

"Miss Somerton, my apologies for intruding like this," he started bowing to me. "I am aware that my presence might be somewhat shocking..."

"Indeed it is, but please be at ease, my Lord," I answered with a voice I did not recognize. "Chatham Hill is always open and visitors are always welcome."

"This is quite a handsome residence. I am very impressed."

"Thank you, Your Grace, but the rain obscures its grandeur and you cannot really make a fully informed opinion. I am proud of my home, I should daresay."

"I hope Mrs. Somerton is doing well," he said puzzled by my indifference. "I would like very much to have the opportunity to present myself and to pay my respects."

"Mother is very well, but she is away at the moment," I continued calmly, while my inner voice was screaming out at him. "She inherited a little cottage on my grandfather's property, and she has gone there to make arrangements for her future residence. I am sure she would be honored to welcome you."

"Thank you very much for your hospitality!"

"It is gladly given. I pray that Lady de Winchester is in excellent health. And now I must ask, what are doing out in this storm?"

He made an attempt to come closer to me, but at that moment Mr. Longwood entered to start the fire and Mrs. Longwood followed closely behind with hot tea. As I watched him, he resembled a wild animal ready to pounce on its prey. He stood in front of me, too tall and muscular for Cyril's shirt and too handsome with his chest exposed. This moment should never have happened! It was not real!

"Please sit by the fire, my Lord," I invited him when we were alone again, but he chose to stand.

"I could not allow the rain from hindering me to come and see you…"

"Your Grace." I was right; he came for the sole purpose to torment me.

"I know about your engagement with Captain Clark. I am sure that I do not accept it, but I am quite forced to acknowledge it."

"There was never a proper moment for me to tell you about it," I defended myself while I had to fight to hide my emotions.

"Yes, of course, and yet you tried to warn me to stay away … and I did not. Do you judge me for it?"

"No sir, not at all. I am judging myself for attracting your attention to me by creating trouble and disturbing your life. There was never any benefit to you for our being acquainted."

"Allowed me to disagree, Miss Somerton. Your presence in my life has changed me in every possible way. The first moment I saw you at the ball, you seemed to me to be so ready to encounter life, to challenge your destiny, and to run toward it. The fact is, I was running in the opposite direction, away from everything that would affect me. And then, there were those moments at the church when our souls connected…"

I lifted my hand toward him as to have him removed from my sight. He had a determined look on his face, one that warned me about his true intentions.

"Please, listen to me, my Lord. I was merely a desperate girl, troubled by misfortunes, with one mission and only one: to find a way to survive. I woke up one morning determined to beautify myself, and I forced myself to acknowledge my family's disgrace and to fight against it. Great opportunities were at my disposal, and meeting her Ladyship de Winchester was the greatest one of all. Among other opportunities, an unequal one rested in the hands of one I believed to be my enemy. In the end, I could not refuse his proposal. I was and I always am truthful with you. There is nothing about me to be desired or accepted by you. I will never deserve you or your love."

"You try so hard to convince me of this, but each time I look at you, I see into your soul, and I see in it different things."

"My Lord, you are so stubborn to deliberately misunderstand me. I am a liar and a selfish person, greedy and unconventional, the talk of the town, and sometimes uncivil ... Why are you laughing?"

Inexplicably, he appeared quite fascinated by my incriminatory speech, rather to accept it as being the truth.

"Because there is no shred of selfishness in you. As of today you are still sheltering two young girls who would otherwise be homeless, and you successfully maintain a property that sustains eight families."

"This property does not belong to me yet…How do you know all this? How do you know about Hannah and Evelyn?"

"From your cousin, Miss Louisa. I had the pleasure to meet her at Miss Catherine's dinner. Of course, some other details I learned from her were very hurtful…"

"Still, your arguments do not make me righteous. On the contrary, I am far from possessing any potentially redeeming quality…"

This time he came to sit on the chair across from me. His close presence made me tremble again.

"Miss Cleona, no one is righteous, apart from our Savior. We dance around each other, but we do exactly the same thing – we each put the other on a pedestal. For the sake of our conversation, you are looking at me from the other side of the rainbow. I am the one not worthy of your attention and I suppose I have been proven correct, since I could not stop you from your engagement."

"What are you saying, my Lord?"

"I am here to convince you to not marry Captain Clark!"

"That cannot be!" My heart beat stopped for that second.

"Please do not marry him." His eyes and voice were imploring. "If you have ever doubted my love for you, I am here to reassure you … I am most serious about us."

My answer to him came from the soul of a corpse; everything in me was dead and unfeeling.

"I do not doubt you, but respectfully, I must deny your pursuit of me. I cannot break my word to Captain Clark."

His eyes turned away from me. I could only imagine how displeased he was about my answer. I closed my eyes for a moment and imagined a time that would never happen: he and I together, husband and wife, sharing our love uncontrollably and enjoying every moment in each other's presence.

But that was only a dream. This moment was reality, and it was so painful to me – and I was so cruel to him. And again, I fervently wished that this moment would have never happened.

"This is déjà-vu. Love and pain are following a vicious circle."

"What do you mean, my Lord?" His word made me tremble.

"I am much aware of the old story of my mother's love for your uncle. She married my father and pretended to be happy all her life. Do you love him?"

"Your question is not reasonable."

"Please answer me – I need to know …" His eyes were

watching me with such intensity; I had to turn away my head.

"Captain Clark is very generous and very much a gentleman. His qualities are worthy and I am grateful for his affection. I owe him everything …"

"And that includes your love? I must say, at the moment, your words say one thing but your demeanor says just the opposite. You are not in love with him …"

"You have no right to judge me! I was hoping to have in you an understanding friend!"

I rose from my chair and started to walk nervously around the room. He made a few attempts to follow me but soon he gave up. My agitation produced much regret in him.

"Oh, my love, I do not judge you! I am too overwhelmed by the great hope that you may be in love with me!"

"If I am in love with him or not, nothing would justify my actions if I were to forsake him …"

"Marrying without love is not an act that is easily dismissed" he said firmly holding his temples with his fingers. "It will torment your soul every day and every moment you spend with that person."

"Love will be born eventually. Not everyone falls in love so rapidly. If you do, there is a tremendous risk of falling out of it without a complete surrendering of your feelings."

"True, but that did not happen to me. If you have no objection, I will dare to confess a very intimate and painful time in my life that marks my marriage as a failure."

I was astonished by his unexpected willingness to open his heart to me, and I agreed to listen. This time I stood still and he began to talk, visibly shaken by his emotions.

"As you very well know, I was previously married. My wife, Lydia, died more than four years ago. She was pregnant with our first child and she was not feeling well at all. She began to have complications in the first three months and then she got worse.

If I had only known ... but she wanted so dearly to have this child.

"I had known Lydia all my life. Growing up, there were certain conversations between our families and agreements were made for us to be married. After a while, you are inclined to accept all the terms without judgment, whether or not those terms are agreeable with your heart.

"I was twenty-two when I thought I was in love with Gemma; at the time, she was only sixteen. I hid it from everyone, including her, because I was not actually sure of it. That was when I realized the fact that I preferred to keep my feelings to myself and keep people to a certain distance.

"But after some time, Gemma had her suspicions and she began to press me for more information. I did not realize that none of my decisions would prove to be right at a later time. Compared with Lydia, Gemma was beautiful, but nothing more. She was like an empty but beautifully painted vase.

"Obviously, Lydia, knew me better than I knew myself and she patiently waited for my return to reality, which I did several months later. Gemma's family was losing hope and patience over my indecision regarding her, and they forced her to marry Lord Winston. Lydia and I married a year later, but there was not a shred of feeling that I could possibly grow for her.

"With all the attempts I made to reconcile and clear my mind for marriage, she gave me her unconditional love, a gift that I could not return for the whole length of our two years of life together. I pitied her and I pitied myself. I was on the verge of despair and self-loathing. I was aware of how wrong my attitude was in the eyes of the Lord and I feared that I would lose my faith. My spirit was tired and I stopped persevering.

"And then, the most horrible moment happened. Lydia was so ill and her eyes were begging for my love and mercy, and only my actions were right. My feelings were useless. Do not think I was a stone – I felt so much compassion and I did what was requested of me to the end. But there was no love there. I became desperately miserable, so shaken by my trouble. I took on oath to never marry again unless I was deeply and undeniably in love.

"I do not have any feelings at all for lady Winston, but her son has developed an unexplained attachment to me. This is the result of the lack of a father in his life. I do not mind the time I spend with him; he is a remarkable young boy, but very ill.

"I am here, now, to declare my love for you, a love so deep that I am losing my mind. I implore you not to risk involving yourself in an unhappy marriage such as mine was.

"Now, you know my deepest secret, the reason for my continuing battle for redemption. You cannot possibly turn me away from your life. I am the most unworthy person to request your love and the one with the most burdens to bear. If you will have me, I promise to buy back this property for you if you desire to have it. Please, forgive me for shocking you, but it was my desire for you to know who I am, so you will stop running from me."

He stopped speaking because I was weeping. Yes, it was a great relief to know that the Duke of Winchester was far from perfect, less mysterious and so much in love with me that he would try to purchase Chatham Hill; but with all of his heartbreaking confession, nothing had changed. His arms pulled me closer to him, holding me to his chest.

"Please, do not be sad my love, I did not mean to upset you …"

Could I run away from him again? Would he accept an uncertain answer?

"Please, my Lord, do not torment me any longer. There are at least two good reasons I could break my engagement. One is that my own cousin is in love with Captain Clark and the other is that in my own mind I owe him a debt that can never be repaid.

But what I wish and what you wish is irrelevant. You must understand; I cannot abandon him. He rescued me from despair when I was destitute. It is not right to forsake him, so please do not make me."

"Forgive me; I will not force you into a decision, but I never wanted anyone so much as I want you. I am desperate; I love you so much!"

"I love you, too!" I answered, and that was an involuntary confession.

"You love me! To hear you say that makes me the happiest man in the world. So, we love each other but we are to be apart!"

CHAPTER 25

WHILE I ATTEMPTED TO EXPLAIN my reasoning for continuing to keep my word of my engagement to Captain Clark, I was being transformed into a pale, beamless shadow.

The Duke of Winchester remained for dinner that evening, and not to my surprise, his demeanor was calm and very pleasant to Hannah. She, however, was so intimidated by him that she could not eat her food. As expected, the only jolly one was Evelyn, who insisted that he see the likeness of me that she was painting.

As I mentioned before, the portrait was all too familiar. My hair was freshly curled and free. The beautiful purple dress I wore was a little to revealing, and my breasts – which I am usually so proud of – were showing a little too much; on the whole, the portrait was too daring. I had no intention to let it remain like that, but Evelyn was so impressed with her work that I did not have the heart to have her alter it, as yet.

The Duke was the first to retire, saying good night to us all. For me, he was saying goodbye, perhaps forever. He saluted each of us individually and he murmured to me: "I shall leave early in the morning if the weather permits. I wish you the best in your life, for you so greatly deserve it. Please do not forget me and that I asked only forgiveness from you."

Watching him walk up the stairs to the guest room was as if my own life became a stranger for me at the moment he released me from his arms.

I cannot remember how long I remained behind. I either walked around the house, or I stood motionless, totally lost in despair. The rain had stopped and only the wind still lingered, whistling around the corners of the house with threatening noises.

As I passed by the hall that led to the library, I could recognize my shadow in the candle light. It so much resembled a ghost that my heart began to beat faster. It was certainly a ridiculous accomplishment to startle myself.

I was still sitting in the chair, crushed and barely conscious when I felt that someone lifted me up and took me up the stairs to my bedroom. I was confused, but my eyes refused to open and see. That sensation of being carried became so comforting.

I was in someone's strong arms and leaning on his bare chest. My body rested on the bed and my head touched the pillow.

The next moments were serene. Someone laid by my side. And he was naked.

His hands found the edges of my nightgown and opened it generously for him to explore my whole body. Soft lips touched my lips, and then slowly they were making their way down onto my breasts. I threw my head back as I felt a tingling sensation from his fingers running down on my thighs.

But tormented between desire and self-control, he collected his clothes and retreated to the bedroom door.

"Good buy my love."

I wanted him so much; I wanted to offer myself to him, the man I love.

"I want you to stay," I said and my hand remained high in the air calling for him. He looked at me for a moment tempted and seduced by my words and then returned.

Without hesitation, his hands gripped my hips and held me down as he gently moved within me. It was wrong but the pleasure I felt coming from our contact, from that part of him that was interacting with my most intimate part of my body, broke any connection with my cruel reality. I lost myself in the moment's pleasure as for the rest of the night he held my naked in his arms.

He left quietly the next morning but I wanted it that way.

In the days to come, my body and my soul were in delirium and agony.

I made love with the man in love with me, but I was the unhappiest creature in the world. Where was the balance? What could I change? I had no strength left in me to change anything.

* * *

On Friday morning I had a surprise visit from my dear neighbor, Mrs. Parker and for her sake, I had to escape the involuntary melancholy that I did not guard against. This pious and charitable lady was such an encouragement for me.

After the Duke's visit, and our night together, my own spirit was torn apart. This immeasurable effort to accept my errors and condemnations expelled any other desires.

Mrs. Parker was happy to see me and she expressed her regret that our prior plans were canceled. She said that she would miss Mother, her dear friend, so terribly. There would be no more frequent visits between them, and promises to visit each other were not always kept.

"Of course, what an extraordinary surprise it was to have your family in the full possession of that which was their right. Mr. Parker and I mentioned it every day in our prayers. We are thankful that the Lord is righteous and that He is constantly fair."

* * *

I waited patiently for her to sit on the sofa and for the tea to be served. One matter that was still troubling my mind for so long might find an answer with my guest.

"I must ask this of you my dear Lady, as you have known my family so well for many generations. Do you remember my uncle, Edward Somerton?"

"Certainly I do. Such a nice neighbor. His death was such a tragedy." Then she continued without my asking. "It was an interesting fact that for a former officer, Mr. Somerton hated hunting; he said so to my husband, who invited him to the hunt numerous times. That day he received a letter to join a hunting party. It has always puzzled me that he changed his mind and consented to participate in such sport. At the time his younger nephew, Mr. Robert Somerton, resided with him after the death of his older sister, your grandmother."

"Oh, I thought he loved hunting and had Uncle Robert accompany him to such events," I said in amazement.

"Mr. Somerton was quite a responsible man; he would never involve that young boy in such a dangerous activity, even some other gentlemen with boys of that age, did. That evening, Mr. Claude Somerton brought him home with a big gunshot wound in the chest. It was quite unclear as to what was the course of events that resulted in such a tragic accident. But that was long time ago my dear, and there is no need to upset your heart with it. Sometimes terrible things happen to good people."

Her rushed account of how my uncle died was astonishing and it raised even more suspicions in my mind about his accidental death. What if someone else had shot my uncle and blamed his young nephew for it? But according to the Duke of Winchester, who was present at the time, it was believed to be the nephew.

And what if my Father did not shoot himself cleaning his

gun, but Uncle George shot him that night during their fight over mother's inheritance? Those sudden and terrible thoughts made me almost to throw up. I could not accept even the notion of a stranger harming my family, and now I had to look closer to my own blood.

Was it possible that Uncle Robert killed Uncle Edward and Uncle George shot Father? But if this were true, my family was cursed, without doubt. Now I must discipline my mind to forget such suspicions.

I must fight fate.

What would it take for my soul to be satisfied?

I needed to stay alive, I needed to live dangerously. I tasted the danger and I liked it. I needed feed my soul and body with something that made me happy. My mind was invigorated again.

I must embrace this new reign of driving force that would take me back to London, where all began. I must confess the burning need and desire to see *him* again.

Yes, I very well knew that I was playing with fire.

CHAPTER 26

LOUISA AND I HAD NOT been alone with each other since I arrived in London. She very seldom exhibited signs that she needed to confide in me, but her frequent trips to London intrigued me. Nothing had changed in my heart for my cousin. I looked at her and I blamed myself for the discord that I allowed to interfere with our relationship, sparked, of course, by the appearance of Captain Clark.

We both loved someone we could not have, we both loved each other, and through all of this, we lost the innocence we once shared.

If I had any absurd notions that crossed my mind that I would be indignant with her about corresponding with my fiancé, all that now disappeared in a second. All I could see in her was my dear friend, closer to me than my own sister, the one who had always been by my side when I needed it.

I could not erase the twenty years we had spent together, and I would not abandon her. I was in a better situation, loved by two men. She loved one of them and she was not loved back. My affection for her made me rise from my chair and in the impulse of the moment I hugged her tightly for a few moments and I unveiled to her the Duke of Winchester's visit and life mysteries.

But it was one moment that I kept silent about – being in each other's arms the whole night.

Even now, in this awkwardness, who else could understand me better, who else would not judge me or criticize me, if not her? Certainly she forgave me for being mean to her in my attempt to erase her feelings for Captain Clark, but we did not have that secret anymore, and I knew her other secret.

That Friday was a day with the greatest amount of stress. Cyril was to accompany Miss Elizabeth to the DeSalles' ball, and Louisa, knowing of my invitation, attempted to convince me to attend as well. Gone, now, was the fragile peace of mind that I had for the past few days, gone with this single event I came back to London for it.

"You must go, my dear," she said. "This will be a good way to cheer you up! Besides, this is the last gathering of the year. As soon winter sets in, there will be nothing left for us to do until spring."

"But what if the Duke of Winchester is there? I do not have the strength to act upon my new social situation and to be indifferent to him. I must respect my promise to Captain Clark and behave accordingly."

"But your presence there will not compromise your engagement! I am sure you can surround yourself in the company of friends and stand your ground."

"My dear Louisa, should I really follow your advice again? The last time I did, it proved to be imprudent."

But there I was, at the ball, against my better judgment. The surprise of the evening was to see how handsome Elizabeth Bowen had become, her face radiating happiness and love. Cyril was quite proud of her and his fear that his weakness for Rosemary would hold him back did not prevail. I received the same impression of happiness and love from seeing my dear friend, Catherine, so delightful and joyous, that Elizabeth had exhibited.

Catherine would not listen to my pitiful excuses of why I had not troubled myself to visit her by now, and I was ashamed. Her only concern was that we were together again tonight.

My first act, when I arrived at the ball, was to ensure that I was in constant contact with my brother's acquaintances and no others. I did not walk around the rooms, afraid of an unexpected encounter, and I continuously observed Lady de Winchester. She was engaged in keeping company with the old Lady Mansfield and Lady Bentley.

And, yes, I could not resist the temptation of dressing provocatively. I was so pleased by being admired by all of the males around me, and being recognized by some.

A few of the ladies who were standing behind me indulged in some gossip which I overheard. They were commenting that I, in my gorgeous attire, was the one who had been dancing with the Duke of Winchester at the earlier ball back in the summer.

One of them mentioned that I was not to be praised for such an unimportant accomplishment, because at the present time I was engaged to an unimportant officer and it was a well-known fact that I was maintaining a peculiar attachment to my former fiancé.

I turned to see who the source of such detailed information was, and it was none other than Lady Winston. As always, her elegance was beyond description and she appeared superior to every lady who was present.

I curtsied to her and she responded with so much indifference and spite that it was like crushing an insect. My face turned red, not because of embarrassment, but because of anger. She was so relieved of my engagement, that she could not contain her contempt. Perhaps she thought that I was out of her way in her quest to capture the heart of the Duke of Winchester and that there was nothing I could do about it. My indignation grew to the point where I left my secure position beside Miss Catherine and I began to walk toward the dance floor.

As I passed by Lady de Winchester, I had to acknowledge her. I was in hopes that she would not cause me to pause in order to speak with me, and she did not. All indications were that the Duke of Winchester was not coming, but Gemma did not seem to be agitated about this. Lady Edwina was being nice, but at the same time, she projected a distant air.

My heart burned with the desire to see the Duke and the disappointment of his absence was cruel. What I wanted and what was right did not connect in my mind. What could I possibly accomplish by seeing him? Only to relive the memory of our passionate embrace.

But I would only be embracing an illusion of things never to happen again. Why was I not running away, as I had done so many times in the past?

* * *

The large beautiful rooms were full of distinguished gentlemen and elegant ladies, and Lady DeSalles was very proud of her home. It was indeed beautiful, but none of the details were important to me and stayed in my memory. I had a battle to fight, and it was against no one but me. Within half an hour of arriving at this ball, I began to regret my presence here.

At that very moment I was so overcome with fear that I had to run into a side room and grasp the back of a chair in order to keep down the contents of my stomach. The thought that he might not want to see me anymore, that he was so frustrated by my constant refusal, found me quite unprepared to accept this possibility. How could I ignore the irony of him avoiding a challenge and me acting like one who was insane in my pursuit of disaster?

Apparently, I had no decency remaining. I was not proud

enough of myself to stay away from these social events, suffering in my misery and not even attempting to avoid scandal. Deep in my heart I burned with shame, and I decided that I must go home.

Suddenly, someone was calling my name. When I looked, it was none other than James Connelly. He was alone and he seemed pleasantly surprised to see me, so I welcomed him with pleasure.

"Miss Cleona I am so delighted to see you! What a wonderful surprise! Are you all alone?"

"My brother is here, too! James, it is such a pleasure to see you again!"

I truly enjoyed our encounter and his presence was more than acceptable to me at that moment. In spite of gossip, he was essential to my surviving the evening.

"I am so grateful to you," I said to him very softly, "for keeping your word to me and not revealing the whereabouts of your sister to her parents. She is so content and is most grateful to you forever."

"I adore her. My parents believe she is alive and hiding somewhere, but they are still unwilling to dismiss her behavior."

"My home is open to her indefinitely. My I inquire about your wellbeing?"

His demeanor changed from relaxed to indifference. Amazingly, I did not see him anymore as the man who broke my heart and abandoned me for fortune, but only as a fatigued young man who could not change the path of his unwanted circumstance.

"I must disappoint you in my personal matter. Regrets about us, are causing me to sink into depression. I continue to live in the memories of the past. Cleona, so many times I declared my love for you openly, but now I ask your indulgence. If I were to be asked today, I would declare to never give you up, no matter what…but I cannot live without you in my heart. I cannot create anything. I am so empty …"

It was a strange silence that followed, for a second. Then he continued.

"I am to be married at Christmas! Miss Linton is at her parent's residence, in the country, making final preparations...But I adore you! My mind refuses to stop thinking of you, or talking about you. What can I do? Will you still condemn me for it?"

"James, please," I whispered in the attempt to make him lower his voice and keep out conversation away from curious ears.

"I cannot help myself. After I had visited you at Chatham Hill, I begin to hope that not all is lost between us. With every breath of my life, I wish I could turn the time back."

"I have left that time behind me, James. My suffering was intense and being angry with you helped to ease the pain, somewhat...I must be sincere and confess to you that I have none of the same feelings for you but ...I will not banish yours."

He smiled and took my hand and laid it on his heart. A few people stared at us, perhaps intrigued by his visible demonstration of interest in my person.

"Please allow me the honor of having a dance with you. And do not worry, we will create no more gossip because they all know us, and they all know that we are both engaged."

"Certainly, but not to each other; you have done nothing to stop all the rumors. James, you are playing with your reputation and mine, even though I do not care – mine is already damaged."

"Dance with me Cleona, please!"

I accepted his offer for a dance. His words, so flattering but so useless, made me feel less submerged in my own regrets. He will marry soon and despite his lack of sentiments for his wife, he will cease to have these feelings for me. But for now, it does him good to be under my influence, at least for the sake of his music.

As we paired up for the dance, I saw Lady Winston staring at us. She would have a mouth full of gossip and accusations for

Miss Linton about this. Deliberately, I lightly flirted with James, trying to spot Gemma and watch her for signs of her indignation. She came closer to us where she could keep us in her sight, but what I saw behind her stopped my heart.

A short distance behind Gemma, the Duke of Winchester was standing there, looking at us as if petrified. His face was severely shocked because of my presence there, or perhaps because of my seeming betrayal with that dance with James. When the dance was over, he disappeared. I excused myself from James and I ran upstairs to hide.

It had happened! He came!

Why did I not go home and save myself from more pain and ridicule? What would he think of me taking cover in the arms of another companion, my former fiancé, like a heartless person? Would he think I was desperate for anyone's affection whatsoever? Was my opinion of myself so low that I really was desperate?

I was not familiar with the plan of the second floor of the house, and I do not remember how many times I went down the same hallway until I stopped. At the end of the hallway I saw an open bedroom and I entered it. I sank down on the edge of the bed and hid, until I decided that all was over. Now was a good time to leave this wretched place with as much dignity as I could muster. As quickly as I could, I rose from the bed to leave the room, but I ran headlong into someone.

When I lifted my eyes to apologize, I saw that it was the Duke of Winchester. I was breathless.

"Miss Somerton, please forgive me…"

He bowed, but he seemed to be somewhat withdrawn.

"My Lord, it is you," I said as I timidly curtsied, but refusing to look at him.

"Yes, I am most surprised to learn that you are in London. I am somewhat in a stupor to see you enjoying the company of

Mr. Connelly. I confess that I must be jealous; please forgive my brutal honesty. Are you all right?"

I did not answer. All I could think of was that I had him here, within my reach, and that I loved him desperately – yes, desperately. I shook my head and I put my finger on his lips.

His eyes were unchanged as they looked at me. I knew then that all was not lost, that nothing was lost. I slowly moved closer to him and I took his hand to place it on my chest, closer to my heart. He was somewhat tense, but soon he relaxed and melted, touching my skin.

"I came to London for you," I whispered into his ear.

He gently took my face in his hands and he began to kiss me, softly but passionately. When our lips touched, there was no way to stop the passion I was feeling. I responded to his kiss and it became more intense, almost violent.

I stepped back for a moment, but then I moved to him again and began to kiss him without restraint. There was no one there in the hallway to interrupt us or to judge us.

I wished he could inhale me into his soul and make me disappear within him forever.

"Cleona, my love! My passion for you is so delirious."

His whole body was shaking and his eyes were shining wildly.

I heard his heart pounding without control. I felt the warmth of his body against mine as it was that night at Chatham Hill.

"Cleona, you are only mine. There *must* be a way for us to be together..."

I shook my head – there was no way. I pulled away from his arms and left him there without saying another word, with tears streaming down my face.

CHAPTER 27

IT IS TRUE: THIS LITTLE forbidden happiness was what I was seeking by coming to London, but in actuality, all I seemed to have accomplished was to hurt the ones I loved even more than I had previously.

Nothing had changed. I was still to marry Captain Clark, even I betrayed him and the Duke was still to empty his heart of any feelings for me. But day and night I could think only of him.

Then, I began to hate myself for interjecting myself into his life again after I declared our union impossible. I had not allowed him to heal. I made him commit the sin of crossing the forbidden boundaries, knowing that I was to be the wife of another.

The Duke of Winchester could not restrain his emotions or his impulses when he was under my charm. Sometimes I wondered if he was evaluating what had happened between us, if he still considered me worthy of so much pain.

Louisa was watching me. All of the bizarre moods I had been having gave her some hint about my state of mind, or to be more accurate, the state of my soul. There was no need to tell her any more than to mention the fact that Lord Evington was at the ball. She had drawn her own conclusions.

On Wednesday morning she unexpectedly announced to me that she wished to accompany Uncle Robert to the south, because he had planned to visit some old friends there. She said that she would not be gone long, perhaps up to three weeks. Caroline and Evelyn would be in good hands under Miss Henry's care, if I should decide to leave for Chatham Hill before her return.

This news was all too perplexing for me to comment on and I simply assumed there was nothing awkward in it. Far be it for me to give any prudent advice, based on my own iniquities. But in spite of my own despicable behavior, I wished I could stop her from going, because my suspicions of her true motives and destination had been aroused.

* * *

After Uncle Robert and Louisa departed that Thursday morning, I left his home to visit with my dear friend, Miss Catherine. Their house was not too far from Mr. Reeves' residence, and it was a beautiful place. But as always, I did not pay too much attention to another's home, for in my opinion, none can compare with Chatham Hill – not even Evington Palace. After guiding me on a tour of her home, she had me to sit in the parlor and to join her in a cup of tea; however, I asked for coffee.

"My dear, please accept my congratulations upon your recent engagement. I am so pleased to know you are going to settle back into your home. I only wish I had learned the news from you and not from Louisa! But I was not the only one to be surprised. Lady Edwina, the DeSalles, the Duke of Winchester, and all of my other dinner guests, were, too."

"Please forgive me for not telling you. Far be it from me to have any wish to offend or deceive you, but I was not certain of it myself. Captain Clark and I were in a very delicate situation, and our relationship was quite fragile."

"I totally understand – you had the right to privacy as you worked through the situation."

"Lady Winston is pleased about our engagement, too! Did I disappoint her in any way? She must be desolate that I did not choose to become a governess!"

Catherine laughed hard. I knew from the moment we first met that this young lady liked me enough to consider me her friend and partly her confidant. I was almost sure I could speak to her freely about the Duke of Winchester without the requirement of having to justify my questions. And her favorite subject was to speak of Gemma's miseries.

"Yes, her amazement was quite unimaginable. But then, she mumbled that you are very lucky to land in the graces of such man and to be properly accepted."

"That does sound like her…"

"She is still very jealous that she cannot compare with you. She knows that no comparison can be made."

"Nevertheless, are she and the Duke more involved now? I am just curious."

"Nothing of the sort! Since you left, he spends most of his time outside of London again, or England. Something has happened to him. Of course, he always acts so strange and appears to be so disconnected from everyone. Do not misjudge my words, my dear but it is a pity that you are not around very much. When he is in your presence, he seems to come alive. There are rumors now that he joined the war again as he can carry the rank of colonel as the Duke of Winchester. This ambition of his does not make sense…"

"OH! This is very dreadful news."

My face was burning. I felt as if there was the lighting of a fire in my chest, and I had to fight for breath.

"Are you all right, my dear?"

"Yes, I am alright, now. I suppose I should not drink coffee anymore!"

"Would you like something else?"

"No, nothing at all, thank you."

The rest of the conversation was done solely by Catherine. On my way home I could not remember another single word she had said. What would be the remedy for my reckless act, what would it take for everything to be whole again? I had no answer because I felt that I was a menace.

I should return to Chatham Hill and never leave again. I should accept my destiny in peace, endure everything that came to me, and accept my fate as my own making. But instead, I was simply a wild heart with inappropriate manners.

I was ashamed of what I had allowed myself to become, and for the first time in my life I was so aware of the damaging effects of my silly conduct.

I stayed in my room alone for days. I did not open the curtains nor did I come down for any of the gatherings or dinner. Anna came up to my room and tried to ascertain if I was truly ill, or was it merely one of my deliberate withdrawals. But I had no appetite and no will to rise from my bed and walk around the room.

Familiar voices were all around me and some questions were asked of me, but I was unable to answer. The pain I felt in my chest was too overwhelming. I was sure I had not died; perhaps I had merely lost consciousness.

Then there was nothing.

CHAPTER 28

WHEN I AWAKENED, DOCTOR COLE and my brother were by my side.

The doctor informed me that I had passed out, and that I had experienced nothing severe. My blood pressure was extremely low, but now I was recovering quite nicely. Then he sent Cyril to the kitchen in order to bring me some food.

"Do you know how long Miss Louisa will be absent?" he asked me.

"I am sorry, Doctor Cole, but she did not give me any specifics. When she and my uncle left, she said that they would be gone for possibly three weeks."

"That is too long."

"Actually, I think that is enough, but she may stay longer than three weeks."

"I need for her to come back here immediately," he said collecting his medical tools. "Miss Louisa needs to be under my constant supervision. I am surprised that you would allow her to go!"

"Doctor Cole, forgive me, but I do not understand you!" I exclaimed, very intrigued. "What is it about her that needs to be supervised?"

"Her illness, of course! Did she not tell you?" My heart dropped to the ground.

"No, there was no mention of anything to me related to her health…"

"She is very ill. Her illness is the same as that of her mother's. Unfortunately, no treatment is known to heal her, but she may have an excellent opportunity to overcome it."

I think I was about to pass out again. This would explain her mysterious morning trips to town to consult with Doctor Cole, as I now understood.

"The same illness? But Aunt Ethel died so young from it! Are you telling me that Louisa will succumb to the same fate?"

"I do not know positively, my dear," he answered warmly. "For now, I need for her to come back to London. As for you, please rest and eat well for the next three days, and do dress warmly when you go outside. You are risking the aggravation of your chest pain and to have a relapse of pneumonia. Good day, my dear girl!"

Cyril was back in my room with food for me before I had the time to fully comprehend what was disclosed by the doctor regarding my beloved Louisa. I was shocked and numb.

"My dear sister, you gave me a fright! The Duke of Winchester was here with you a moment ago…"

"What did you say?" I screamed desperately. "That the Duke was here?"

"Yes my dear. He held you in his arms for a while."

I did not want to be alive. I wished that he would have let me die in his arms.

Life without him would be almost unbearable, and to die would be an easy way to end all of my troubles. Apparently he wanted to go to war where his own life was in danger. How could I go on? How could I ever be happy? And now, the cruel news had come to me that Louisa's life might be cut short because of her illness. Please Lord, help me ...

"Cyril, you know I want the best for you," I said barely holding my tears.

"Of course," he answered, while placing the soup on my bed tray.

"You must take a stand a resolve your situation. If you wish to marry Elizabeth Bowen, please do not procrastinate, because we have no way of knowing what tomorrow may bring!"

"But why should I be rushing into this marriage?"

"Forgive me, allow me to explain. I just was made aware of some terrifying news regarding our Louisa's health. She kept it a secret to protect us, but I am afraid her illness may be terminal and her life could be cut short. This is not fair! She is so young!"

"This is most dreadful news indeed!" exclaimed Cyril, truly concerned. "You, my dear Cleona, need not worry anymore. Please, lie there on your bed and just rest."

How could I rest? I was baffled by this new chaos on the horizon.

* * *

Friday I returned to Chatham Hill, leaving London's elite society perhaps in more turmoil than last time. Mother had written me that she was back at Chatham Hill for a week, only to collect some belongings. Then she informed me of her deepest wish, to return to her cottage with Mr. and Mrs. Longwood and their niece, Betty. I could not say "no" to her, but the thought of losing those beloved people whom I had known all my life agitated me more than I already had become regarding my own matters.

There was much about the past few days for which I should have been sad, perhaps forsaking the man I loved, again and again, only to find myself once again in his presence and being mortally wounded in my soul.

But this time it was different. Cyril's engagement to Elizabeth Bowen was a most happy turn of events, but I could not hide the frightening news of my cousin's malady from my mother, and that would bring an extreme shadow of worry into her heart.

My intense inner suffering began the moment after Mother left Chatham Hill, accompanied by Mr. and Mrs. Longwood and Betty – and Hannah! Hannah welcomed the invitation from Mother to move into another safe place, and suddenly, Chatham Hill had lost all meaning to me.

I felt abandoned there, and I buried myself deep in my emotions.

In the first days of my sudden loneliness, the two persons I loved occupied all of my thoughts and concentration. I prayed for days that nothing Dr. Cole had said was true about Louisa and that she was not ill, and I felt nothing for myself any longer. That was good. I also could not stop wondering why life was so unfair to Duke of Winchester, tormenting him first with a marriage with no love and then being unable to marry the one he loved.

He and I must simply stay apart and our love must dwindle into nothingness.

One cold evening I burned his letters in the fireplace; it would not have been proper for me to keep them anymore, for my own sake, as well as that of Captain Clark's.

I watched the flames in silence as they consumed his declarations of everlasting love for me.

Winter was settling in, with an unseasonal early snow and a strong wind. There was nothing for me to do anymore, except to wait for some sort of absolution. The fear for Louisa's life and her well-being was haunting me each day.

A letter arrived from her, a carefully crafted account and very sensuous description of all the little adventures she had experienced in the south. She discussed the people she had met, the kindness of Colonel Weston's wife to her, and with no embarrassment, her encounters with Captain Clark. His visits with her had become more and more frequent. Louisa found him to be in good spirits, still quite charming, and still a good dancer. Everyone there loved him and Uncle Robert, happy for his engagement with me, welcomed him into the family.

These were all good things, except I felt totally abandoned by her for not reaching out to me more intimately. There was no mention of my request for her to return to London sooner than she had originally planned. I was uncertain if she was so readily open to the idea of not disturbing me with such news, or if she was simply prepared mentally to ignore it. As I was contemplating my own reactions, I determined that I must not address it directly, but I must be prepared to follow her lead in this matter.

My fiancé's letter was a somewhat shorter than Louisa's. He praised my dear cousin for her efforts in ensuring him an open door into the family, and for his introduction to our friends. He said that he was so grateful to her for the wonderful attention she had given him. It had been a great delight to have her there, and time would pass by more pleasantly until his first visit to Chatham Hill in March. Perhaps we should plan our wedding for the early spring.

He leaves this decision to my convenience.

On Tuesday, I left Chatham Hill in order to travel to Forestdale for a visit with my sister. Solitude was not what I needed, then, and finding myself all alone at Chatham Hill frightened me too deeply. The house seemed to die right before my eyes and I refused to be trapped in it, having as company only the unseen spirits of my father and Uncle Edward.

When Father was alive, this place was majestic, and it was freshened daily by his powerful presence. After he had passed, Mother became the strength of the house, and through all of her sweetness and sensibility, she brought to it a feeling of comfort and continuity. I thought that nothing would ever change, but she eventually abandoned it for the safety of her own shelter.

There was no one remaining here to empower this place, and I felt broken, with no roots. This house would be mine again, one day, but I did not feel that I belonged here at the present time.

I wanted to lose the memory of making love with *him*.

CHAPTER 29

WHAT A CALMING FEELING IT was to be in the company of my sister, Cecilia! I arrived there in the afternoon, and to her surprise, I had brought a lot of luggage with me, allowing her to hope that I would stay longer than on my previous visit. Their house was not large, and its architecture was not grandiose. On the contrary, it was rather old and uncomfortable.

The room that she arranged for me to have was one of the largest in the house, and it had a great deal of old, heavy furniture in it. After she showed me to my room, she left me alone in order to allow me to rest. When she was sure that I was comfortable in the room, I could sense her impatience in wanting to have some private time with me. I assured her right away that my desire to spend time with her far outweighed my need for rest.

In the parlor, little William, now three years old, ceremoniously saluted me with a deep bow. I held him in my arms, amazed and pleased by his sweetness and good manners. After we had renewed our acquaintance with each other, he left in the company of his nanny.

"Oh, my dear Cecilia, what a handsome boy! He is growing so quickly and he looks more like you. I am so happy to be here; perhaps you lost any hope of me keeping my word to you."

"Cleona, my dear sister, I never lost hope to see you," my sister said embracing me and had my take a sit by her on the sofa. "Will you ever forgive me for my insufficient support of you in all of your dramatic struggles of late?"

"There is nothing to forgive," I rushed to assure her. "Your letters and the affection that was contained within them supported me and provided me with much inner strength. I have so much to tell you, most of which you may know by now, but first I wish to be civil and pay my respects to your husband."

"Oh, I forgot to mention to you that he is away until next week, with Colonel Radisson. They are somewhere on the Isle of Skye, in Scotland but he shall return soon."

My sister's face was luminous and happy. I could only assume that her husband's absence was quite beneficial for her well-being. I was even more relieved that I would not be required to talk with him than I showed in my outward appearance. Still, I could not resist my comments to Cecilia.

"It is certainly quite a loss for me to find your husband away."

"I detect a little sarcasm in your voice, my dear, but I shall ignore it," she said smiling so beautifully. "I have found his absence to be beneficial at times, and this is the perfect time for us to visit without any interruption. Please, my dear, tell me everything."

Where should I begin? How was I to tell her all that I have been through? How did I begin to tell her about Louisa? How long should I wait until I revealed my true love for Duke of Winchester, and not for Captain Clark, my fiancé?

Cecilia, so kind and beautiful, so wise and mysterious, had her own share of sorrows, but they were hidden by her perfect manners and pleasing attitude.

I had forcefully persuaded Mother to reveal her secrets, but I would be more subtle with my sister. I would have her reveal her troubles and worries to me, in order that I might find some solace in overcoming my own. There was no doubt in my mind that she did not marry Mr. Sutton either for his love or because she loved him. Her marriage to him was more of a desperate and inexplicable attempt to define a life that had to be more secure and comfortable.

"I should give you some time to prepare for all I have to tell you...I would rather start with some good, unbelievable news: Cyril is engaged!"

"This is such wonderful news, indeed. His last letter to me was confusing and I did not understand it all...I am sure Miss Bowen is a wonderful young lady."

"She is one of the sweetest girls I have met in quite some time, and as you know already, she is the niece of Lady de Winchester. And, yes, Cyril was confused for some time. He did not realize at first how deep her affection was for him, but as of two weeks ago he saw her true light. He proposed to her, and now they are engaged. I was determined to not allow our misfortunes to destroy our family. Of all the things that I had planned in my mind to prevent that destruction, this was the one to come true!"

"Did you actually plan for Cyril to marry Miss Bowen?" Cecilia was quite in awe. "Oh, my dear, you are a very gifted match maker."

"I planned it, but I had to force him into it. There were times when he was very hesitant to accept her sincere affection for him."

"Wonderful! And what about you, my dear? I cannot even imagine the level of your suffering."

"Yes, my dear sister, you can! You are the only one who can!"

Here I was again, a guest for only one hour in her home, and I did exactly what I had tried to avoid: asking her to air her confessions. My compassion for her should have made me more cautious, but I did not have the time to wait. My own life was too miserable.

"Cecilia," I continued, "I run a very great risk here of being rude to my own sister, but before I can open my heart to you, I must know that this is not a one way conversation. Perhaps it is the age difference between us, and I do not deny it. I was never mature enough for you to confide in me, but now I am prepared. I have an intense desire to know why my beautiful and extraordinary sister married Mr. Sutton, such an unworthy, despicable man, who, after all, became the agent of alienating us to our enemy?"

My sister looked at me, visibly surprised and disturbed. She was quite taken aback by my comment. Her hands were shaking when she quickly picked up her embroidery and instantly began to sew. Oh, Cecilia, why did you marry that insufferable man? What made you accept him, of all the other nice gentlemen who asked? Looking back, I can only assume the existence of different kinds of feelings from her towards William Henry.

With my adult mind, I could not exclude a seed of lost love as a symptom of her behavior, after William Henry moved away to the north. It came to me, after reflecting for only for a minute on recent memories, that there was a connection between Cecelia and William that produced a most outrageous marriage with Mr. Sutton.

I could not concentrate well enough to remember all of the details – only the gloomy day of their wedding and her silent, almost unsentimental acceptance.

Being sixteen years of age and still affected by Father's death, I never wondered if William would have been a good suitor for my sister. It never occurred to me to ask if William would ever dare to become romantically involved with Cecelia, and why Father might be against such a relationship at all. William's absence from the ceremony saddened me, but it was a different sort of sadness from that of my sister.

A few gentlemen attempted to win my sister's hand, and I have to admit to being in love with one of them. Mr. Walters was a handsome, athletic young man who liked to climb in trees and jump on his horse to amaze all of the girls who were present. Because he was not encouraged by Cecilia, he lost interest in pursuing her. But more suitors came after her rejection of Mr. Walters.

Edgar Sutton was the most bizarre choice of them all. I did not understand why Cecilia chose him, and I wished that it had never happened. He is the son of a very powerful family in Canterbury, with a large fortune. Edgar's father, Sir John Sutton, Baron de Gilbert loved his son and Edgar was indulged very much.

It was anticipated that this indulgence and spoiling would result in a fashionable gentleman, but Edgar did not produce the expected results. He spent his time and money with a not very good class of people and he was on the way to building a bad reputation for himself.

Sir John Sutton took a more severe approach to Edgar's upbringing and he sent Edgar to join the military, against his wife's desperate protests. There, Edgar met and was befriended by Colonel Radisson, the commander of Edgar's company. Edgar's father intervened again and bought him the commission of a Colonel. The ten years that Edgar spent in the military did nothing to uplift his character.

Sir John had received consistently bad reports about Edgar's behavior. When Edgar's mother became seriously ill, he asked his son to come home. Edgar did so gladly, but only to return to his old habits as a rogue and a rake. He was thirty-eight years of age and still without a wife and family. At the time of his mother's death, he promised her he would marry. Slowly working through his grief, Edgar began to search for a mate.

Again, it was his good friend Colonel Radisson who mentioned to him that General Somerton had a very beautiful daughter. With his father's help and encouragement, Edgar bought Forestdale, a property five miles west of us and immediately came to our house, presenting himself as a neighbor. Father received him politely.

From all the information I have gathered and from some that I could barely remember, I was undeniably convinced that an evil spirit was burrowing into my family's affairs, endangering our lives and our wellbeing. At the age of sixteen, how could I know that a father's untimely death, a young girl blinded by love, and an extraordinary marriage acceptance, would lead to an unspeakable attempt to ruin a family forever?

* * *

"Cecilia, please forgive me. I need you, my sister. I need to know how you overcame your pain, so I can apply it to myself. I do not have the will to live anymore…"

She put her work aside and came to sit beside me.

"What are you trying to tell me my dear? What has happened to you?"

I could not talk, then. Perhaps she did not have the answer. Perhaps the solution for her was not the answer for me. I had no means of escape and no plan to redeem myself. There was nothing for which I could dare hope.

"I married Mr. Sutton because he would have me," was her sudden reply to me.

I was aghast when I heard this answer. "Please repeat what you just said."

"You are correct about your being too young for me to confide in you at that time. No one else knows what I am about to tell you, not even Mother. When I married Edgar, I was pregnant with William, my son. Mr. Sutton had always wanted to marry me but I refused him the first time he proposed to me."

"Was there a second time that he proposed?"

"Yes there was, and I accepted, then. I could not bear the thought of ruining the reputation of my family."

"Cecilia, I am still confused…"

"You must understand, my dear, that Edgar is not the father of my son!"

It was my turn to be shocked. This was more than even my active imagination could comprehend.

"It all happened that summer when you were in London, at Uncle Robert's. Do you remember William Henry?"

"Of course I do."

"He and I fell in love when we were very young. We loved each other very much, but when Father learned about our relationship, he made it known to us in no uncertain terms that it would be an impossible union. I had to let William go to continue his education and to make a future for himself. It was the first time that we had been apart for such a long period of time. Each time he came to visit, I would fall more deeply in love with him. When Father died, it was extremely painful for me. I had lost a man I loved, and I did not want to lose another.

"That August, while William was still at Chatham Hill, we foolishly ran away from home. Poor Mama! She desperately attempted to prevent our escapade, but it was Colonel Radisson who gave us shelter at one of his country estates. But after a week of unstoppable passion, we both came to our senses and we decided to return home, in order to avoid a scandal for the sake of my families. Our hopes were that later we would find a way to be together and we would receive Mother's approval. Unfortunately, when we returned home our lives changed forever, because there was so much guilt pressing on our consciences.

"William decided to accept employment in the clergy, and I

had to live knowing that I had betrayed my mother's trust and that I had disgraced my good reputation. It was only after William left for his pastoral assignment that I found myself pregnant with his child…"

"Cecilia, what are you saying?" I asked quite confused.

"What we had done was not proper behavior for a general's daughter."

"I am astonished! Oh, my dear sister. But why would Mother have been against William, especially when she learned of your condition?"

"She did not know about my condition; she merely wanted to honor Father's wish for me to marry into a reputable family. I understood, of course. A week later, to everyone's surprise, Mr. Sutton renewed his marriage proposal. I accepted the proposal."

"Why would you not wait for William to come back – to you and to his son? Why would you not tell Mother? I am certain that in that circumstance she would allowed the legitimacy of your marriage."

"As of today, Mother does not know anything. William's words to me before his departure were about rethinking our past mistakes and his deepest regret that he had was his negative influence on my life. He said that he was giving me the freedom to have the happy life that I deserved, and not a life of limited poverty that he could only be able to provide."

"What about his child? Was he completely indifferent about his son?"

"At that time, he was not aware that I was pregnant. He left before even I knew about it."

"Cecilia!" by this time, my sister's story left me partially numbed and shocked. "How did you deceive Mr. Sutton?"

"I am not sure, but he unknowingly saved me from humiliation. The truth is that Colonel Radisson kept him rather intoxicated for most of our first months together…"

"Colonel Radisson? I do not understand! He is our family's most cruel enemy. Why would he be of any assistance?"

"I do not know, my dear, but at the beginning of our marriage he was quite attached to me, and he was very friendly. What could possibly have changed in his demeanor? I do not know the answer to this, even today. This is my story. This is a portrait of your rebellious older sister, imperfect and uncivil, who does not deserve any high regards from you. Now, if you are satisfied with my confession, you may see why I kept it secret from you, my dear. I pray that your fate in marriage will be better than mine."

"Are you quite unhappy?" I asked her uneasily.

"No, not at all! I do have my son, the fruit of my love, to fulfill my life. After all, he is to inherit this estate and the barony."

"What about William Henry? Does he know all of this by now? Do you still love him?"

"I will discuss that with you later. Will I be made to wait any longer for you to confide in me, my dear?"

"I will not make you happy when I tell you this. I sought an answer from you, but I see now that there is none to be found. My suspicion was that you had married Mr. Sutton out of spite, because of your impossible love for William. I wished to know how you coped with the pain of going through life in the absence of the one you love. But you have a son to compensate … and I have nothing."

"Cleona, you and Captain Clark are still engaged, am I correct?"

My sister's face was becoming increasingly worried. Her one fear for me was becoming a reality.

"Yes, but I do not love him. I am deeply in love with someone else!"

CHAPTER 30

CECILIA HAD A WEALTH OF information to assess and to process. For the past four days we had been together, through the long hours of days and evenings, and she had listened to all my stories – about Captain Clark, my love for the Duke of Winchester, his love for me, our forbidden and passionate encounters, Louisa's illness, and her love for Captain Clark. She learned of Hannah's impending marriage to a much older gentleman and her refusal to become a part of this travesty, about James' regrets regarding his own engagement, his love for me and our late friendship. We discussed Mother, her inheritance, and Colonel Radisson's love for her.

I, in turn, exhausted all of my energy in my attempt to discover a reasonable explanation for the behavior of my sister, and Colonel Radisson's involvement in all of our lives.

I would never have thought of her as being superficial in what she had confided to me, but how dearly she had paid for the little happiness she now possessed. And Mama, always so proper and kind, had not approved of Cecilia's first love. And Colonel Radisson, who, I had no doubt, brought Mr. Sutton into Cecilia's life for her rescue.

For some time, now, I felt a strange feeling, of living in a parallel life, with strange things happening to me, as in a dream. Dreams, at most times, are unreal and disconnected from anything that has to do with reality, and that was how my life was spinning throughout its mysteries and the past's riddles. Beyond everything I knew, there was so much concealed from me.

I was incapable of accurately understanding my family's secrets, and all of my attempts to do so brought about only half truths or partial disclosures. At this moment I felt hollow and numb, and I prayed that I could keep this feeling for the rest of my life. I held secrets too.

I played one of James' sonatas for Cecilia that evening, and it was indeed beautiful. James' only escape to find true happiness was through his music, and the restless spirit of his creation of those gorgeous sounds.

"I am sincerely astonished by his composition!" said Cecilia. "I believe that through this composition he will become widely recognized. My dear, what a precious gift of talent for music and composition he has. Just imagine what the two of you might have accomplished if you had married. Oh, but I am so sorry, dear Cleona. I speak foolishly!"

"Regrets are not on my mind at this time. It is true, he did hurt me, but I have no desire for revenge, not anymore. By now, his sister Hannah is to be, perhaps, part of our family. She is so close to Mother, and Hannah never leaves her side. I have pity for James and Hannah because they have such heartless parents. Tell me, were you ever upset with Mama because she was not open to your marriage to William?"

"I was, sometimes. And I often wonder how my life could have been with him…"

"And…"

"Knowing William's tumultuous character, I came to the realization that his love for me would make him suffer from the failure to offer me the social status I desired. This was a great obstacle. After it all, he accepted that my social life was better with Mr. Sutton. Do you judge me by my actions?"

"Not at all. I never thought of you as being so bold and adventurous ... and you do deserve to be happy. You, Mama, and Cyril are all established, now, and I am not, as yet. My future is with Thomas Clark and I have no objection to him. He is above everything that I deserve."

"My dearest!"

* * *

As I practiced to perfect the sonata, I heard a great deal of commotion outside. Dogs barked, geese honked, and horses neighed – signals that someone was arriving for a visit, but I ignored it. I would not be interrupted here. My sister's old fortepiano was in a back room that was located behind the dining room, in a very secluded part of the house.

I admit in this journal that I spent a great deal of time there that afternoon, practicing and repeating the sections of the music of which I was not sure, until I was aware of a presence behind me. I thought that perhaps it was a servant who had arrived to call me for dinner, but no one said anything, so I continued to play. But perhaps, too, I was wrong – the servants would come into the room sometimes just to listen to my playing.

"A fantastic performance", said the voice, and it startled me. It was a male voice, but it was not Mr. Sutton's. Mr. Sutton had just arrived home, along with his despicable neighbor.

I turned around quickly and this person, so like a gentleman, bowed to me, and without presenting himself, left me there quite astonished. He did not need a presentation! I knew instinctively that it was Colonel Radisson. This was how I encountered my fiercest enemy for the first time – and my future relative.

It took me a few minutes to reduce the speed of my heart to

nearly normal and to make the connection that it was, indeed, Captain Clark's uncle. I began to laugh nervously. It had crossed my mind that in coming here, I would inevitably meet him, but I could not decide how I should behave in his presence.

Should I be hostile, as he so richly deserved, or should I be indifferent to him? After all, I am better when I am charming, rather than when I am uncivil. But what grade of civility would be necessary to face such an intolerable man who was so aggressive and so heartless, without regard for anyone? My opinion of him was well established, regardless of my sister's strange account of him. His ruthless act of destroying my family was not to be forgiven, ever, even if I managed to live and tolerate his presence.

Colonel Radisson did not remain for dinner. I was relieved, but regretful at the same time. My attempts to unveil the secrets of my mother and sister would not stop me from having a sincere conversation with my future uncle. As revenge, I would make it clear to him the proof of my mother's highly despising of him and our family's rise to regain our fortune.

I was not welcomed by Mr. Sutton at all. He was apparently already tipsy, and he began to drink more as soon he arrived home. His presence changed my sister radically. Now she was so quiet and withdrawn, barely responding to her husband's questions.

Dinner was very nearly a disaster. The servants became almost invisible, avoiding their master as much possible. My sister was the first to leave the table in order to attend to William for bed. Suddenly, I felt the need to leave and go somewhere myself, far from his sight.

Later in the evening, he was quite intolerably confused. He called me by my sister's name, all the time addressing the rude remarks he meant for her to me. His entire demeanor was a warning of more unpleasantness to come. Oh, my dear Cecilia, how long must you endure this man?

While he was still drinking I retired to the music room, but I changed my mind and I did not play, afraid that my brother-in-law would be too close by and be disturbed by it. I heard him calling me, addressing me as Cecilia again, and asking where I was hiding. There was so much unpleasantness about his voice that I decided to truly hide from him, and I went into the kitchen. Only the cook was there, and I asked for her silence.

From the kitchen, a long corridor connected the main house to the servant's rooms and to the back door. Someone was coming towards me, and a very familiar face came into view that I recognized as being none other than that of William Henry. I stopped and turned toward him.

How could this be possible? I ran after him, calling his name, but he did not respond, instead going outside and into the stables.

I followed him, intrigued by his appearance at Cecilia's home, and my need to prove to myself that such a notion was impossible. It was extremely cold outside and I was not prepared for it; my house dress was inadequate for such a task. There was no snow on the ground, only frozen mud from the rain, and the darkness was thick. My only guide was the whinnying coming from the horses, and I entered the barn, still sounding William's name, although this time I was only whispering. No one was there except the animals, who were nervous by my entrance into the barn, and I was trembling.

Eventually I began to regret my little adventure and to blame myself for this inexplicable curiosity that could have easily been solved the next day. If who I had seen was William Henry, my sister could answer the question of why he was here.

The door opened with a loud crash, sounding like the percussion in James' new symphony, and Mr. Sutton came in rapidly, holding a candlestick. He was looking at me with fiery eyes and trying to stay balanced, with much difficulty.

"Cecilia, what are you doing here?"

"Mr. Sutton, it is me, Cleona!" I screamed hoping he would see me.

He came closer and set the candlestick on the ground, almost falling as he kneeled down.

"Do not lie to me! You are here to meet him, are you not? I heard you calling him!"

I began to step back, immensely frightened by his rage.

"I am not Cecilia, you are confused…"

"Do you think me stupid? I know better! I know everything about you and the stable boy. You are not going to see him, ever, for as long as I live, do you hear me? I will kill you and I will kill him, too…"

I ran in the opposite direction, and at that moment I believed my life to be in immediate danger. A monster was chasing me with the intent to kill, and I was in his path of his vengeance. Whatever he knew about my sister and William, I was about to pay the price for it. My fear of him was indescribable. He proved to be quite fast for a man who was intoxicated, and my attempt to escape from him was unsuccessful.

He caught me by my dress and pulled me back to him with a force I did not think was possible from him. I attempted to struggle away, but his big heavy hands were holding me too tightly. Then, he pushed me down on the floor and clumsily lay down on top of me, laughing loudly and suffocating me with his heavy weight. His face was so repulsive, and his alcohol leaden breath was forcing me to lose my dinner.

I turned my head and began to scream for help, but who would hear me at this late hour, and who could help? This was not the way I envisioned that my life would end, in the hands of a mad man. I prayed that the Lord would help me.

My call for help resumed at the end of my prayer. Edgar's body was incapacitating my movements and his hands were squeezing me tightly around my neck, pressing me hard until I gasped for air.

I closed my eyes and I wondered how much longer I could remain conscious. I did not know how much longer I could breathe, but I knew that soon my life would end here, strangled by my brother-in-law. I supposed my wish of dying was about to become true.

A moment later I felt him struggling, as if he was fighting with someone, and his body became lighter, its weight lifted off of me. I was not sure if I was still alive, but my body was free at last. Someone was calling my name and shaking me forcefully.

When I opened my eyes, Colonel Radisson was holding me in his arms and pressing my wrist to check my pulse. I was barely breathing, but he was still holding me closely.

"Mr. Henry!" I heard him calling. Yes, it was none other than William Henry who responded to his call, his face frightened and as pale as death.

"Miss Cleona, are you all right?" William asked me with much concern in his voice. "Oh, my Lord, forgive me ... I had to do it, sir. I could not get him off of her, and he would not stop choking her..."

I looked down beside me. Edgar Sutton was lying face down and bleeding from the back of his head. It was a sinister scene and I was far from understanding exactly what was happening. A noise like a groaning came from him, but Colonel Radisson shook his head.

"He is gone!" William exclaimed. "He is not breathing and I cannot feel his pulse. Sir, what I am to do now?"

"Quickly, put him on his horse and take him to the river," Colonel Radisson ordered him.

"Sir?"

"It must look as if he fell from his horse. The animal will come back to his stall alone. In the morning, send for me. I will search for him and bring him home."

William was not responding, obviously hesitant about the whole plan of covering up Mr. Sutton's death.

"I need you to do this, Mr. Henry! *We* are both responsible for this act! What has happened here will die with us and we will be silent about it forever. Do it for Mrs. Sutton…"

They both lifted Mr. Sutton's lifeless body onto his horse and William went to the door. He took a look outside, mounted another horse, and they disappeared into the night.

I was left behind, alive but in the company of my enemy. I wish I could say that I regained my composure quickly, but that would not be true. Instead, I was in shock, almost unable to function.

My dress was torn and ripped, but more than that, my soul was torn between recognizing that Colonel Radisson was my enemy and the acceptance that he had undeniably saved my life. He had helped William Henry to commit murder on my behalf; yet, his voice was so pleasant and comforting when he addressed me with what seemed to be sincere concern.

"Please forgive me for arriving so late to your rescue. I deeply regret what has just happened to you. Edgar Sutton was not a gentleman! Are you capable of walking?"

"Yes, sir, I am … Colonel Radisson, why are you here?"

"Please take my coat, this weather is freezing! I could not depart from your presence. Halfway to my home, I turned back. My heart was burning with the desire to make myself known to you, to explain my actions, to have you understand … I saw you entering the barn and in your shadow was Edgar. I decided to investigate, and once inside, I saw Mr. Henry's attempt to incapacitate Edgar. It was clear to me what I had to do."

"Colonel Radisson…"

I was trembling and I was close to passing out. I had no energy to hate him, or to listen to his heroics, but at that moment, my enemy and I were allied.

"This is forever our secret, Miss Somerton. Do I have your word?"

I agreed.

"Please, go inside to your room and rest. Do not worry about anything. I will take upon myself all of the consequences."

CHAPTER 31

THE DEATH OF MR. SUTTON was a surprise, but it was not regretted by many, with the exception of his father.

As he promised, Colonel Radisson came the next morning to Forestdale to inquire about his friend and to investigate his absence. My sister had not heard from him, and she could only report that he did not return home that evening. Colonel Radisson's visit that morning only caused Cecilia to become confused.

When Mr. Sutton was found dead, Colonel Radisson suggested that he had been intoxicated and had fallen from his horse by the frozen river. Of course, Cecelia was the only one who was not involved in the true story of Edgar's death. She could not understand why her husband would be on the road to visit the Colonel at that late hour. But the officials and the doctor accepted Colonel Radisson's explanation because it came from a trusted source.

So, Edgar Sutton's remains were buried in the family cemetery.

I was unwell, spending all of my nights agitated and immersed in nightmares. I was agonizing over the memories of Edgar's attack on me, fearful that his death would haunt me forever.

Finally, the chilly weather and the events of that night caught up with me, and I spent most of the time in bed fighting a severe cold. The same strange pain in my chest was causing me some agony. Cecilia rarely left my side all during the day, and she was there with me each night. She quietly and efficiently moved into my room, a welcome thought for both of us. I watched her as she nursed me, and to my amazement, I saw that her mind was still affected by Mr. Sutton's influence. She had not yet accepted the freedom that came to her with Edgar's death.

Cecilia moved around the house almost fearful that the reality of her husband's demise was not yet absolute. There was no need to ask any more questions. I totally understood that her guilty happiness came from the man she loved, being in the home and employed as its caretaker.

But it was over, now. Her quality of life would improve and she would be free to marry William Henry, the father of her son. Her fate was to certainly be happy for the remainder of her life. In the midst of such a horrible tragedy, there was a light shining for her, even though the path was paved by the sin of murder and deceit.

My situation improved on the fourth day of my illness. Cecilia brought me hot tea and announced to me that I had a visitor.

"It is Colonel Radisson, my dear! I fully understand if you do not wish to see him, but he is most persistent to be accepted …"

Just for a short moment my mind was outraged, but I became aware of the reality that he and I were bound by a terrifying secret. He might be a murderer, infamous and evil, but in spite of all the disgust I held for him, a troubled spirit of curiosity within me overcame rational thought.

"It is all right, Cecilia. He does not frighten me anymore…"

"I must leave you with him and go write a note to Mother. But remember, I am in the next room if you need me."

Everything that I had told myself was true. When the Colonel entered my room, my body did not react adversely. It had been such a long time ago since this man, unknown to me, entered my life by ruining my family and my future. I hated him, his name, and all that he represented – passionately! For so long I had been awaiting a day of vengeance. And now, as I foresaw it, my family had prevailed. We had escaped annihilation and we found strength and fortune in the most unlikely of places.

Colonel Radisson was at a loss here, and I had no intention of allowing an unmerited gratitude to grant him forgiveness – not even for saving my life. But the man standing beside my bed was neither proud nor resplendent. I must be accurate, however, and describe him as a gentleman whose past handsomeness was still visible and dominant.

He bowed to me respectfully and his face was grave. I was impressed by him, but I was determined to not be intimidated.

"Miss Somerton, thank you for allowing me to present my services to you and to inquire as to your health …"

My response was silence.

"I know we that do not share an amiable …"

"Colonel Radisson," I exploded, "you are wrong if you think that there is any merit in your coming here with a high expectation of improving our relationship. That will never happen. My question to you is, why you are here? You conspired to despise and ruin my family. You actually turned against your own nephew upon his engagement to me. Everything about you is a wide open book, and your vicious character and lack of respect for others is quite readable …"

"Miss Somerton, please allow me to explain," he pleaded, a bit intimidated by my forceful words.

"It is useless, Colonel Radisson. I can never forgive you for turning my life upside down and transforming me into this uncivil and insensible person that I have become. In addition, I now have to fight against the knowledge that my Mother loved you once."

"Please believe me," he pleaded kneeling by my bed. "My soul is full of remorse and no day passes by that I do not regret deeply the pain I have inflicted upon your family. You have every right to be bitter and to be impolite with me ..."

"No, Colonel Radisson, I have no *right* to incivility. This was foisted upon me by ..."

And then I realized that something in me was changing. Contrary to my previous thought, I did not find any pleasure in this superficial attempt to bring my vengeance upon him. This phase of my past must end, here and now, without me carrying around further anger and worthless feelings of resentment. I had poisoned my soul and my spirit enough with it.

"I did not mean to create this much havoc," he continued hesitantly. "As I look back on what I have done, I now see that I have acted quite foolishly and I am being greatly punished for it. By now you must be aware of my love for your mother, and of our unfortunate circumstances.

"It was only a month after my engagement when I met your mother, and I fell in love with her immediately. I could not fight against it. Many times I tried when I was away, but it was impossible. She took over my heart and I loved her passionately, regardless of my situation and the prospect of a future wife whom I did not desire. But I could not keep my fiancé ignorant too long. Soon I had to boldly disagree with my parents' choice for my wife and I broke our engagement.

"Your mother did not find my actions to be proper or fair, and she ran away from me and my love. But I never lost hope to regain it. Later, she married your father and I married, too. You know, it is said that time heals the wounds of the heart, but mine never healed. I wrote to her every week; it was the only way for me to stay alive. At first she returned my letters but then she responded to my suffering love. She destroyed the rest, so your father would not find out about us. He had some suspicions and on one occasion he violently threatened me about it. Twenty years later I was still in love with her more than ever.

"She came to me one day and asked for my help with your sister's elopement, and it was an amazing time in my life. I had the opportunity to spend some time with her, to hear her deepest worries, and to mourn the death of her husband. For that short time, I was her hero, her savior. It felt like I was a part of a real family: I, your mother, and your sister.

"What can I say? I was stricken by love and I was furious that I might lose her again. My wife was still alive and your mother had gracefully retired back to Chatham Hill. After all the matters were resolved and Cecilia married Mr. Sutton, your mother withdrew from my sight again.

"I knew then that I would arise each morning for the rest of my life, awaiting a disaster to happen in order to be accepted by her and to have her back in to my life. I had to do something drastic, to change our fate, so we could be together.

"As you can see, my motives were sincere, even if my actions took a disastrous turn. I did not mean for any of this to occur. My wife's illness was terminal, and my plan was that after she died, I would find your mother and she would accept my proposal to marry me. She would move into my house, and I would give her everything that she deserved and I possessed. By that time, she would have no other choice except to marry me, and I would save all of you. Cyril would have inherited one of my many properties.

* * *

"Ironically my nephew, who was unaware of my plan, ruined everything by falling in love with you and asking for your hand, assuring your mother the very shelter that I had planned to offer her. My refusal was not against you but against his plans. He was so much in love with you that not even the prospect of our broken relationship would change his mind. I did not blame him. I saw you for the first time at Cecilia's wedding and you were the living image of your mother when she was young: so sweet and innocent.

"You are absolutely correct – my foolish actions resulted in some extremely undesirable outcomes. Please forgive me for what I did. I accept my fate and I must pay for my mistakes.

"I wanted so much to redeem myself somehow, but I could see no way out. Even more, my sins were so numerous and they were growing in number. Although I do not expect any forgiveness from you, I must let you know that I have no regret regarding what happened to Mr. Sutton, even though morally I should. I owed my dear Cecilia to undo a great mistake of the past. These are the best of my life's accomplishments, since I have become a menace to all who I love."

Colonel Radisson struggled to wait for my response to his pathetic speech, but I was still quiet. I was right – it was love that drove him to this madness, and I did not want to linger in this interminable chaos anymore. But I understood him very well. Love and madness were my wrath as well.

However seductive I may have been transformed on my outside, my inside had become a place of festering sores, a place where I could no longer live. But I was the old me, the one who needed to be real and sincere, or die forever.

"Colonel Radisson, your visit was acceptable," I said trying to calm my nerves and surpass all my old feelings of hate for this man. "I pray that one day you will find peace within yourself."

"May I ask a tremendous favor of you, my Lady?" he asked getting up, ready to retire.

"You may," I agreed politely.

"My nephew, Captain Clark, is on his way here to visit you.

Please, say a good word on my behalf, I beg of you. I am so pleased to see your union coming to fruition. My life's desire will finally be accomplished in your marriage. He is a true gentleman and he deserves to be loved. Please, be gracious to him, he loves you very much."

"I understand. He is very much loved." *But not by me* – I thought.

CHAPTER 32

THOMAS CLARK WAS COMING TO visit me? What an unexpected surprise! Perhaps he might have written something about this visit in one of his letters that I had not yet read. My fiancé was coming to be with me and my mind could not even conjure his image. I could not remember how he looked.

The next morning the snow began, and it was almost noon when he arrived. I left my bedroom that day, dressed more elegantly that I had in weeks, my looks improved after my illness, and I made an intense effort to receive him well with an amiable outlook. He was sincerely pleased to see me, although I must admit that he seemed to be less enthusiastic than when we had last met.

Nothing had changed about him – he was still charming and polite. We spent that afternoon together making neutral conversation about the most recent events, his slight disappointment in not finding me at Chatham Hill, a great deal about Louisa, and news of a few more of our common acquaintances.

After dinner, I played the fortepiano for him and something changed in his demeanor. Suddenly, I realized that he came here visibly content and relaxed, but as his uncle did over and over with my mother, he was about to fall in love with me again, a love that had diminished a bit by our long separation. That temporary gap of feelings towards me did not displease me at all.

Beneath his lovely manners I could sense a struggle inside him of which even he was not aware. He felt infatuation for me, but perhaps, a stronger feeling of admiration for Louisa. If he could not bring himself to make a decision in this matter, I would make one for the both of us. The opportunity came the next day, after tea.

"Captain Clark, I regret cutting your visit so short, but tomorrow my sister and I will depart for Bristol Cottage. I would suggest that you find in your heart the desire to visit your uncle, Colonel Radisson. There is no reason whatsoever for you to forsake your family. In these days, family is all we have."

My request came as a surprise to my fiancé. At first, he was not inclined to believe that I was sincere.

"I am serious! You cannot persist in this separation, regardless of your uncle's remarks and his behavior. I truly believe that he is in need of your acceptance and support, especially following the loss of his wife. Would you not agree with me?"

"Of course my dear, but I am astonished that this request is coming from you. I dearly covet your opinion, and it is not my desire to offend or bring harm to you regarding this sensitive subject …"

"There has been no harm done at all. Captain Clark, I have no right to mislead you into discord with the one family member who you held so dear at one time. I have no satisfaction in it and I wish you to …"

"But Miss Cleona, what if he does not care for my intrusion?"

"Your visit with him will be no intrusion, I assure you."

"All right! There is nothing that I would not do for you, my dear. I am more than astonished by your sympathy and your regard for my uncle, and I am so impressed by your beautiful spirit.

My dear, I must confess again my impatience in fulfilling my happiness, and I wish to propose that our union take place immediately before my return to Port Dover."

"Thomas…"

What right did I have to keep this man, a man I did not love but who was so loved by my cousin? I could not love him nor could I pretend to, especially for the rest of my life, when it was undeniable that I loved another.

My culpability tormented me. I must put an end to this now, this very moment, if not for Louisa, and then surely for the Duke's love for me. A change must happen … I must make things right.

"Oh, my love, please agree!" he exclaimed, taking me into his arms. "You are so wonderful, talented, beautiful and sensitive. I know you deserve a prince, someone like the Duke of Winchester. I have watched his eyes on you when you were dancing. I was so worried that in my absence he would make himself loved by you and I would be forced to kill him. But you chose me, of all men. I have spent so many nights dreaming of you, of our wedding day, and of our life together, and I melted each time. I felt that I was going insane each time I thought of holding you in my arms just as at this moment. There have been times when I was crazed with passion for you, but lately I have been desperate just to adore you … I cannot wait any longer."

My hands pushed against his chest and I released myself from his embrace.

"Captain Clark, please listen to me carefully. What I am about to say comes from a deep conviction and my need to be as realistic as possible, and this is long overdue. It is time for us to separate. Our union was created by our own consciences, and it was forced by certain events and opportunities. I hereby free you from all of your promises."

He blinked, perplexed, while his hands remained in the air

pointing to me.

"But, Miss Cleona, I am madly in love with you."

He reached out to me and pulled me back into his arms. Our lips touched and I allowed it. I needed to know for sure – and I felt nothing. But he became even more daring and for the first time I felt I was in danger to be in his presence.

His fingers were caressing my face and my neck, working their way down to my breasts.

"No, Mr. Clark. You idolize me more than I deserve and from your admission, I can only conclude that my influence on you is more like a spell or mesmerism. Your friendship with Louisa has truly affected you in a positive way, and although you may not be aware of it, you have a great deal of compatibility with her tender spirit. She loves you much more than I do …"

"Miss Cleona!"

He was not totally convinced by my arguments. To him, at that moment, they all appeared to be rather like a test, not fact.

"But what of Chatham Hill?"

"Chatham Hill is now my past, but it is your future. It is only proper to tell you the truth and to accept my loss. All the time of our engagement I was driven by the wrong motives, one of which was to keep our family estate intact. Please forgive me for this."

I felt his pain and uneasiness about my declaration to him. I sensed the battle inside his soul, the difficulty of accepting my words.

"I am speechless, my dear Cleona. I had never foreseen this development. Is it because of the Duke of Winchester? Is he in love with you? That is it, isn't it? I love you more than he ever could, please believe me … I do not want to lose you …"

"I do believe you Thomas but I must do what is right. You and I will have a bit of a joyless time ahead, but then, all will be become tolerably pleasant, I am sure of it. Do not delay your return to Louisa; she is the one who loves you very much."

"I must be honest and declare that lately I somehow possessed sincere feelings for Miss Louisa, as she resembles you very closely; however, those feeling are different. Deeply and undeniably my heart belongs to you. Please forgive me if I have given you doubts; I cannot let go of you! I will never release you from my heart, and never be so devoted to anyone else."

"Please, you must! It is for both our sakes."

"My deepest desire is for us be united in marriage as I have always dreamed, as it was supposed to have happened."

"Mr. Clark, my decision will not change. I offered my heart to someone else and I crossed the boundaries of our engagement. You are one of the finest gentlemen I know. I trust you will now leave in peace."

Captain Clark stared at me for a few moments trying to speak, but he could not find in me a willing listener. I turned to face the window, pretending to look outside so he could not see my own struggle to remain calm.

"Please, do not refuse me. I would not hold it against you if your heart was not committed to me."

He positioned himself to face me and attempted to kiss me again. I kissed the Duke of Winchester because I loved him and I kissed Captain Clark because of my guilt for breaking his heart.

My own judgment made no sense to me but I was accustomed to that by now. But when his hand pressed against my breast in an attempt to unseat it, I pushed him as hard as I could and ran to the door.

But he did not follow me. Instead, he got on his knee, holding his head.

"At this time I am not capable of thinking clearly," he said in distress. "I was so close to having you all for myself and now that is all gone. How can I control my passion for you? What you ask of me is impossible, but I will leave as you wish."

"Captain Clark, please think," I pleaded with him. "My

cousin Louisa loves you so much and she is the one who is right for you. If you marry her, we will become cousins and my door will be always open to you. Thomas, please, you must understand."

"I cannot understand," he whispered, rising to his feet and clasping his hat. "However, I shall do what you wish of me – but this matter is not resolved, nor will it ever be. Good bye for now, my dear."

"Good bye, Captain Clark. I wish you well."

* * *

My sister, little William, and I departed for Bristol Cottage the next morning. I had not told one soul that I had ended my engagement with Captain Clark, yet; there was time enough for this when we reached Mother's home.

I was a bit worried for Captain Clark. He left visibly shaken and his last attempt to make me change my mind was desolate. Rejecting him was painful for me, too. It was my Mother's and his uncle's story all over again. I did feel remorse, but I stood my ground. The time had come to correct my mistakes, but his love and devotion for me would haunt me for some time. All I could do was to pray that he would follow my advice and marry Louisa. After that, his life would be effortlessly restored.

Each in their turn -- Mother, Hannah, and Cecilia came to encourage and console me. I listened patiently to all of them, exasperated by their excessive attention. It was a constant reminder of my past behavior. Unlike other times, I was not in need of sympathy and I would not cry or dramatize those events to the same extent as before.

As I was a year ago, I was on the same path but with a different goal and no expectations. This road that I traveled was without an end or destination. I took refuge in this place in my life; time was irrelevant here, and over and over I awaited absolution.

"Now that you have regained your freedom," said Cecilia, "I must warn you that the likelihood is that you will be the subject of ridicule and parlor gossip – and they have you dead and buried by now."

"Yes, I have some expectation of that sort," I said, quite undisturbed.

"This kind of news travels rapidly, and soon it will be common knowledge. Of course you must be prepared that half of the talk will be untrue and the other half will be their side of the story. Just imagine! Some rumors are spreading now that Edgar was murdered. As I said before, humans delight in speaking of such misfortunes, is beyond the understanding of any rational person."

"I will not be offended by it, for it is all too mediocre, and this will also pass. Tell me sincerely, how did you find the strength to marry Mr. Sutton? I must confess that regardless of my grateful feelings for Thomas Clark, at last I could not force myself to marry him and spread more deception."

"I did what seemed to be appropriate at the time," answered my sister with her usual sad smile. "I admit that I wanted little William to have dignity and a future. I did not want him to be just the son of a clergyman."

"But now you and William Henry can be together…"

"No! William and I will never be husband and wife again."

"There is nothing there to stand between you. Does he not deserve to know he has a son?" I asked astonished.

"William and you are the only ones who know it, and I urge you my sister to keep this secret for the rest of your life. William left me once but I did not stop loving him and he loved me too. He came to Forestdale when William was two years of age and requested employment. Mr. Sutton did not recognize him. He gave up his calling for the church and his future in order to be near me and his son. We were lovers.

"But little William was very much loved by Edgar. He treated him like a real son, and William is to inherit both estates and his grandfather's barony upon his death; he is to be the next Baron of Gilbert. But if it was learned that little William is not the son of Edgar Sutton, Sir John will disinherit him and the fortune will pass to Sir John's younger brother. Mr. Henry is in complete agreement with me – to keep this in absolute secret for the future of his son. Please, we must not discuss this anymore, ever."

"But Cecilia, this is not right, my dear!" My persistence in this matter seemed to cause my sister to become furious; I had never seen her like that before.

"I am content with this situation, Cleona! William and I still love each other. But I am also taking seriously now my role as a widow."

"But your son deserves to know the truth," I said, still in shock over her outburst.

"Perhaps, but it will ruin everyone's future. I cannot allow that. Please, do not tell a soul. All must be kept a secret. Our family has suffered enough ridicule, do you not agree?"

Cecilia smiled to me again, and in that moment my heart almost fell out from my chest. The striking resemblance between her and Colonel Radisson was so obvious, I had to sit down pretending to read so I would not stare at her excessively.

This could not be true; certainly it was only the stretch of my imagination. But what if was true? Mother has admitted that she still holds secrets.

Yes, it was true. My sister Cecilia was Colonel Radisson's daughter. I was sure she knew it, too.

CHAPTER 33

FINALLY, A WEEK AGO, CATHERINE wrote to me, responding to my letter to her, expressing her surprise of my recent development. Then, she revealed the exciting news of her pregnancy. In other news, Lady Winston's son was unwell and unfortunately his illness was progressing. Among my London acquaintances, she was the only one who did not criticize my broken engagement.

But at the same time, Catherine reported that she was in possession of good news from the Duke of Winchester. He was back in England, but at his country residence. In her opinion, he might be wounded, but some secrets are kept in regard to his condition. Besides, she added, the whole of London knows that he is in love with me – the infamous country girl whose former fiancé still loves her and whose current fiancé, (now former himself), didn't know she had a lover.

I was the subject of intense and pleasurable gossip to the receipt of the highest rate of popularity. Unfortunately, there was no way to know precisely if the Duke was informed of my new situation. To him, I still might be lost to Captain Clark.

I must write to him as Cyril advised me and declare my love and invite him to visit me. I would tell him myself about my own sacrifice for us to be together. This was my future. I would pursue the man I love and try to break the unfortunate fate of my mother and my sister, both of whom lost the chance for happiness by fighting against their feelings.

I would not banish love, nor would I live my life haunted by a lost love, rather than with the man I love.

* * *

My sister brought me tea this morning and she found me reading another note from James. He was angry and hurt again over my constant refusal to return his affection.

He requested permission to come and visit me and his sister so he could restore his broken spirit. Then he continued as always, lamenting about his unhappiness in his marriage and the supreme need to be close to me. I was the only one for whom he had passion and love in his heart, and I was the source of his inspiration.

Otherwise, he would be better dead. Without me his life was meaningless.

I accepted his visit because I knew I must force him to remove these unhealthy feelings he possessed for me as soon as possible. I was equally guilty to have them escalate by my own irresponsible logic. He would arrive sometime this afternoon, quite in a rush, but I should be lenient and understand his hidden reasons.

"Are you all right my dear?" she asked setting the tea cup on my desk.

"Poor James," I said handing his letter to my sister. "Surely he will not consider these matters as hopeless and doomed as he puts them in writing."

"I was not certain about anything anymore. Now, dear Cleona, I must confess something to you and there will never be a better moment as this. I am sure you will be petrified by it, but

I must not hide it from you anymore. Please forgive me for what I am about to say."

"Cecilia, there is nothing that could possibly astonish me anymore."

"But this revelation will! Colonel Radisson has asked Mother to marry him and she has accepted. This evening, at dinner, they will officially announce it. Captain Clark is among the participants."

"It is not entirely unexpected." I said, unwilling to comment on Colonel Radisson's action in any way, not to his daughter. Indeed, Colonel Radisson disrupted our lives and I hated him fiercely for it but I could not deny the fact that I would have never met and fallen in love with the Duke of Winchester if I had not lost Chatham Hill and Mr. Connelly.

"How wonderful for you to have Captain Clark and Mr. Connelly for dinner," I said. Ghosts of my past love were rising back to life.

"The two gentlemen who still declare to have lingering feelings for you. Don't you find that a little dangerous?"

"Perhaps, but I will make amends to them and certainly they will be found acceptable."

"Your words are silly, my sister," laughed Cecilia loud. "They will not accept anything less than absolute return of affection from you. Will you commit to that? You are in a peculiar situation my dear, though perhaps not as peculiar as Colonel Radisson and Mother."

"There is always hope, my dear. I almost lost the man I loved but I was fortunate enough to find him again. I wrote to the Duke of Winchester and he agreed to come visit me. Cecilia – I am so happy. He does not know that I have forsaken Captain Clark for him. You must only imagine his surprise. I will become the new Duchess of Winchester. Oh, my dear, I still wish to encourage you to disclose the truth about your son and his father, William, to Mother and family."

"You cannot be serious, Cleona! You must know by now that in that circumstance, my son will lose his inheritance. Here, drink your tea and do not worry too much about me."

"That is not a sufficient reason for you to refuse the father of your son. I will help you explain, I will be there for you. Trust me, my dear, they will all understand. I want you to be happy and get married, too."

My sister watched me in an awkward silence, as I started to sip the strange tasting tea. I read to her the letter from Louisa that had arrived yesterday morning.

"My dearest Cleona,
Is has been such a wonderful and emotional time, to be back at Chatham Hill. I am content beyond description, and so pleased. I never exhaust my constant delight of your great kindness…"

When I visit her in the summer, I will urge her to diminish this unnecessary expression of gratitude. But the end of her letter was intriguing.

Remember those boring books that Uncle Edward wrote? I know you are very fond of them. Thomas will be there at Bristol Cottage tomorrow, to bring those books to you as a gift, along with my love and gratitude. He is beside himself with joy to reunite with his dear uncle again under such pleasant events.

Cleona, I must confess this to you. There is something wrong with my husband's mind — he thinks that your phantom is in the house. He thinks that he sees you everywhere. Please talk to him, my dear; I believe he is still deeply infatuated with you."

Louisa Clark,
Tuesday, April 17, 1810. Chatham Hill.

My sister shook her head in disbelief and left without saying a word. I watched her leaving the house and entering the stables, most likely to talk to William Henry.

I did not judge her for her motives to keep William close. She needed his love, but they must marry for the sake of little William. I could not imagine being raised by a different man other than my father. And still, my Mother and my sister were loved by more than one man – and I was no better.

What have I done? Cecilia was right. All three of these men were deeply in love with me. I captured their hearts, upset their lives, and now, did I expect that they would find it easy to heal, without recurrence of desire?

James Connelly, Thomas Clark and the Duke of Winchester – all fought and lost at one point or the other to be the keeper of my soul.

This past year of my life has been a long and emotional journey for my soul. Soon, all these memories will surpass the hurts and they will vanish into nothingness. Life will go on. It will slow down and become a settled reality.

Soon I will unite with the one man I truly love and lose myself into happiness. Everything around me will quiet down and become normal. But how will I ever know what normal is? I will be always famous for being engaged three times in one year.

I felt the need to go outside and breathe fresh air before the arrival of the guests, and especially before the arrival of the Duke of Winchester. I was so ready to see his wonderful and beloved face when he would learn the truth.

I was about to cross the alley toward the river when James Connelly arrived. He called me to come back, and as I turned I saw that he looked very thin and pale, quite pitiful, with a wild and deranged appearance.

"My dear Cleona," he said bowing to me, "it's so gratifying

to be here with you, at last. My soul was hollow and dry from desiring to be in your presence."

"Mr. Connelly," I said, trying to keep a safe distance, "I am glad you arrived. Please go inside and wait for my return. May I ask of you to keep in check your feelings that you have for me. Tonight I have special guests for dinner. I am certain that my happiness is important to you."

"What about my happiness?" he asked, desperately looking into my eyes.

"What you ask is impossible. James, you are a married man and I shall marry the man I love, quite soon. But we shall have a more pleasant conversation later," I said, smiling peacefully as I tried to retire from his presence. I curtsied and left him there while Mr. Henry carried his trunk inside.

As always, I took a stroll by the Thames River to clear my mind, before the arrival of the others. An unexplained fear invaded my soul and as I struggled to dismiss it, dread overtook my whole body. I was shaking.

The pain in my chest had returned, and it was very unpleasant, but I was certain that it would pass. This encounter with the miserable James Connelly produced more turmoil in my already devastated soul.

Through the sweetest sound of the multitude of singing birds I heard a voice calling my name, but the evening shadows impaired my view of the cottage. As I strained my eyes I thought I saw Mr. Henry's shadow.

The sound of horse's hoofs coming from behind startled me, but it was only Captain Clark. I had not seen him since he visited me at my sister's house, when I freed him from our engagement. He lifted his hat to salute me and jumped down off his horse.

"Captain Clark, what a pleasure to see you again," I said, but my voice trembled under the memory of our past together and the influence of Louisa's words in her letter.

"Thank you my dear cousin," he said, quite calm and a bit indifferent. "What an interesting turn of events in regard to my uncle and Mrs. Somerton. I suppose they were meant to be together."

"Indeed", I responded looking down at the grass.

Captain Clark came closer to me. I stepped back but he continued to follow my movement until I stopped on the edge of the river. He took my hand and kissed it. His expression of affection was all too familiar – and then he attempted to kiss me on my lips. I turned my head to the right, frightened by his intentions, and he caressed my hair.

"We are relatives now, Miss Cleona, please forgive my manners," he said, backing away and trying to counteract his indiscretion.

"I expect nothing less than excellent manners from you, Mr. Clark," I said coldly as a sudden feeling of nauseous overwhelmed me.

"I was surprised not to be the only guest," he said getting back on the horse. "I think I saw the Duke of Winchester passing me earlier and heading rapidly to the cottage."

"Wonderful," I said, incapable of hiding my joy from learning that news. "The Duke was invited by *me*. We shall have great news for everyone tonight."

"Oh," he said biting his lower lip. "My dear cousin, would you like me to accompany you back to the house?"

"No," I rushed to respond. "Please proceed without me. I will see you at dinner."

I turned my back to him but the next moment I felt a deep and sharp pain in the middle of my back. My legs became numb and I felt on my knees, out of breath. I heard Captain Clark's horse fast gallop in the opposite direction.

I didn't have the strength to call his name. Perhaps was just the chest pain that transferred to my back. It took me quite a bit of time and effort to overcome this ordeal and stand up again. The fresh air made me feel better, but the next moment I started to shake and sweat.

I should have returned immediately and welcomed my lover, but the magic of the river kept me hostage a little longer. Besides, I did not want the Duke of Winchester to see me in Captain Clark's presence any longer.

He came! Indeed, he came for me; he was at the cottage right that moment. He still loved me and wanted me. The happiness I felt rushing through my heart brought me to tears.

I bent down, touched the water with the tips of my fingers and washed my face. I had seen my reflection in it, as I was there, on the other side of its mirror. The water was silent and refreshing. Suddenly, my whole body was submerged in the water; I tried to fight it but something was holding my down.

I begin to UNDERSTAND. *I was not alone.*

The pain of losing my breath was not prolonged. The water embraced me as in a dance, softly at first, but moments later, I lost my consciousness. My body floated up to the surface and although my eyes were still wide open, I could not see …

I had crossed over into the dark.

CHAPTER 34

DOCTOR CLIFTON COOPER HAD READ my story a dozen times by now, but he was still unwilling to make any comment in this regard to his aunt, Lady Cooper, even though the good lady was inquiring as to his opinion every day. I could only conclude that he was extremely disappointed in all the revelations about me, my family and my reckless demeanor. But I had tried to warn everyone about it. This was not easy to bear.

One morning he came into my room as usual for his consultation. When he bent a little to listen to my heart, I laid my hands on his head and I gently raised his face towards mine. My gesture left him astounded for a moment, but I could sense that he was thrilled. His eyes opened wide under the effect of the unexpected change in my demeanor.

His affection made me happy, but this was all too familiar to me. This path would only bring affliction to this man to whom I owed my life. I could not allow for another soul to attach itself to me, although at this moment in my life, I had no identity among the living and surely his sincere interest in me could only be beneficial.

I must make an effort to break my silence and escape my own demons.

"Thank you, Doctor Cooper," I attempted to say and in the beginning my voice was a weak rasping whisper.

"Miss Somerton, you are speaking," he jubilated, holding my face into his palms. "How wonderful it is to hear your voice."

Doctor Cooper took my hand and as he called for his aunt, he walked me to the parlor where Lady Cooper was quietly drinking her tea.

"What is the matter," she asked, bothered by the commotion. "Is everything all right, Clifton?"

"Miss Somerton is speaking," he said, very excited, still holding my hand, a gesture that did not pass unobserved by his aunt.

"I am grateful to your Ladyship," I said, overwhelmed by this visible progress of my road to recovery.

"You are so welcome my dear girl," responded Lady Cooper, successfully rising from her chair with no assistance. "What an improvement, indeed. Not that I ever doubted my nephew, but I had lost a bit of hope."

I curtsied to her, unable to retrieve my hand from Doctor Cooper's possession.

"I am totally aware that by now you formed a conclusion about me from the pages of my journal," I continued, holding my head down. My words were forming slowly. They were somewhat altered, sounding more like someone who was learning to speak English. "You probably should discuss it between yourselves and make a decision in my regard. Whatever you will decide, I will gladly follow your lead."

"Miss Somerton, there is plenty of time for such a task," Doctor Cooper said, losing his smile and relinquishing my hand.

"There is no time, Clifton," Lady Cooper admonished him. "Miss Somerton is right." Then she turned to me. "Would you mind leaving us for a moment, my dear? I am certain my nephew will see that you are entirely correct."

I curtsied to both of them and I began to retreat to my room.

But half way up the stairs, I changed my mind. I came back down and I silently hid behind a curtain in the living room. It was not curiosity in regard to my future that prompted me to such incivility, but the suspicion that their conversation would shed new light on the events that culminated with me drowning in the river.

"You have avoided talking about this matter long enough," I heard Lady Cooper say. "I know your reasons and it is not a surprise to me that in spite of Miss Somerton's complicated past, you still desire her."

"I only concluded that her reasons and decisions were not always wise," Doctor Cooper defended me. "I will not attempt to make any judgment. I have sincere feelings for her and I pity her, especially after such a tormented conclusion in regard to her family."

"Aha," said Lady Cooper. "There are mysteries to solve – not one, but three. We have three murders that somehow managed to escape suspicion, but you and I can pursue the truth. Miss Somerton did her part in the investigation, and now is time for the truth."

"Let me start first with the older mystery, the death on Mr. Edward Somerton. This is easy. I believe that he was killed by the hand of the old Duke of Winchester."

"But, Clifton, the Duke himself was a witness that Mr. Somerton's nephew, Robert, accidently shot him. At least this was Lady de Winchester's recollection about the demise of her old friend and lover. Even Cleona entertained this possibility."

"She had very many doubts, but not suspicions, my Lady," answered Clifton in a very confident tone of voice. "The Duke knew about his wife's love for Edward and that was a good motive to eliminate a rival."

"Perhaps, but if you refer to motives, Claude Somerton, the older cousin, is a good candidate. He was absolutely certain to inherit the Mansion, so he acted upon it."

"I must disagree. It was not Claude nor Robert Somerton, who had absolutely no motive, but the Duke. If you recall Cleona's conversation with Mrs. Parker, her neighbor who knew Edward well, she denied that he would take Robert to such events, and that he hated hunting. The day he left for hunting, he received an invitation from the Duchess to come to the court. Instead, he was met by the Duke of Winchester, who saw an imminent danger in his presence around his wife, and decided to take advantage of the situation and take him down. Then he returned to his palace with the news that Edward had died by accident."

"This is a quite stretch. Why he would blame it on a young boy who was not even there?"

"He told that lie only to his wife to entirely eliminate him as a suspect in her eyes. He did it because of love. For everyone else, it was just an accident they did not bother to investigate. Such things happen all the time in that sport. You are not yet convinced?"

"You could be right," answered Lady Cooper a bit hesitant and I was conflicted between the relief of eliminating my uncle as a killer, and accepting this new suspect and the coldness of his act.

"Of course, I am. Now is your turn, my dear aunt. Who injured Colonel Somerton, Cleona's father?"

"Let's agree on something we know for sure," Lady Cooper began. "He was shot during his trip to Miltonville, to confront his brother-in-law and settle a disputed inheritance on behalf of his wife."

"And we do not believe it was an accident, although the Colonel declared he was polishing his own gun when it happened."

"Precisely" she agreed. "An experienced man with guns, like the Colonel, would not make such mistake or choose to do the task when he was not at home. But my question is: if his brother-in-law shot him in a moment of anger, why would the Colonel would keep quiet about it?"

"Perhaps to not upset his wife with such terrible news. Besides, he must not have thought it was a dangerous wound."

"That could be, but I do not believe it was George Milton who shot him," said Lady Cooper lowering her voice a little. "As much as we could find out about his character, George was a tormented spirit who desired to do things right by his sister. He would not keep quiet about it, but attempt to make amends."

"I am not sure about that," said Clifton. "Look how long he kept the secret about the inheritance and how dominated was he by his wife. I think that he did it, but they agreed to keep it a secret from Mrs. Somerton. Even Miss Cleona agreed to keep a secret from her sister concerning Mr. Sutton's death."

"They kept it a secret, all right, but because the shooter was none other than Colonel Radisson."

From where I was hiding this new revelation made me gasp. But I waited for the conclusion, half suffocated by the heavy curtain covering my face and body.

"Do you have any proof?" asked Doctor Cooper. "That would be quite unbelievable since not even Miss Cleona could find any circumstances to accuse him."

"But many times she suspected him. Anna remembered clearly that the Colonel returned wounded from a trip to Miltonville, but he also did something unusual – he took his gun for the road and most likely with the intent to go to Galveston. Also, Joseph confessed to Cleona that after his father argued with Colonel Somerton, he left that evening to meet with other officers at a hunting club. I assume he found Colonel Radisson's letter to his wife and went to confront him. Miss Cleona was not aware that Galveston is Colonel Radisson's residence. After all, they were friends for a long time. Most likely they had an old fashioned duel and one of them was shot. Colonel Somerton agreed to keep it a secret and return home with a story."

"It does make sense," said Clifton and I realized that Lady Cooper's conclusions were sound. My father would never agree to bring this embarrassing family matter to light or upset mother further for any reason. Although I always suspected him, I cannot believe that this man deceived me and Mother in such a manner that now he became part of our family. "The Colonel never fully confessed, but he allowed the shadow of guilt to be there. All these men, killed for love."

"Indeed, but it is not over. We have one more mystery to solve. However hard it will be for Miss Cleona to accept that her lover's father killed her uncle, and her mother's lover shot her Father, she must face the fact that her own encounter with death was provoked by someone."

There was silence for a few minutes before they started to analyze my own unfinished demise.

"We have quite a few suspects for the job," started Lady Cooper. "Miss Somerton is very beautiful and she has that seductive charm that captivated the will of the men in her life to gravitate hopelessly to her and be at her mercy. I must confess that her story is more than I could artificially create in my own characters."

"But let's begin with the former fiancé, Mr. Connelly, the one still desperate for her love. As you recall, he arrived at the cottage about the time Miss Cleona left for her walk. He could have easily followed her at later time, and in a moment of desperation, stabbed her and pushed her into the river."

"Indeed," said Lady Cooper, "he could be the one, but I do not believe so. I truly believe that he needed her in his life in order for him to create music and counteract the unhappiness of his marriage. Regardless of his desperation to be closer to her or have her share his affection, James Connelly had no power or inclination to kill the only women he loved. He only had use for her alive. I would rather tend to accuse the Duke."

I wished to leave my hiding place so I would not continue to listen to my hosts, but my weakness was too great and I could not move. How much more pain could I endure? My own soul was a cluster of darkness with thoughts that made me wonder, for the thousandth time, if it was worth saving my life. I had made so many people unhappy and I had turned one of them into a killer.

But if it was the truth that the Duke of Winchester killed me, so be it. At least he was the man I loved – to my last breath.

"It was not the Duke," said Doctor Cooper.

"I believe you are not thinking logically, Clifton," said Lady Cooper to her nephew. "The Duke was madly in love with her and on the verge of losing her forever to Captain Clark. At the time of his visit he was not aware that Miss Cleona was free from her engagement. As his Father did before, the Duke of Winchester's only choice was to kill the woman he loved, so no one else could have her."

"On the contrary," argued Clifton, "I tend to believe that he must have known something of her broken engagement. It was impossible for some rumor – if not the confirmation of fact -- not to reach him, even on his estate in Winchester. And it was Captain Clark's account to Cleona that the Duke passed him in a hurry to reach the cottage. So, he was aware of her freedom and perhaps her wish to accept his offer. The Duke's love for her stands against time and reason. I am certain of this fact."

Behind the curtains, I covered my face with my hands and cried in silence. I was relieved but puzzled over their conclusions.

Then, who killed me?

CHAPTER 35

"It must be shocking for you, my dear aunt, to be entertained so highly by a story that rose so far above your expectations and was not told by you. That is because Miss Cleona was poisoned, stabbed in the back and drowned and she lived to tell the story. Except that she wasn't told the whole truth."

Behind the curtains, I almost lost consciousness again. Poisoned and stabbed before an attempt to be drowned? Oh, the offal tea was poison and the pain in my back was not at all the reflection of my old chest pain.

"And she will learn of the whole truth, as soon as we find out who is to blame for her poisoning," Lady Cooper continued. "Now that we have eliminated two lovers, unfortunately it could only be one person responsible for all this. There is one other person with strong motives and much to lose if Miss Cleona revealed some family secrets – her own sister, Mrs. Cecilia Sutton."

I moved the curtains aside, gasping for air. It was unclear to me if I had heard them correctly.

"You are correct, my dear aunt," I heard Clifton say. "Cecilia Sutton appeared to be very angry over Cleona's insistence that she reveal her son's the true identity. She was not willing to have anyone know the truth and put her son in danger of losing the estate and the barony. Cecilia and William Henry were lovers, a situation with which they both were content. She has the money and he was well kept, with a son as future baron. She brought her sister that strange tasting tea in an attempt to make her sick before the dinner and keep her quiet about her business. Cleona was fortunate that as she hates tea, she didn't consume enough."

"Correct, my dear Clifton. I also suspect that Cecilia didn't intend to mortally harm her sister but to incapacitate her ability to participate at that particular family dinner and risk her make inappropriate remarks. She was buying time for herself."

"And of course," continued Clifton, "now we can blame Captain Clark for stabbing her. This is the only logical conclusion after reading Cleona's journal."

"Yes, it could be," agreed Lady Cooper. "He was a soldier trained to kill in cold blood and he was mentally disturbed, influenced by the fact that he had lost the woman he worshiped and was infatuated to the point of having hallucinations. But killing her, even in a moment of rage over the news that she was engaged to the Duke of Winchester, would not fit his skills. The wound she suffered was as superficial as it was absent of intent. It would not have killed her."

"I have an explanation for that," rushed Clifton. "Apparently, Captain Clark dressed up for a very fancy dinner in the presence of his uncle. In that regard, his sword was one of ceremonials. It wasn't sufficiently sharpened to produce a fatal wound."

"All right, dear nephew! I guess you deserve the honor to decipher the last mystery. Who had drowned her?"

"Thank you my dear aunt. As a matter fact, this riddle is quite easy. Everything started when Cecilia confessed to Mr. Henry her concern over her sister's intent to reveal their most terrible secret and embarrass the family even more.

'His love for them was strong enough to motivate him to kill Cleona and keep Cecilia's secret secure, and there is no doubt that Mr. Henry would have done this for her. Mr. Henry was outside when Cleona left for a walk. At first he called her name with the intention of talking to her and asking her for her cooperation. But he changed his mind when he realized how easy it would be for him to simply eliminate their problem. After the murder of Mr. Sutton he was convinced that he could easily get away with yet another murder. Once Cleona was gone, Cecilia would be safe. She would keep the estate and keep him, too. They were merely protecting the future of their son."

The magnitude of this theory deeply astonished me. Although my mind refused to absorb the possibility, I was conflicted with doubt and shame.

My family tree was replete with killers. My mother's new husband had shot my father and my own dear sister poisoned me to make me sick and her lover pushed me into the river, holding me down until he believed me dead.

My sister and my mother both kept spare lovers – and so did I.

We were cursed.

My past, as disturbing as it was, would not compare with my uncertain future. I was at the mercy of two strangers who knew everything about me, and perhaps even pitied me, but would they want to keep me?

"The old curse of unfulfilled love," nodded Lady Cooper. "Every female in Cleona's family married someone other than the man they loved, but not her. But one matter still stands as Miss Somerton awaits our decision. Of course, she cannot go back home. Cleona is welcome here with us and we shall keep her secrets secure, but is this the best course of action for her? I can read your thoughts, Clifton, and I am aware that she is dear to your heart. But that would be the beginning of another curse. Will you keep her here with you in the hope that she will share your affection, or will you let her go where she belongs? Will you be willing to stop the curse?"

Before he had the opportunity to answer, I decided to come out from my hiding place, and I walked directly into the middle of the room. Lady Cooper and the doctor turned to me, surprised and chagrined. They had no doubt that I had been listening to their conversation and that I was fully informed about their discussion. They watched me in silence with concerned looks in their eyes, but I struggled to smile.

"My gratitude to you is immense," I said "along with my genuine affection. I am not bitter at all over your findings, but I must ask you to not be overly concerned over the right decision for me and my future. I have been educated and I possess some talents that would help me survive and sustain an income."

I took a deep breath and focused my attention on Clifton.

"Doctor Cooper, it would not be fair for me to encourage your feelings when I have no room in my heart for a renewed relationship. In any other circumstances, I would be honored to be noticed and desired by you."

Clifton Cooper stared at me for a few moments and appeared to be unnerved by the cruel reality of my words.

He bowed to us, exited the room, and I did not see him at dinner.

* * *

A month later, on a Monday morning, Doctor Cooper and I took Lady Cooper's carriage and traveled to Winchester. I had taken Lady Stella's advice and before my departure, she adopted me as her niece and gave me a new name: Kiara Cooper, after her beloved sister.

When the carriage turned into the immense circular drive, it was still unclear to me how I arrived at the palatial entrance of the Duke's estate; the entire ordeal of the trip was shrouded in a deep fog, both outside in nature and inside my mind.

The immense old palace, covered in dark brown stone, appeared threatening and unappealing to me. I felt small and insignificant under its shadow, so much so that it made me hesitant to take my first step as I approached its entrance.

"The Duke of Winchester has returned from the battlefield," said Dr. Cooper, holding my hand and helping me to step down from the carriage. "My sources have informed me that after your disappearance, he tried very hard to be sent into the most deadly battles. When I wrote to him and requested an audience, he accepted my visit because I am a physician. That makes me believe that he may be injured, but I cannot be sure. He does not know about you, and I did not make him aware that you would be visiting him with me. Miss Cleona, I could not take away your right to give him the good news – he very much deserves it. I am well aware that this was your last wish before the *accident*."

"Thank you, Doctor Cooper," I responded, while my heart and my own emotions were about to provoke me into fainting. "But are you sure I should go to him? He belongs to my past. What if he accepted my demise and decided that his grief should end? I cannot just suddenly appear on his doorstep as if I were a ghost, when my own family thinks me dead."

"I am absolutely positive that his grief has not ended," Dr. Cooper encouraged me as his voice trembled. "He loves you, even now, I sure of it. I will be waiting for you for some little time, but if you do not return to the carriage right away, I will know that you are in safe and loving hands. The curse will end here – you are free of it."

"I am grateful to you. Goodbye, Doctor Cooper; be blessed," I said, leaving my savior behind, perhaps forever.

* * *

Mr. Pattison admitted me into the house, somewhat confused by my solitary presence, but he was polite and had me wait for what seemed like an eternity in one of the many parlors. I stood motionless in the middle of that expensively decorated room like a lost child, hoping that someone would come and rescue me.

When I was finally allowed to see him, my legs seemed so heavy that my feet seemed to be moving through thick muck, but my heart was racing. The Duke of Winchester received me in his private master apartment, and not in the parlor, as it was proper to meet with a female visitor. Perhaps he was expecting Doctor Cooper.

When I entered the room, he made an attempt to stand, perhaps believing that his senses had deserted him and that a phantom had entered his apartment. My eyes gazed at his body in an attempt to discover if there was a wound that would cause any disability; the fear of seeing something dreadful made me shake uncontrollably. But I could not see any injury.

Indeed, he was a bit slimmer and his features had lost some of their softness and vigor, but to me he was still the man I loved.

The Duke looked shocked at first, although he recognized me, and then he seemed to withdraw into himself; his demeanor denied me that delirious feeling to be in his presence once again. His hesitation was a direct answer to the fact that he was totally convinced I was gone forever.

"For a moment I thought I was dreaming," he said, and his voice trembled. "Is this you, Miss Somerton or just your ghost? I believed you to be dead."

I walked across the room and sat on his bed. He followed me with his eyes.

"Yes, it is me, my Lord," I answered slowly and with a slight accent. "I am not dead – fortunately someone saved my life after I fell into the river that day when you arrived at Bristol Cottage. They gave me shelter and protection. The healing was slow and dreadful. No one else knows that I did not perish. Are you well? Please forgive me, Your Grace, but I must know if you are wounded!"

"I am not wounded, just fatigued. Please forgive me for my clumsy manners but your presence here, alive, is overwhelming. When you did not return to the cottage, we began a search for you throughout the night, until morning. When we found evidence that you might have fallen into the river, everyone concluded that perhaps you had drowned. I was on the verge of going insane. I was so distraught that I went to war hoping to die, and I left elite society behind to its own misery. You are so pale and fragile, my love, it took me a few moments before to recognize you. May I touch you?"

This time he came to sit beside me and touched my face, hesitant at first. My heart was holding out the hope that soon I would be the mistress of this room, a rightful companion in his bed.

"Perhaps you are aware by now that I could not marry Captain Clark. Our engagement was terminated before Christmas, but I had no knowledge of your whereabouts."

"Is it true? In truth, I was making plans to kill Mr. Clark before your wedding, I swear. I was prepared to kill him and Mr. Connelly as well, for that matter. I was so angry, and my jealousness knew no bounds. I could not allow you to become his wife. You belong to me!"

I smiled, and he did too, but for different reasons. The discovery that his father had killed my uncle to protect the woman he loved was still fresh in my mind. But that was just another secret, among many others that had been revealed to me.

"I am yours," I said, looking into his eyes with passion. I could not risk losing him again just to act aloof, based on propriety and decencies. "I love you, and only you. My Lord, will you have me?"

"Are you asking me if I still want you to be my wife?" he asked, holding me closer to him. His hand was caressing my hair.

I nodded. The Duke of Winchester seemed to lack a clear understanding of simple words, or perhaps he was in doubt that I wanted him to be my life's companion.

"I understand if you hesitate, my Lord. I suppose this moment is as right as any for you to know the truth about my family, and then decide if *you* still want me," I said, taking a deep breath. "Indeed, I was pushed into the river by my sister's lover out of fear that I would not keep their secrets. Also, he is the one who killed my sister's husband. My sister tried to make me sick with poisoned tea to keep me quiet about their affair. Years ago my father died from a wound inflicted by my mother's lover. Now he is married to her and is a part of my family, the father of my older sister and an accomplice to her husband's murder.

"Because of these things, I cannot make myself known to anyone, especially to my family. I shall forever be apart from them. I can only conclude that they have accepted my "passing" by now and they are content. My reputation was quite infamous before my "death"; you could have never married that Cleona Somerton and not ruined your reputation. Now, the only proper conclusion for you to function in society is that I should remain dead and perhaps unrecognizable. You are a royal; I am merely an unattractive ghost. Can you still desire me after knowing all of this? If not, I shall return to my saviors and forever remain lost to you."

"Cleona, I never stopped loving you, not even when I thought you were dead," said the Duke taking me in his arms. "My love and desire for you is like a curse you cannot escape – I wanted to follow you in death. My sweet love, to me you look so beautiful and mesmerizing. Now, we both can be alive again. We will travel together, away from here, and marry in Paris."

"Further, away than Paris," I whispered in ecstasy. "And my

name is now Kiara. Remember, Cleona is gone forever."

His shirt was open and I touched his chest with my fingers; his skin was tan and so pleasant to touch.

"Kiara, my love," he whispered in my ears.

He kissed me softly with no intention to rush; time was on our side. I was not leaving to go anywhere. Soon his lips were burning my neck and slowly his hands began to undress me.

I wished he would rip off all my clothes, but he was quite gentle. My breasts were the first to enjoy freedom. Soon they disappeared into his hands, followed closely by his lips.

Our desire for physical love was natural, not lustful and predatory.

Lovers and killers, we all have our moment in time.

EPILOGUE

A MONTH LATER WE WERE married in Wien, Austria. I made my debut to the court as royalty in early March, being introduced as the new Duchess of Winchester. No one there who had known me in my past life seemed to recognize me as the "dead" socialite. Cleona Somerton's "demise" was the subject of continuing debate, but it was accepted as the fulfilling of an old curse.

A year later, the memory of Cleona had vanished from everyone's mind. To them I was a complete stranger, the new bride of Lord Grayson Evington, Duke of Winchester.

The tremendous ordeal of surviving both the "drowning" and the pneumonia had made a radical change on my body. As a result, my speech was affected and my hair was darker and dull. I was slimmer and I had lost that sweet angelic look that had characterized my face. I appeared much more mature now, and my fair skin had changed to a darker complexion. But it was all to my benefit.

* * *

Many were astonished by the Duke's unexpected choice in his

marriage, but all were charmed by the mysterious new Duchess. Unlike Cleona, I did not present myself as a keyboardist nor did I create sensational garments – I had no further use for those accomplishments.

Lady Stella Cooper rejoiced over the fact that she was so closely *related* to the young bride. She used her unique talent as an author of fiction to create a credible past for me: I was her niece, an orphan raised in Austria by her husband relatives. To my surprise, nobody contested the authenticity of my biography.

Lady de Winchester was very much surprised by her son's unexpected marriage and she stared at me for days, as if there were something about me that she almost recognized but could not quite bring to the surface of her mind. But she received me with grace and kindness and treated me like a royal; somehow I reminded her of someone who she cared for and enjoyed, but who died so young. She never asked me about anything from my past, but she was jubilant over her son's new found happiness.

* * *

I could only assume that my "passing" affected my sensitive brother, Cyril, deeply. He had married Miss Bowen and had retired to one of her country homes. He, too, appeared to be puzzled by my appearance when he accompanied his wife to a ball we held in the spring, at the Evington Palace. I hid my tears, because I wished with all my heart to embrace him, but I kept my secret and played my part as a hostess. He was content and happy.

* * *

I have seen my dear Louisa at a court ceremony for the officers. I kept a safe distance as I suffered quietly the loss of my best friend and confident, a true sister to me and so dear to my heart.

She was pregnant, looked well, and that was a great joy. The pain of my "death" drew her and her husband, Captain Clark, closer to each other. As it did to the other members of my family, my "death" was also beneficial to them, in that regard. Now – they only have each other. Evelyn was living with them at Chatham Hill.

I hold no grudge against Captain Clark. Only the Lord knows how much pain and suffering I inflicted on him. I killed his soul first, before he killed me.

* * *

Our main residence was in Winchester. I came to terms with the massive old palace and to love it almost as much as I loved Chatham Hill. It became my real home and my shelter. We avoided London as much as we could, but when we were there, I had a favorite friend in Catherine Cleaves, who named her first daughter in my honor – my old name. But she could not comprehend my sudden attachment to her, from me, a foreign princess.

* * *

On many occasions I continued to visit the St. John's church with my husband. Rev. and Mrs. Warren always maintained steadfast devotion to their congregation, and the Duke and I supported them to the fullest.

* * *

James Connelly was found by my husband in a small apartment in London, all alone and ill. He never returned to his wealthy wife after my "death". My husband invited him to spend some time with us in the country. Each evening he would play his music with pain and passion. To my amazement, my dear husband hired him to teach me and my three nieces, the daughters of his brother, who became permanent guests into the palace, to play fortepiano.

After the disturbance produced by my physical similarity with Cleona faded away, he slowly opened up to me and started to confess about his lost love. I encouraged him to continue to write music as his beloved Cleona would expect him to do so. He had a new purpose in life – he celebrated her memory and impressed a beautiful Duchess who was interested in his art.

* * *

But not much stranger than my new identity was the fact that James Connelly was also my source of information about my estranged family. His sister, Hannah, married my cousin George Milton, the same spring and now she was living in my Uncle George's home. My mother moved out from Bristol Cottage to one of Colonel Radisson's grand mansions.

I understood why she would not want to reside at the cottage anymore. She loved me and she never knew anything about the terrible secrets that surrounded her – her own secrets were torment enough. The cottage was now empty and abandoned. The curse required its third soul.

* * *

My sister, Cecilia Sutton returned to her home at Forestdale, and I was certain my "death" affected her a bit. But I would never know to what degree she would regret giving me that tea, or that late afternoon conversation with William Henry. Now her son was safe to inherit the barony and her lover was still her caretaker, a situation with which she was so strangely content. William came into our home as a young boy with a bright future, but instead, he became a killer.

But I refuse to judge them – the Lord will do that.

* * *

Although Lady Winston's opinion was that the Duke of Winchester married me only because I resembled so closely the woman he loved, but died, no one contested my rights to our marriage.

Kiara Evington, Duchess of Winchester.
Winchester, 1812.

The End

ABOUT THE AUTHOR

Camie Gregory lives in a suburb of Atlanta, Georgia with her family, and is an executive in a bank.

Made in the USA
Lexington, KY
23 August 2015